THE CATALYST

'Please, sit down.' She joined him, clenching her hands between her knees as if they might be out of control. 'Look,' he went on, 'I have to stay here for a couple of days – '

'No problem, really, no problem.' She was smiling down at her hands.

'You don't understand,' he said, standing to take off his coat, keeping his elbow tight over the gun, 'I have to. And you have to stay here with me, incommunicado.' She looked round at him, fear and bewilderment beginning to suffuse her face. 'You aren't in any danger. I haven't done anything. At least I haven't done what they, the police are going to believe. And that's bad. Very, very bad. I just have to figure a way to get out of here. I can't check into a hotel or wander the streets. I need a safe place. I'm sorry it's yours. really I am.' She was biting a knuckle and her eyes were screwed up, watering. He could see the bewilderment, the mounting panic. 'I really need you to believe me. I really haven't hurt anyone despite what you'll read and hear – '

About the author

Ron McKay has worked extensively in Lebanon, Libya and Northern Ireland as a journalist and photographer. In 1980 he was the first reporter to be arrested and charged under the Prevention of Terrorism Act, for allegedly withholding information. The charges were subsequently dropped.

Ron McKay lives in London. THE CATALYST is his first novel.

The Catalyst

Ron McKay

NEW ENGLISH LIBRARY
Hodder and Stoughton

Printed and bound in Great Britain
for Hodder and Stoughton Paper-
backs, a division of Hodder and
Stoughton Ltd., Mill Road, Dunton
Green, Sevenoaks, Kent TN13 2YA.
(Editorial Office: 47 Bedford Square,
London WC1B 3DP) by Clays Ltd St
Ives plc.

British Library C.I.P.
McKay, Ron
  The catalyst
  I. Title
  823.914 [F]

ISBN 0 450 54979-8

For the Sister of Mercy

'You couldn't help it that you were born without a heart. At least you tried to believe what the people with hearts believed – so you were a good man just the same.'

Kurt Vonnegut
Jailbird

MONDAY, 10.30 a.m.

He woke with a slight headache and remembered that he couldn't remember the last five years. He froze, before tentatively inching a hand across the bunk. He was alone. One thing he couldn't stand, along with the total amnesia, was that early morning ritual of making love to a total stranger you had made love with most of the night before.

He stretched, his toes crackling on the cold reaches of the sheets. The air felt damp on his nose, the seeping misery of another November. He braced himself and leaped out of bed, scrabbling on the faded linoleum for the socks and pants – he'd rather not think how long he had worn them – and then the jeans and the bobbly grey sweater someone had knitted him in another incarnation. His eyes caught the drift of mail spilling from the moquette bench seat. At the hatch, another small shower had gathered. He swept the pile up with both hands, glorying in the burst of energy, and threw the collection at the unmade bunk. A thin, square brown packet caught the wooden surround and bounced off, on to the wreckage of the weekend papers. He stared at the detritus of financial and personal neglect. 'Responsibility,' he told himself out loud, as he tended to do when he felt an aphorism particularly sage, 'is the ultimate achievement of the terminally unimaginative.'

He pulled on the musty sweater. It smelled of oil and past promise. Then he slithered into the underpants and socks and flopped down on the bench, letters sticking to his bare legs. At his right stockinged foot he saw a knocked-over whisky bottle, a couple of inches of the golden malt still surviving. He picked up the crusted coffee mug, the one with the Pope Paul motif, and poured out the whisky.

'I don't know how it's come to this,' he said out loud again. 'In fact,' he remembered, 'I don't even remember.'

Walnuts have no memory either, he thought, realising the pickling effect of strong drink on the brain had gone further than he imagined. He shuddered slightly, recalling the quantities of brain he had seen, in differing stages of damage and dislocation from the cranium. Marie Curie had kept shards and gobs of her dear departed's precious matter in a pouch on a belt round her waist, having retrieved the useless, if still warm and quivering mess from the gutter after a hansom cab had rolled over her beau's skull and exploded it like a . . . walnut?

The glow of the malt burst in his stomach and he settled in to compose. Memory, he searched for the phrase, is the inevitable and pitiable result of alcohol deprivation. He was beginning his first chuckling toast to himself when the ship-to-shore telephone rang. Let it ring, he thought. Only those you don't want to hear from make the effort to reach you. He felt the familiar tension mount and then, cursing his enslavement, he picked up the receiver, saying nothing, which to those who knew him was a clearer identification than a voice print.

'This is your alarm call.' A voice, an accent that he couldn't place yet which gnawed at the edges of his memory. It was a soft accented voice and the cadences were becoming familiar – and then the line cleared and the static howl cut in. He peered at the mouthpiece, stupefied. Then he got up, moved to the weeping glass of the cabin's main porthole, pulled apart the caked curtains and peeped out like a wronged neighbour. The view was depressingly familiar. And unrevelatory. Nothing but mud flats, rusting metal and the winter sun glowing venomously on the petrol film of the river. He felt a turn in his gut. Panic? He thought about it. It didn't feel so, although after all these years he could accept that he wasn't properly in tune with his feelings. Feelings? a hazily glimpsed shape under the ice.

The Irish voice – it was Irish he realised – knew he hadn't opened his mail. That wasn't possible. It also wasn't possible that he had got through on the line directly, but he had. Alarm call was right. Calm down he counselled himself as he walked round the chart table three times, and a fourth, anti-clockwise, for enhanced luck.

The whisky was beginning to flame the embers of his courage now. He tore open the letters and packets, the bills and unrepeatable offers, the solicitors' letters, the final demands and the rest of the normal coercion of commerce. And debt shall have no dominion. Finally, somehow knowing, the manila, malleable, flat seven-inch cardboard packet, ripping back the gummed flap of the envelope smudged in felt-tipped capitals with his name and address. A record, with a sepia sleeve of men in faded trenchcoats, rifles – Lee Enfields, more like fouling pieces nowadays – and one man, a hat, a fedora at a jaunty angle, cradling a Thompson sub-machine gun. Nothing else. He looked at the record label, in green and orange of course. The Broad Black Brimmer. He stared at the sleeve. The men of 1916 stared back. He walked over to the Dansette, switched the bakelite knob over to 45r.p.m. Scratched the ball of fluff from the needle with a nail, and, making a mental note to run the engine to recharge the battery, he took out the record trepidatiously. A small, oblong scrap of paper fluttered to the floor. He snatched at it, catching it at the third attempt in the wind eddies. A bank pay-in slip, his bank, made out to his account, with ten thousand pounds lettered in blue ink along the dotted line.

Just don't think about it, some old psychic sore told him. The record deck spun. He put on the record and dropped the arm.

. . . but when men claim Ireland's freedom, the one

9

they'll choose to lead them, will wear the broad black brimmer of the IRA . . . Penny whistle, guitar, banjo, a deep, hectoring voice – the rhythm and romance of the death rattle.

And then the years came flooding back – violent, raw and screaming. He put his hands over his ears and slumped foetally into the armchair, for some, arcane, reason remembering a line from James Cameron about the first astronaut – cosmonaut – Yuri Gagarin . . . The first man in space went out of the world as he came into it, with his knees pressed firmly against his chest . . .

MONDAY, 7.15 p.m.

He spent the afternoon constructing plausible scenarios, typing out lengthy hypotheses, only to pull the paper brusquely from the old Underwood, crumple it and start again. He hovered over the telephone. He showered. He shaved. He made the bed, tidied the cabin and as the light went he realised that he hadn't eaten. He was pulling on a denim jacket and deciding on a vindaloo garnished with whisky when the phone rang again. He grabbed it, knocking over a dead glass on the table.

'Eight. In the bar of the Two Brewers in Elgin Avenue,' – the same voice, what was it about the accent that concerned him? – 'the ten thousand is only the start . . .' The line was dead again.

He stared at the buzzing phone, dropped on the chart table and, to quell the mistral feelings, tried to consider his options. The neglected phone began to whine. Take the money and run? A mistake, dangerous, possibly fatal, given the likely source of the cash. The pitch seemed to be rising. He had been fatalistic for years, but ten thousand would go little way to constructing a new identity. With a fair wind, about as far as Calais, he thought. And clearly he couldn't go to the police. Fines, alimony, an outstanding assault charge, failure to answer numerous summonses, they would love to know his whereabouts. The only noise he could hear now was the banshee receiver, octaves higher. He had spent years living outside the law, totally ignoring its remit. A girl, all suppurated passion, had once called him a crook. 'No,' he had replied archly, 'I'm an outlaw.' It was a line from a long-forgotten film. Fix on a minor sore when you're in

11

Ron McKay

terminal pain, he heard himself think. Anyway, he hated
police. All damp clothes and ill-fitting minds. Which left
just one option that he could see. Face what was undoubtedly an elaborate and probably dangerous set-up.

He felt the warmth of exultation tingling in his nerve
ends. Or was it the malt? But, whatever, it felt good
again. It was what had been missing, he appreciated –
danger, the glorious, uplifting adrenalin rush of it. But,
this time, someone else was measuring it out. The narcotic
dose. And, he told himself, be aware that you are also in
less than prime condition.

He picked up the tortured phone and put it back on the
rest, staring into the greasy mirror. Consider yourself.
There was a thickening to the chin, flecks of grey to his
temples – he stared closer at his reflection – but the eyes
still have it, he noted approvingly. Wintry. There was still
no thawing of the soul. He laughed at himself in the filmy
glass. He hadn't been graced with much of one to begin
with. Soul. Remember, he remembered, keep putting
your faith in paranoia.

Then he sat down at the typewriter again and hammered out on the big, round, chipped black keys. 'To
whom it may concern . . .' There was no one to be
concerned, but no matter. 'This morning I received an
IRA record in the post. Together with a note that ten
thousand pounds had been paid into my bank account. I
have been telephoned and told to turn up at the Two
Brewers in Elgin Avenue at 8p.m. I may never know why.
If not, good luck with finding the answer.'

He got up, feeling watched, took the shiny record from
the machine, found the sleeve and the pay-in slip, tucked
the slip inside the sleeve, and then put the pack behind
the paper in the typewriter carriage, as if to stiffen his
message, wondering briefly if he should make a call.
Could you tap a radio phone? It was probably a lot easier,
with a bent bit of wire and a receiver, than getting a

warrant and clamping a plug on a what's-it at the telephone exchange. Not that they bothered with warrants now, of course. But, better be safe and follow the twisted path of paranoia.

Then he went to the head, grabbed a torch and a tin of Vaseline from the cabinet, pulled the donkey jacket from a hook and left the cabin, taking care to switch off all the lights to conserve the battery. Outside in the cockpit he opened the tin, gouged a small lump of the gel which had been used for other conspiratorial things, and filled up the Yale lock, wiping clean the brass ringlet. He smeared a thin sheen of grease on the door handle and, feeling sea damp in his bones, climbed up the weed-covered iron ladder in the darkness and ran down the wet street to the lock-up and the car, apart from the boat, his only other valued possession. His points of reference and departure.

His footsteps ricocheted behind him, along the cobbles, off the walls. He got to the lock-up and the dirty old car pulled up in front of the sprayed, autographed door. He paused for breath, waiting for other steps. Then, taking deep draughts of air, he went down on his knees beside the old Jaguar, feeling the damp tarmac through his trousers and, conscious of the insane spectacle he would be making if there was anyone around to see, he spread-eagled on the road and rolled under the car, switching on the torch to check the chassis. He didn't quite know what he was looking for . . . fuck it, this is what you were supposed to do – but it looked clean. Well, filthy, but undisturbed. No magnets, suspicious bumps, trailing wires. Then he crawled out, brushed himself down, and opened the heavy door of the car. The leather smelled comfortingly uncontaminated. He released the bonnet catch and ducked out to look at the engine. Clear. Then he got back in, pushed in the ignition key, felt his stomach turn in time with the engine which coughed several times and then caught. It was fuelled on neglect and abandonment.

He was sweating, he realised, the wheel was slippery; he rammed into gear and set off. Bar some undiscovered mercury-delay device, or a nearby psychopath with a model aircraft control unit, he was safe. Rather, untouched. He felt good. He felt the present recede in his exhaust and he briefly wondered why, through everything, he should have kept the car, maintained the payments on the lock-up. And after rejecting notions of talismans, style anti-statements, convinced himself, or at least told himself, that it was just another means of exit.

MONDAY, 7.52 p.m.

The Two Brewers seemed to glow atomically in the wispy damp air. He drove past and parked the car two streets away, sure he hadn't been followed. He walked briskly to the pub, glancing behind, keeping wide on the pavement, paces away from ambush. Inside, the decor seemed to be fashioned from melted acrylic and formica, the carpet glowed a dangerous green in a sodium light which brought out bilous tinges in the faces of the patrons. Or maybe it was the beer. There was a new fashion in architecture, he thought, post-holocaust chic. He ordered a double whisky and looked about.

Clearly there is one thing certainly to be concluded, he told himself, my Irishman is no aesthete, given the choice of venue. He scanned the faces, searching for some tell-tale characteristic of conspiracy, for eyes that avoided his. But then they all did. He sat down on a scarlet plastic bench seat which farted under his buttocks, back to the wall, facing the door. By ten past eight he had finished his first drink, and was trying to order another from the bored and puffy barmaid who mouthed silently, almost penitentially, to the jukebox, her only visible sign of a functioning nervous system.

'I drink to forget,' he said as she dropped the measures from the optic into his used glass.

'What?' she said disinterestedly.

'I forget,' he said and spun a five pound note into the puddled bar.

'What?' she said, this time with what he was pleased to note was the faintest tinge of anger.

'No matter. It was a joke. I wanted to be a Scottish

15

stand-up comedian once, but someone else beat me to the goalkeeper's jersey.' He smiled pleasantly at her, lifting the glass from the bar. She slapped the change down. The bar rippled. 'That's what I hate about progress,' – he had noticed with hideous fascination that a money spider was scampering across her sprayed confection of a hairstyle – 'with the old money, pound notes, it used to be that at the end of an evening you could wring out your pocket and pass a very comatose Sunday on the residue.' Her anger was now visible, burning through the rouge.

As he turned away, he noticed that he was moving lightly on his feet, that he was enjoying himself.

By eight thirty the second whisky was almost gone, and he was still alone. He began to smile inwardly, and then started to chuckle, aware that he probably appeared a doolally. An old toast had just popped into his head. 'Here's tae us? Wha's like us? Damn few and they're aw deid.' He drained his glass '. . . to the dead,' he muttered.

The tide of progressive architecture had not reached the toilet, which still reeked of the passed, from a thousand loins. He looked at the predictable graffiti. Why hadn't anyone done a coffee table book on it, he considered? Sure Norman Mailer had put together some typically macho frivolity about New York spray paint vandals artistry on subway trains. But then anyone who had written an essay called 'The White Negro' had to be seriously questionable. Particularly when, driven no doubt by the moral certainty of a pint and a half of Jim Beam, Mailer couldn't even take out his eight-stone wife with a .44, or was it a six-inch switchblade? He drank to the puzzlement. The best bit of graffiti he had seen was two carefully pencilled rectangles and the legend, 'balls to Picasso'. Clever, but it would have been even more subtle if the pencilling had been in blue. He considered the blue veining of his penis as the steam rose.

When he got back to the table there was a fresh glass at his place, and through the clear honey liquid he could see a folded piece of paper under the base. He moved aside the drink gingerly, like a chess piece. 'SORRY,' the note said, in block capitals 'WE COULDN'T MEET. RETURN HOME IMMEDIATELY. WATCH THE 9P.M. NEWS. BE IN TOUCH.'

Well, he thought in growing elation, he, they, are not infallible. It was, what?, two years since he toe-ended the television from the bookcase over some great electronic affront, probably the sight of the prime minister patting the head of the nation, or something really important, like Partick Thistle losing at home to Kilmarnock. He pocketed the paper, picked up the glass and went to the bar. 'Who ordered this?' he asked the barmaid.

'I've had enough of you and your jokes,' she said. Her ironic smile, he thought, has all the characteristics of some dreadful gastric disorder.

'Who?'

'You've had too many. Who else? You! No one else is drinking whisky in here.' The corners of her mouth arched mirthlessly and she moved away.

It was four minutes to nine when he stepped down on deck, the old boat lurching now on the tidal water. One of the drawbacks of living on a boat was that you couldn't make an unannounced arrival (and, often, you had to wear a lifejacket to go to the toilet). No point in the old burglar's gambit of walking up stairs, legs widespread, treading on the steps only at the junctions with wall and bannister so they didn't creak. He didn't even need to check the Vaseline evidence, wedges of light bled evidentially from windows and door into the night. He ducked down into the cockpit beside the hatch and listened for movement, and heard none. The loudest noise, over the creaking of the shifting wood, was his heart racing. In the dim distance a car horn sounded. Then he put the key in the lock, turned it ten degrees and pushed open the door, still from his crouched position. Nothing. He considered rolling fast into the cabin, but what was the point, he was unarmed. Anyway, there were six wooden stairs down. He'd probably break his back. He peeped quickly round the door from three feet up and saw on the table in the centre of the room a television, silent but flickering, casting pools of changing colour onto the typewriter beside it.

What is wrong with the entirely reasonable urge, he asked himself, to run screaming into the night? But he breathed deeply through his nostrils and moved down into the boat, testing each footfall with a cautious touch. For some incongruous reason, the thought of the drain on the battery swam into his head. Ridiculous.

The place was empty, he could feel that. No untoward odours, no disturbances in the atmosphere. Just the silent witness to the breach, the television. He watched the ridiculously overblown computer graphics herald the news and found the volume switch. God knows how much life was left in the battery. Or your own, he thought sombrely.

'Good evening,' the announcer intoned earnestly – news presentation depended on ersatz earnestness – 'news is just coming in of a large explosion in a public house in west London. No one has yet claimed responsibility. And according to first reports, the bomb went off just minutes before we went on the air at the Two Brewers in Elgin Avenue. A telephone caller, using a known code word, gave police a warning. Just seconds after the building was cleared a large explosion devastated it and the force of the explosion also shattered dozens of windows in the vicinity. Several people are being treated in hospital for shock and minor cuts and bruises. We will bring you more news later in the programme when we have it.'

Through the roaring in his head he heard the jangle of the telephone. He snatched the receiver, knowing intuitively who it was, and said 'Fuck you' into it.

'And good evening to you too,' the Irish voice said

18

mockingly. 'Now, obviously you now know the serious-
ness of our intent. And I'm sure I don't need to tell you
under whose seat the bomb went off?

'And that mouth of yours . . . tut, tut . . . well, I nearly
said it would get you into trouble one day. But it has. The
barmaid will certainly remember you, won't she now? I
should say that even as we speak she's sifting the mugshots
and helping the police put together a photofit of the
leading suspect. You. The joking Jock. The comedian of
carnage *The Sun* will probably call you.'

'What do you want?' He was fixatedly looking at the
television, which was now following the progress of a
duck on a skateboard. It seemed apposite, somehow.
'Why me?' he said.

'Why not?' And still, annoyingly, he could not place
the lilt and what it was about it that disturbed him. Silence
ached. 'There's no need to tell you that you are in the
gravest of situations. You are known to the police. You
have suddenly come into a windfall, the source of which
can be traced, with just enough difficulty to be convincing,
to a Belfast bank account which has exceedingly dubious
connections. That will provide the security services with
all the circumstantial proof they need. Which is more than
enough for them to convict you, without the unnecessary
recourse to the courts.'

He could feel the smile, the triumph in the voice.
'How long do you think you've got?' Another pause for
effect. 'Well, you have precisely as long as it takes me to
decide when to make the anonymous call about your
whereabouts.'

'Why me?' he heard himself say again. The TV picture
was now jumping with action and insanity, an outside
broadcast from Elgin Avenue, smoke rising from debris,
flashing police lights, people in yellow overjackets sifting
the rubble and, in front of the wreckage for maximum
dramatic editorial effect – God preserve us from the

sanguinity of the BBC – a reporter delivering his breath-less, concerned, glib, harshly-lit piece-to-camera.

He smelled the remembered tang of smoke. He could see dismembered, torn bodies, gutted buildings, the hooded corpses on bleak wasteground where even final dignity eluded them and dogs nosed at their resting, twisted blackened cars, fragments of flesh on telephone wires. And always, the tears, the wailing.

'You are necessary, that's all. You have little time. But I repeat myself. Pack a bag now and check into the Admiral Hotel in Lancaster Gate. There's a reservation in the name of Emmett, as in Robert. And I'll be in touch . . .' Again the deafeningly empty burr in his ear.

He sat down, throwing the phone on the table, its tone changing to a high-pitched warning scream. He turned off the television, making a mental note of things to pack, there weren't many, then caught sight of his last testament in the typewriter, the note for posterity. At the end, the words erratically hammered, an additional paragraph had been added: 'In life you make your own luck. Otherwise . . .' and circling the line, in red ink, was a perfectly drawn noose.

Opposite him an old man debated with himself, the slurry from the argument making a sheen on his chin. After every muttered phrase he shook his head vehemently, a punctuation rictus in some undiscoverable conflict. Cities are awash with lunacy, he thought.

He looked around the carriage, studying all the faces, trying to pick out his man. Man? It didn't follow that it would be a man. It didn't follow that he was being followed. He had taken some fairly elaborate steps to avoid it, switching trains, jumping on and off buses. A bicycle, he thought, was the surest method of avoiding surveillance. It was the perfect vehicle for the environ-mentally-conscious evader. Too slow to be trailed by car or motorbike, too fast to be followed on foot, perfect for avoiding motorised shadows – and you could go up on pavements, across grass, through crevices and the smallest hole in any net. So why didn't you see this in movies? Bond on a bike. He began to chuckle, answering his question; tension cannot survive titters.

The old man opposite smiled back at him in a conspiratorial way, then snapped his head down into his turmoil.

Now a young woman was moving through the standing passengers, bumping apologetically as the train rocked in the bends. 'Excuse me' she said to him, pushing a wrinkled card briefly under his eyes. She had a pleasant, guileless face, clean of make-up, with a dust of freckles round her nose and eyes, her head framed by a rough woollen headscarf. The smile was serene. The conclusive mark of a spiritual casualty, he thought, selling sanctuary. She produced a collecting can. 'No,' he said, shaking his head. The smile didn't splinter as she moved away.

Well, he mused, whoever it was wouldn't be black, which ruled out half the passengers. There hadn't yet been a black Volunteer. The odd Protestant, very odd, an American or two. And certainly at least one Scotsman.

When the tube got to Victoria he pushed impatiently and deliberately through the slow-moving crowd in the arcing underground corridor – one such person is an inconsiderate, a second is definitely a follower of the inconsiderate, he thought. Looking back he was reassured to see that no one was elbowing through the swell after him.

On the escalator he looked back, trying to catch a familiar face. Fruitless. He went through the barrier and trotted to the top of the short flight of stairs.

The photo booth was empty and apparently functioning. He pulled the curtain shut behind him and spun down the rotating seat – the average British traveller was five revolutions smaller than him he noted – and randomly twisted the picture selection dial. He fished in his pocket for a pound coin and peered out through a slash in the curtain for anyone stationary outside and studying the booth. The coin dropped down and the machine gurgled. The passers-by seemed calculatedly unseeing, in a bemused sort of concentration, looking around and up at the VDUs and departure boards. There were the usual groups of backpackers, the stumbling winos with their hands out, the purposeful business men and the snaking luggage trolley, but no observers.

A bright explosion in his peripheral vision brought him whirling round to catch his reflection in the mirror. His unguarded expression, menacing was the only way to describe it, unsettled him momentarily. Well, he told the mirror, what would a watcher make of this. It certainly wasn't the action of a man in a hurry. He tried to look more composed, less malevolent as the other flashes went off.

He waited outside the booth for the prints to arrive. Was there a negative, he wondered? Would additional prints be produced in evidence? Or published posthumously? He banished the train of thought. The green walls of the booth felt cool on his palms behind his back as he gazed around. Finally he felt the strip drop down into the basin, picked it out by its edges and there he glistened, quadruply, four frames; in the first pose, looking startled, in semi-profile, almost looking back over his shoulder. Very symbolic. In the other three, he was pleased to see, he looked merely thuggish. He began to walk to the station exit, cupping the pictures in his right hand and shaking the strip to dry it off.

It is ridiculously easy to get a false passport in Britain. To get someone else's passport. What he had done, in the thickets of one of his periodic bouts of psychic disorder when he knew that only a new identity could save him, or at least preserve him from the financial posse, was to go to the newspaper library at Colindale and search through the bound and yellowing copies of local newspapers – the *Hackney Gazette* had been one – for the death notices of infants who would have been, had they lived, around his age. He smiled to himself. In Britain the dead can truly travel.

Winter, William Edward. Called to rest on Sunday, July 3, 1952 aged 11 months. Beloved only child of John and Claire. Funeral Service St Aidan's. Wednesday July 6 at 3 p.m.

This was his parallel identity. He had checked back to the earlier birth notice, thirty-year newsprint staining his fingers, and then he had gone to the registration office on the corner of Kingsway and, armed with the name and place and date of birth he picked up a copy of the birth certificate, the bona fides of a new identity. Then with that, two pictures, a forged endorsement signature on the back and ten minutes filling out a form, he had his passport credentials. The only possible snag could have been that the child was already on a parent's passport, but there was no cross-checking like that, he knew. And anyway, babes in arms of working-class parents did not nip off on package tours to Benidorm in the austerity Fifties, when the stamps were on ration cards, not passports.

Winter is coming, he thought, as he left the station and crossed over to the Barclays bank on the corner. He had a safety deposit box there. And a new identity locked inside. Then he would take the tube to Bond Street and the short walk to those very obliging people in the American embassy who provided you with the visa free, and in six hours, provided you weren't some international terrorist, former member of the Communist Party or dope fiend which, he supposed, in almost all qualifications, he probably was. William Edward Winter, however, unless he had been a terrifically precocious child, was none of these.

*

23

Ron McKay

He had checked into the hotel after dark, buttoned into a large overcoat and wearing glasses which threw out the planes of his face. The night clerk had been bored, barely sparing him a glance. He had used room service for his meals, making sure he was in the bathroom when the waiter arrived, running the water in an attempt to disguise his voice timbre. All that would be remembered about him, he hoped, would be that he was a hygiene fetishist. To minimise his exposure to the front desk he even carried the room key with him when he went out.

The lift door wheezed open and he walked a few paces across the faded patterned carpet. He unlocked the room door, spinning round it quickly and throwing on the light switch. It was an anonymous room – he hoped he melded in – with pink hues, plastic noise-excluding curtains, and a TV and mini-bar. On top of the bar a vase of paper flowers, camellias, somehow only added to the utilitarian decor. The double bed had been made, from the tangle of damp sheets which he had fought out of in the morning. On the maroon counterpane a tabloid newspaper lay like a window from obscurity. As he moved towards it he first saw the huge headline 'FIND THIS EVIL BOMBER,' with an artist's identikit drawing abutting a photograph of the embers of the Two Brewers. The drawing, close eyes, vicious mouth, two-inch forehead, he could say with relief and unaccustomed modesty, bore not even the slightest – slighting perhaps – resemblance. He picked up the paper, and absently noticed a package under it. Quickly he read through the story, spirits lifting with each snappy one-sentence paragraph. There was no trail to him. Yet. On an inside page the barmaid, Kate Marshall, spread large over three columns (and she needed them), gave her account of their meeting and, for some dark reason, he laughed raucously. She had been just as uninterested in him as her manner had suggested. The conversation she described, and his appearance, bore very little relation to reality.

24

He picked up the unaddressed manila envelope. It was weighty, sellotaped round the seals, stiff and about half an inch thick. He spun it between two index fingers, shook it gently and squeezed it, feeling for any internal mechanisms. 'Oh, well,' he said, and he tore it open. Money, dollar bills, fluttered onto the bedspread. He shook out the contents onto the bed. A quick riffling count showed more than 2000 dollars. An airline ticket, an open return, first class, to New York, in the name of T. Gale. He riffled through the mess of paper on the ribbed pink bedspread and turned over a two-inch square cellophane packet packed with cloudy white crystals. Cocaine probably. And another passport. British again.

He picked it up, shovelled aside the expensive mess, lay down on the bed and examined the passport, opening at a valid business visa for the United States. He flicked to the inside page facing her Brittanic majesty's requests and requirements and saw that he was Thomas Gale. Winter. Gale. He smiled. More identities than Professor Moriarty. But when he turned the page his mirth gagged. There he was, in what was clearly a formal passport pose, gazing out. Neatly shaven, wearing a white shirt and tie. The picture could have been taken any time in the last two years. But that was impossible. It hadn't been. Nevertheless, this was no doppel-ganger, there was no doubt that the picture was of him. But it just couldn't be. He started to shiver, staring at himself, glossy and embossed, looking back.

The ringing of the telephone in his left ear brought him back. He swung round to sit on the bed, knowing before he answered who it would be. Who it had to be.

'Yes.'

'Hello,' the amused voice said.

'Well, the candy man.' He picked up the cellophane packet.

'What?'

'Nose candy.' He tore an edge of the plastic in his

teeth, a fine milky mist sprayed on to his crutch. Cradling the phone between his shoulder and chin he licked his right index finger, plunged it into the packet, and then he licked off the deposit. The numbing metallic taste of cocaine. Against his shirt he could feel the voice drumming.

'No,' he said at last. 'No drugs.'

'A moral aversion Mr Doherty . . .' The address jolted him. It was the first time in years he had been called by his proper name.

'God,' he said, 'you are pompous.'

'You'll be our go-between,' the voice continued. 'There are some gentlemen in the States, of Mediterranean heritage shall we say, who are anxious to meet you, to do business. We have some rather excellent Peruvian connections who can supply their needs. And they have the wherewithal to provide for ours. Perfect synergy, don't you think?'

'Why me?'

'Oh. A certain qualifying experience. An unknown face. Whatever you like.'

'And if it doesn't work out, I'm the one that gets shafted.'

'Well, indeed.' The mellow Irish laugh made his teeth set.

He looked round at the striped confines of his room, wallpaper like prison bars he thought. 'No.'

'But yes. You'll be paid well, you won't be called on again. You'll be set up financially . . .'

'For what . . .? I have what I need.'

'I can't even countenance the alternative. You'd die, of course. Slowly. But first, as an earnest of intent, we'd probably arrange something unpleasant for someone close.'

He sighed slowly. 'There is no one close.'

'There is a girl in Belfast still, that we both know . . .' He let the silence hang. 'Our reach is long, our will unremitting. We could arrange for you to be turned over to the others, to an outfit like . . . like the Shankill Butchers. Remember them. I'm sure you wouldn't relish your last meal being your own cock . . . The grave's a fine and private place. But none, I think, do there embrace.' A sneering laugh. 'Marvell.'

'I do. I'm awestruck.'

'Andrew Marvell.'

'I'll bet you do a rousing graveside oration over your dead Volunteers.' His funeral, he thought, would be the only one where the corpse outnumbers the mourners. 'Well,' he said, breathing out resignedly, 'so long to the inglorious arts of peace.'

'You do know your Marvell. "The Horatian Ode Upon Cromwell's Return From Ireland", isn't it? Very apt. The call to the youth of England to reject poetry and take up arms. Just. If unlikely. So, be on the plane. In the meantime, don't go out again. Stay in our sight.'

He felt a surge of elation, they were not infallible, he had given them the slip this afternoon.

WEDNESDAY, 9.20 p.m.

The foot patrol flattened round the corner into the Falls, the lead man dropping down into a crouch in a shop doorway, bringing up his SLR rifle against the bright and blank yellowed window. The rain was on again, gusted into swirling clouds by the wind. Then the three other soldiers came past, the last man shuffling backwards, squinting back down the dark road for a shadow movement, a curtain shimmer, a giveaway chink of light.

Mary Cavanagh saw the patrol ahead and automatically crossed the street. Falls Road was quiet, just one black taxi coming down from Andersonstown which flashed its light at her as it came past. She pulled up the collar of her leather jacket, the water was already making cold rivulets down her back and her black hair was pasted in abandoned tails to her face. The file she carried under her arm was now sodden. She unzipped her jacket and shuddered as she put the damp paper against her dry blouse.

Then she heard the shout and the running behind her, but she continued to walk, with her head pressed down against the weather. She felt a hand on her shoulder and she was spun against a wall.

'What's that inside your jacket?' He was an officer, she could have told that from his public school accent, even if she hadn't known the rank from the pips on his epaulette. He was very young. And on edge. Good, she thought. His sergeant was a pace behind him, his finger, she noticed, curled inside the trigger guard of his rifle. The two other soldiers had moved wide to give cover and were crouched into smaller targets.

'Open it.' His fingers moved towards her throat, to the zip.

'It's only a file,' she said. 'Papers. Private.'

'Open.'

She unzipped the jacket and handed over the wet file. The lieutenant tore apart the card covers, droplets of water dripping from his cap badge onto the typewritten sheets. Over his shoulder another black taxi came past, headlights hooded.

'Sinn Fein,' he said, looking up from the papers. He was about her height she noticed. She said nothing. He jammed the papers back inside the folder and waited for a response. Finally he said: 'Name and address.' She guessed him to about twenty-three, the same age as her brother. The countervailing force, she thought. But she gave her name and address in what she hoped was a tone of insouciant scorn. The sergeant repeated it into a hand-held wireless.

'Sinn Fein,' the lieutenant said again.

'It's a political party,' she said mockingly. 'But we don't go in for kissing babies, so you'll be all right there, son.'

She noticed him tense and she steeled herself not to flinch at the blow. But, instead he put his face into hers – she almost laughed at the incongruous odour of diluted aftershave – 'Slag,' he said 'slag.'

'They all are,' the sergeant added, further off.

'Turn round and put your hands against the wall. And spread your legs. You'll be used to that.'

'Look,' she said, trying to defuse the moment, 'I make it a rule never to carry Semtex when I'm wearing trousers, it just accentuates the panty line.' But she turned round, put her palms against the rough brick and opened her legs. The sergeant slung the rifle over his shoulder and began to frisk her body, his hands running down her chest and cupping her breasts. 'Just don't press the nipples,' she said into the wall, 'or you'll blow us all to kingdom come.'

The hands moved down below her waist, grabbing

29

roughly at her crutch. 'Will that keep you going until you get back home?' she said as his palms ran on down her legs. 'Assuming you get back home.' She felt fingers dig into her shoulder, but as she turned the officer said 'Sergeant,' and he relaxed his grip. The sergeant was chubby, mustachioed, jaundiced in the yellow street light.

'Can I go?'

'When the check is complete.'

But she sensed that they were now anxious to be off. Too long in one place. Did they feel in their backs an Armalite bead?

She heard static from the hand set. 'Yes,' said the sergeant 'black hair. The address checks.'

'Don't bother calling round. Me ma doesn't let me go out with Brits.'

'Sir,' the sergeant was saying 'her brother is Brendan Cavanagh.'

'Brendan Cavanagh. Well, well.' The lieutenant was smirking. 'By the time he gets out PIRA will be issuing him with a walking stick, not a gun.' He had a gold filling, she noticed, in the grin.

At least he's safe, she thought, and then, God forgive me. 'When you Brits get out you'll be issued with shovels so you can take the rest of your army back with you.' He grabbed her by the mouth, fiercely, his face so close it was out of focus. She could taste blood on her tongue. 'You disgust me,' he said. 'You look like a woman but you're an animal. Animal.' He released the hold.

She tried not to show the pain. And she thought she might say that with his public school background he'd probably be closer to the animal kingdom than the opposite sex. But she smiled bloodily instead.

'On your way.' He handed her the file.

She zipped it into her jacket, knowing that its colour would bleed into her blouse. But she didn't care. At the corner of Leeson Street she looked back. But the patrol had gone, or at least merged into the monochrome background.

She saw him immediately she came through the door, but she passed her eyes over him and walked to the bar. The low ceiling, the blue-grey blear through the smoke compressed her longing. The Jameson's was on the bar as she fished in her tight right hand pocket for the change. Her eyes stung and watered, but she blamed it on the atmosphere.

'Ta,' she said, running her fingers through her hair. And she thought, it's interesting how gestures are greater signifiers than speech.

Unzipping her jacket again, she noticed, as she removed the file, the damp ochre stain on her chest, on the blouse. The old silk was irrevocably stained, even on the fluting round the pearl buttons, touching her grandmother's stitching. She shivered involuntarily and made her way towards the table, skirting the explosive arms, the forlorn legs and the man with the slick-shiny hair in a private dance of his own. Danny had his head down over a paper, pretending he hadn't noticed her. The young, she thought, should have less of a sense of themselves. She touched his hair and he looked up. She tried to smile, and was aware of the pain. 'I know,' she said 'bee-stung lips.'

'Who?'

'It doesn't matter. A Brit.'

'Is that all?'

'Praise the marks and pass the ammunition,' she said, reaching for her drink. The glass touched her bottom lip, which felt puffy and vaguely foreign. 'I'll never pout properly again . . . And as for blow-jobs . . .' The alcohol stung her mouth.

'The regiment?' he said. And she wondered how it was

that he could take over her hurt and transform it into his mortal wound.

'Oh . . . the Eton rifles.' He had introduced her to The Jam, although she was more of a contemporary, and the first time she heard the song she had thought it was about eating trifles.

He began to smile, his coal eyes for the first time looking at her. 'I know them. That's the mob that wear stripes on their bums, not their arms.'

'The very same. And they don't live in barracks' – she took another sip of the whisky for dramatic effect – 'they just camp.'

They both smiled, at ease. In the background, singing had swollen with the band, a disjointed five-piece led by an accordionist and an intense singer who coat-trailed the struggle, moving effortlessly from Sean South and 1916 to The Boys Behind The Wire, with barely a stout gulp for sustenance. 'Jesus,' she said, 'we better get out now. In half an hour we'll be waist-deep in British corpses.'

'If the Second Battalion had as many volunteers as songsters,' he said, picking up her file from the table as she drained her glass 'we could ignore the Brits and declare war on China.'

'I know,' she answered. 'And then half an hour later you'd be needing another one.' She felt awkward in her pause, a recognition that he wasn't as bright. 'Like me and men, really,' she said into the gap but he stopped and she knew she had to soothe him. 'Chinese meal. Always at war, is what I meant. Or, the sweet and sour of love.'

Danny slapped the file at her. She caught it in a cradling motion. 'No need to ask,' she said as he led her by the hand 'what's on the menu now . . . origami?'

Mary lay awake. She could hear the movements below and the hissing of muffled voices, occasionally the higher sound of a child's voice and the squeak of chairs and the clatter of breakfast. Danny was still asleep, his hair petrified still by her longing tugs. In the night he had shrugged down the bed covers on his side and although the room was cold, there was a film of moisture on his torso. On his stomach she could see the white puckered mark of the bullet, a stigmata of the conflict. She touched the scar lightly and he grunted, curling away into a tighter ball. He had told her about it, an internal feud with the Officials, the Stickies. There he had been lying on his bed at his parents in the early morning when he heard shouting at the bottom of the stairs and then running, coming for him he knew. Somehow he had stumbled out of bed and had got himself against the door, 'bollock naked', just as the first one was coming through, with a sawn-off shotgun in a gloved hand. He had hit the door hard, jamming the arm and the gun inside and the screams and curses outside. Then one of the others – there had been four he later learned – fired through the door with a short, a pistol. If it had been anything of a heavier calibre he would have been dead. Then, he guessed, he must have slumped down against the door, semi-conscious, a dead weight against them. And they had panicked and run away. 'Fuckin' amateurs,' he had called them.

She had told him then that she didn't want to know any more, about his past or where he went. And there had been no more. He came and went as he pleased. They went days, weeks without seeing each other. His absences, never spelled out, were to do with the Movement. Whether he was active still she didn't know. But when he wasn't there and she heard news of an incident, a shooting, a bombing or a bank robbery, she wondered. And when he wasn't there she worried; although, of course, she never told him.

Sure, she could have found out exactly his rank and what he did, but she preferred not to know. When others started on about him she shut them up. But when she walked out with him she knew, from the deferential body language of passers-by, that he was respected, feared, that he was obviously a senior member of the army.

There is, she thought, in the communication of gestures and glances, the muttered asides, a street language of oppression which is without vowels and consonants, which is almost telepathic, and which is certainly indecipherable for an outsider. Constant surveillance, the high-technology war had forged it. And it could never be cracked.

She got quietly out of bed, shivering as her feet landed on the linoleum and the raw chill of the room enveloped her. She dressed, tutting at the dried stain on the blouse, like a mapwork of dried, washed-out blood, and then went downstairs into the now quiet living room where a fire burned in the grate, the dishes still lay on the table but the occupants – who they were she didn't know – had gone. She looked round the small room, the walls with the Long Kesh decorations – the calendar painting of a hooded volunteer with rocket launcher at attention, the wooden memorial plaque to the dead of the Second Battalion, their names picked out on a tricolour in silver – and the ubiquitous crucifix. On the table, a boiled kettle still steamed. She noticed the newspaper, *The Irish Press*, and she picked it up, idly scanning the front page, 'Police are anxious to interview . . . in connection with Tuesday's bombing of the Two Brewers public house . . .' There would be panic in England now, fears of a new campaign. She smiled to herself. But inside she felt a deep chill which she couldn't explain and she clasped her arms round herself and then moved to the fire to poke at it with a long toasting tong from the grate.

NEW YORK

The jet was in a holding pattern over the city. As were his thoughts. The only way he could fly now was in a state of suspension – he smiled at the unconscious irony – induced by large draughts of alcohol and a stern, if somewhat erring, concentration on in-flight movies, MOR music through the ears and trash novels. He was by now only mildly drunk and he had pulled out the earphones when the pilot, an earnest mid-Westerner, had cut into the Sixties revival channel to tell passengers that they could listen in to the landing chat between plane and ground control. He would rather, he thought, that catastrophe was presaged only by an unexpected plummet, the stomach hitting the mouth, not the hysterical mounting of voices in crackly stereo.

He was surprised to find that his fear of flying had receded to a mere manageable terror. Perhaps it was finally the triumph of rational thought. He thought about it. No, his fear was entirely rational. When he had travelled constantly the tremors had built until finally, full-scale terror set in on the flight – it was more of an escape – out of Beirut at the height of the civil war, when the Middle East Airways airliner had skidded out of the airport in one of the periodic, unexplained lulls in the fighting, banked furiously to outdistance the small arms fire and the threat of SAMs, and then levelled off to passenger whoops and claps and grateful handshakes. He was ashamed to notice that his teeth were chattering uncontrollably. The hardened, unfazeable war photographer had to bite on the sick bag to stop the rattle. Embarrassing. Since then it had been elaborate and tissuey excuses to avoid flying. And when there had been no alternative he had simply relied on high-octane alcohol. Others would time their flights, arrival times, compute time zones and jet-lag effect. His measurement was the whisky quotient. Glasgow from London, about four hundred miles, was half a bottle away. Which meant that to New York he should be insensible by Newfoundland, where they knew about these things. But here he was, gazing down the Statue of Liberty's cleavage, with only a mildly muzzy vision.

The jumbo banked once more, he slopped on to his Ivy League neighbour again, and the plane began the approach run. He closed his eyes and settled back in the seat. Only immigration control now. He felt fatalistic. At least capture would put an end to it all. At Heathrow he had shuffled up the short queue unable to decide whether he actually wanted to be picked out. But there had been only a cursory glance at the fake passport and although on the long walk along the moving metal corridor to the plane his back tingled, anticipating the heavy touch of Special Branch, he boarded uneventfully and the 747 had eventually lumbered out into the gathering darkness and struggled into the air.

The jolt and the scream of engines in reverse thrust brought him back. As the plane taxied up to the TWA terminal with its long, round arching tunnel which, he thought, was like walking into the gullet of some giant, earth bound bird, he recalled the last conversation and the instructions. Check into the Dartford Hotel off Times Square. There is a reservation. Act like a tourist for a couple of days until you are contacted, his mocking Irishman had said.

Tourist. It was the accent, he thought, what he probably said was terrorist.

*

Why do their officials dress like cops and ours like bankers? He was looking down at the balding head of a middle-aged man in a dark blue uniform who was, in turn, looking down at Gale, on the passport.

How long was his stay? Less than a month. His resources? More than sufficient. The man clipped the immigration form to the visa page and stamped the passport. 'Enjoy your stay.'

'Yes.'

He took the subway into town, the train for the plane, which was marked out from the other rolling stock by having graffiti only on the exterior. The presence of the large cops with loosely holstered howitzers was a powerful disincentive to underground art. He got off at Times Square and went into the neon daylight of sex bars and cinemas, with pimps and prostitutes in dark doorways and glittering cars, wider than goalmouths, cruising the circuit. The Dartford was one of the warren of hotels which serviced the burrowing and beavering of the area. His room was surprisingly clean – he had expected to find the bed still warm. He tipped the large black man with the blank eyes five dollars. 'Take care,' the man, said, 'which means, lock the door.'

He took off his shoes, lay down on the bed and the sounds from below washed over him: the raucous, competing music, the far-off hullabaloo of a police siren, the undecipherable jabber of street talk. Tomorrow, he told himself, I will submerge. And then sleep closed over him.

It was still dark when he woke. It was tomorrow for him, but morning in America, as some president had put it. His head was sore and his shoulder ached from where he had lain on it. He looked at his watch, calculated the time difference. It was now 6a.m. Probably. He spun the hands on his watch to local time. Then he undressed wearily, washed and shaved, took out a clean shirt and a pair of jeans from his travelling bag, found his wallet in the discarded crumpled jacket on the chair, slipped it into his back pocket and pulled out a leather jerkin from the rumple of his packing.

In the rain and the streetlights the city looked glazed. In the water, another reflected city. Promises of the most unlikely sexual pleasures shimmered in the puddles. He began to walk aimlessly, collar drawn up against the gentle drizzle. In doorways and alleys, in disintegrating cardboard boxes, the comatose drunks, the homeless, the diseased of the alternative city were rousing. The light was beginning to come up and New York was drowsily coming to in the city that never sleeps.

He was walking uptown. Manhattan island was spreading. He sensed he could smell grass from the park, and not at this hour the hand-rolled stuff. The buildings were pricked by lighted windows and the clamour was building, the thrum of engines and the clanking of garbage cans in echoey back courts. Somewhere in the garment district, where the peddle of machinery had already begun, he went into a coffee shop. The white lettering on the window for the three-dollar breakfast was already criss-crossed by rivulets of condensation.

'We got eggs as you like 'em.' The short-order cook had meat hock arms and a blue sprouting jowl.

'Just coffee, please. No cream.'

'English, huh?'

'Partly.' He couldn't be bothered explaining his convoluted ethnic origin. 'I live there.'

Meat hocks splashed coffee into a chipped white mug and slopped in milk anyway, then wiped up the steaming spots from the glass counter with the end of his apron.

'Buddy, over here we're all partly. Partly Jew, Polack, Italian, Irish,' – he ran out of nations – 'you name it. Mongrels, that's us.'

'I'll remember that.'

'Sure.' He was looking round to another customer who had come in. 'Have a nice day.'

Doherty moved into the farthest corner of the room, to a table hard up against a wall of studded glass and browning sellotaped pictures of baseball players, with peaked caps and chubby grins and brilliantined temples. The coffee burnt his tongue. He winced.

'I'd kiss it better. But these days, with HIV, you never know.'

The voice was coming from over his shoulder. He put the cup down on the table and looked round. She couldn't have been more than twenty, with huge black-lined eyes, (he looked intently, ritually for drug signs – the comfort of strangers had to be chemically-induced) and small white hands coming out of a wallowing dark coat, cupping a mug of coffee, sitting at the adjoining table. He hadn't noticed her. She sniffed noisily.

'Look, no offence . . .' She was wiping her nose with the back of a hand '. . . two's company, but one's cheaper.'

'I don't fuck for money.' She smiled unabashedly. 'Try me on fame. Or highballs.'

She was smiling, staring into his face, staring him down. 'I'm sorry. A suspicious foreigner in a far city. Sorry. And it's too early for highballs.'

'Yeah? What time's that?' She had picked up her coffee and was moving towards his table. He thought, overwhelmed by the coat, as she sat down. 'My real name's Leaf – you know, Californian flower-power parents, Children of God missionaries – but everyone calls me Lee.'

'Everyone called me Crippen.'

'Come again?'

'He was a famous English murderer. A doctor.' Her eyes narrowed. 'But I'm perfectly harmless,' he added quickly. 'My real name, I am embarrassed to admit, is Jeremiah Habbakuk Doherty – parents Scottish religious maniacs. I used to be called Doc – '

'As in – ' she put the first two fingers of each hand up against her ears, curled back her upper lip ' – what's up, Doc?'

'Exactly. I was a pretty mean football player. Soccer. I specialised in amputatory tackles. So one afternoon, after I had seriously interfered with the ambulatory functions of some poor wretch, a spectator shouted out "Doc fuckin' Crippen more like." It stuck. Except I dropped the fucking.'

'That's a pity,' she said. He noticed her perfect white teeth in the smile. And, he thought, it's a long time since I've been discomfited.

'What do you do?' He said, moving across the silence. She smiled. 'Work at, I meant.'

'Well, I was studying drama. Stanislavski. Method. You know, imagine you're a plum falling off a tree. Bullshit. Also the tutor was a dork. Who was working his way through the female students – male, too probably. Did Monroe have to put up with some menopausal fat asshole putting his great hairy gorilla paws up her jersey each morning in the name of art I asked myself? Probably. But fuck that. Before that I was travelling.'

'After the was. The is. What now?'

'Well. I could tell you that I had a part in a small off-off-Broadway play, which is true. But I guess you'd realise that doesn't pay the rent. So, I sell drugs.'

She looked levelly at him and smiled. Then she wiped her nose again, caught what she was doing – 'It's a cold. Honest.'

'You're kidding.'

'No. I'll show you the prescription.'

'You know what I mean,' he said. 'You're dangerously honest.'

'It's the flower-power parents in me. I figure you're not a cop.'

Assuredly, he thought. 'What makes you so sure?'

'You didn't proposition me as soon as you walked in. And I heard you with the Hulk. You sounded bemused.'

'I only got in a few hours ago.'

'Besides which, I am clean. No chemical nirvana on my person.'

'Not even an aspirin?' He noticed under her coat, at the neck, a silver crucifix. 'I have a headache.' He had, he realised, a thick, generalised pain in the cranium.

She stuck both hands down into the pockets of the tweed coat. 'Well, I've something for period pains. That ought to do it.' She had a way of looking directly at him, which he found not so much flattering – disconcerting certainly – but which made him examine his estimation of himself. 'Mind you, it won't stop the internal bleeding.'

She pulled a half-bottle of brandy from her pocket, unscrewed the top, and sloshed huge measures into both their mugs. 'Medicine for the Doctor.'

He clinked his mug with hers and downed the contents in one gulp.

He looked down at her asleep in the bed. The television, sound turned down, lit the room. Changing patterns of colour played across her face. It took him back to London. He had looked away as she got undressed, which made her chuckle. He watched the disrobing shadows on the wall, enlarged and lowering, sexual shadow puppetry. From the chair he watched her wriggle between the sheets; she smiled blearily and then was asleep almost immediately. He had waited until her breathing had slowed into a deep pattern before kneeling down beside the bed to be aware of the signs of deceit. Imagine you're asleep. Stage instructions by Stanislavski. But she was definitely asleep. Occasionally she whimpered. He wanted to lightly brush her lips in consolation, cuddle her. But instead he waited a few minutes and then picked up her coat and jeans and went into the bathroom.

He turned out the pockets. Her jeans held five dollars, a couple of subway tokens and a pawn ticket. He rustled through the coat. A large can of . . . hairspray? He pulled it out. Mace. Take out a punk at ten paces. A strip of pills, predictable, a letter and a wallet. He went through the wallet. Credit cards – he discovered her second name was Garrison – condoms in tinfoil – sexually she was certainly well-armed – a driving licence, photobooth pictures of a wan youth sucking in his cheeks, a library ticket, a few stamps and a scrap of paper with a telephone number. I am, he said to himself, a desperado of love – this is a fairly disgusting thing to do – but then death isn't exactly dignifying.

He went into the main room and punched the numbers from the paper into the phone, a digital scale. It rang out. He returned to the letter, sitting on the toilet as he read it. It was an anguished appeal from Gary – concave cheeks? – asking her to come back. Dwelling on passion, sexual healing, the ache of parting, the redemption of his suffering. Doherty started to grin. It was either the perfect cover or she was innocent. Well, hardly innocent. But uninvolved. Anyway, a Volunteer would have to be commanded to sleep with him. Carefully he replaced her possessions then he switched off the light and went back into the bedroom and began to undress. It was barely noon, but he was ineffably tired. He was now down to his underpants. He considered taking them off, decided against, and climbed into bed beside her, careful, for his own equanimity, not to roll against her nakedness. She whimpered again, then turned away.

Doherty woke suddenly with his heart pounding, damp with sweat and dark dreams swirling away. He sat up in the bed, alone. The TV was still on. A Woody Woodpecker cartoon played soundlessly. The rush of running water carried from the bathroom. His heart began to slow. He thought back to yesterday, checked his watch and realised that only four hours had passed, it was still today. Why had she started talking to him? What did, does she want? On the evidence, old son, not your body.

The bathroom door opened and she came in shrouded in steam, like the arrival of a stage villain. Except, she had a towel tied like a sarong round her waist and she was towelling her wet hair. Her upper body was naked. And she smiled.

'Thank you,' she said.

'What for?'

'Most men would have, you know . . .'

She stood before him without any sense of shyness. She was slight, milky, he felt he could put his hand right through her. Her breasts, he thought, were perfect. 'Catalepsy is no great turn on. Anyway, you know how it is, when you're saving yourself. Or maybe you don't.'

'Are you married?'

'Not recently.'

She sat down in the basket-work chair and began to absently towel her hair again. 'Most men of your age are, that's all. Involved?'

A telling question. 'Not sexually.'

'Who are you, Doherty?'

'An odd question.'

'Go on.'

'I can tell you what I have been, who I used to be – '

'Cop out.'

'Does it matter?'

'It might.'

He sighed. He could describe the circumstances, but not the substance. 'I had a friend – '

'Had?'

'Had a friend who wrote scripts, screenplays, anything. He always opened with, quote, the setting is unmistakably Acapulco, unquote.'

She waited. 'Am I being obtuse?'

'Unmistakably. Dreams. The perfect tomorrow. I preferred the imperfect today.'

'You're being very delphic, Doc. Not to say pretentious. Answer the question.'

'I live on an old boat. I move around. I take pictures. That's it. I used to be reasonably well-known. Fortunately not now.'

'Well-known for what?'

'Taking pictures.'

'I've never heard of you.'

'Therefore I must not exist.' He rubbed his hands over his face. 'That's good. It was all a long time ago.'

'What kind of pictures?'

'Wars mostly. Death, famine, pestilence. The progress of the horsemen. It's very well paying. Cadavers are a cash crop. You can live off them for years. I have.'

'That's sick, Doc. Damaged.'

'The dope dealer calling the ghoul damaged. Hypocritical. But well aimed.'

She had stopped towelling her hair and he fancied he saw her shiver. The sarong towel had split showing a slope of right leg. 'We'll come back to me. But you. You don't do it any more.'

'No.'

'Why not.'

'No good reason. The fun went. Fear. They don't do wars like they used to. An overcrowded market. How the fuck do I know?'

'Touchy. What was it like?'

'Exhilarating, mostly. Uncomfortable a lot. Damaging?' He stretched and then cupped his hands behind his head. 'I stopped, that's all. I was working in the darkroom, on a print of kid, a famine victim in Sudan. It was for an exhibition called The Caring Eye or some such shit. I had worked on the print for ages, burning in skin tones, dodging out parts of the background, getting the perfect image for the wall, for the visitors. I looked down into the developing tray and watched the kid assemble perfectly in the dish, his eyes looking up beseechingly, the dust on his spaghetti limbs absolutely in focus down to the tiniest mote. It would have brought a tear to a glass eye. And I thought, he's dead. And this is no job for a grown man.' They looked at each other. 'Maybe,' he added, smiling.

She shook her head and then gave a vigorous towelling to her hair. He noticed that it was longer than he had thought earlier when it was tucked down into her coat collar. It reached past her shoulders. She picked up her jeans, let the towel fall and got into bed beside him.

'I still earn out of it. A subsistence. Through an agent. I let him handle the moral consequences. Which suits both of us excellently. You'd be surprised how death doesn't date. Part-works on wars, compilation albums on great disasters of our time, encyclopaedia, stills for TV.'

'And now?'

He smiled and rolled on to an elbow. 'That's up to you.'

She slapped his leg under the bedcovers. 'Pictures, I meant.'

He gazed at her breasts. She was sitting up in bed with the sheets lapping her belly button, hair damply tangled. He reached over and gently touched her right nipple. She moved a hand under the bedcovers, onto him. 'Ah,' she said 'so that's what's up, Doc!'

Then, with her other hand she grabbed the discarded jeans from the bed, pulled out her wallet. 'What are you doing?' he said.

'Precautions.' She took out a silver packet and tore it open.

'Last time I saw one of these they were stitched out of pigskin,' he said. And then: 'I haven't been with anyone for so long it doesn't matter.'

'No,' she said, moving her hand under the blankets again, 'but I have.'

*

'What do you need,' he was saying, 'to buy a gun here?'

'Apart from the cash and a serious personality problem?'

'Apart from that?'

'Why?'

'Did I ask why drugs?'

'For the money. Simple.'

'Answer the question.'

'Uh. Driver's licence, I think.'

'No permit?'

'I don't think so. Look, Doc . . . Look I can't keep calling you Doc or Crippen. What can I call you? And why the gun?'

'Because this town makes me feel very unsafe? And you can call me Jimmy. Where I come from everyone does.' He smiled. She looked puzzled. 'It's a joke. A Glasgow joke. You wouldn't understand.'

'Glasgow, Scotland?'

'Where men are men and the women are too.'

They were sitting at a scarred wooden table in a basement bar off 52nd Street, owned by an ex-fighter. Blue cigar clouds hung overhead. The walls were glittered with photographs, of large men, stripped to the waist, usually black, but always glistening, squaring up to the camera and addressing mean sidelong glances around bulbous, misshapen noses. The custom, too, looked like it had stepped down off the walls. Mostly men, as wide as they were tall, whatever their height. More meat than the Ponderosa, he thought. And ran his thumb and forefinger thoughtfully down his nose.

'I'm not going to rob a bank, shoot myself or anyone else, I hope. I need your help. Trust me.' He gripped her hand.

She released it. 'When a guy asks for trust, I check my gold fillings.' She sat back in the chair, straightening her back. 'Look, I don't know you. I don't want to be mixed up in anything bad, worse than I am now. You want a

46

gun . . . you want to shoot somebody! Why else? Or
threaten to. And I'm the accessory. Well, no thanks.' Her
right hand toyed with the schooner glass, beaded with
condensation. 'I'll stick to the comparatively healthy
business of purveying chemicals to the needy, desperate
and wealthy of this city . . . I think I want to go,' she said.

Doherty thought, how can it be that you can make love,
entwine, share all that heat and passion and tenderness
and then with a few words make the memory misshapen?
'Believe me,' he said, watching her eyes, 'I don't want to
hurt anybody. I'm in the worst kind of trouble and there
are men out there who would cut off parts of me that you
have grown . . . if you see what I mean . . . and grown to
know, if not love – just for light amusement. I don't know
anyone else who can help. Please!' he said. 'I'm desperate. Help me.' And then, and he knew it was a mistake:
'I'll pay you. How much? Please.'

'You can't buy my compliance. You're insulting me.'

He sighed and looked up at the ceiling. He felt tired,
light-headed, defeated. 'I'm sorry' he said. 'I keep apologising. And I'd forgotten how to,' and he reached for her
hand again. 'Why should you involve yourself? Forget it.
Don't go.' He was looking at her again, waiting to see if
she would come back, emotionally.

She looked at him again. He felt a tentative squeeze of
his hand. 'I dunno. Must be all those acting classes. This
is a fucking play. Actions without consequences.' She
said: 'I have a gun. And the personalilty disorder. So tell
me what it's all about.'

'I can't. It's too dangerous. For you.'

'Fuck that, Doherty.'

He got up and went to the bar. The bartender, an ex-
pug, probably a bantamweight under the flesh and the
years, had a distended right eye, scar tissue and rough-
sewn lacerations pulling it out of shape. His hair, oiled
and swept straight back, glisteningly reflected the overhead lights. And his movements, as he swept two beers

from the ice shelf and popped off the tops in one motion, were graceful, remembered. It was impossible to tell, Doherty thought, from the equality of hand treatment, which fist he had led with.

'It's a question of belief,' he said when he got back to the table, the two Buds effervescing out of the bottles. 'Yours in me.'

'Yeah? That word again. Mine all evaporated when I heard that Lou Reed was into jogging. Time was you could trust in a decadent.'

'And you hardly know me.'

'And I hardly know you. And I don't know Lou in the slightest.'

'Tell me,' he said 'do you normally go to bed with men you hardly know?'

'Very often,' she replied, ignoring the glass and swigging the beer straight from the bottle. Then she rearranged her seat so that she was at right angles to him, her dark hair spinning in the motion, her left elbow and forearm slapping down on the table in a defiant, curtailing gesture.

'What kind?'

She turned back vehemently and leaned forward over the table. Her teeth were clenched. 'Just the usual. Bisexuals, intravenous drug users and ageing foreigners down on their luck in a hostile town.'

'Gun, I meant.'

She giggled. From over his shoulder he heard a Brooklyn voice drifting past '. . . shoulda stood in bed and it never woudda happnt. In tree. I ast ya . . . shoulda stood in bed.' She stood up, leaned over the table and kissed the tip of his nose.

'Just your standard Saturday night, blow-their-balls-off-if-they-come-within-penis length special.' She made a gun shape with her right hand and drew a bead between his eyes. 'If the shells don't get 'em the shock waves will.'

'Lee. Second name Enfield, right?'

'I told you, didn't I?'

'No. That was a joke which . . . ehhmm . . . misfired. Lee . . . Enfield. As in rifle.'

'Joke? Like are you pleased to see me or is that an Armalite in your trousers?'

'It was a revolver.'

'Not in my neighbourhood, buddy. Black. You know!'

'That's an offensive racial stereotype,' he said, grinning.

'Offensive. Nnhh, nnhnh!' She shook her head and smacked her lips. 'Now, that kind of statement, that's a stereotypical shrivelled white male reaction.' ·

'If you could just drag your mind back up to between your ears Ms Garrison.' He held his right hand out, palm up.

She slapped it. 'Garrison, Doherty.'

'Distinguished sounding. Garrison Doherty. Poet, tragedian – '

She cut in. 'Who shoots his critics.'

'Yes,' he said, blowing her a kiss. 'The gun.'

She made a knocking away gesture with her right hand. 'Doherty. How do you know I'm not some sort of federal agent trying to get you in entrapment?'

He began to laugh, almost hysterically. 'Haven't we already been entrapped?' he said eventually. 'But seriously, that would be a relief.'

She got up, took his hand and began to pull him to his feet. 'Come on. Explain that one to me later. There is work to do.'

She lived in a surprisingly cared-for brownstone, the smell of disinfectant in the hallway almost completely masking the putrescence. The door to her apartment was dark, stout, carved with sexual graffiti, and carrying more locks than Leavenworth. Doherty studied the chopped messages in the wood as she clanked open the locks.

'You are certainly in demand' he said. 'Pablo in particular seems to be carrying a mighty torch.'

'Looked more like an Indian club, last time he flashed it' she said sweetly, while turning the last key.

He closed the door behind them and she, automatically, slotted in a chain lock. Then she picked up mail from the floor and he followed her down the dark hall as she shuffled through it. The main room was large, airy, with explosions of colour on bare white walls – posters, theatre openings, movies, a *de rigeur* James Dean, a red and ochre Mexican rug, and on one wall a gallery of pictures he presumed were family. Above a fireplace, which framed a huge bowl of dried flowers in the hearth, an oil painting, a nude, of her, hung. He stood looking at it, hearing noises of her from the kitchen. It was a stark, unerotic painting, full-length and she stood looking sagaciously at the artist, hands clasped behind her back in a pose beloved of British Royals, with her left knee slightly bent. Her left breast looked slightly larger than the right. He tried to remember if it was. No, he thought, probably the artist's astigmatism.

He felt her arm round his waist and her mouth nuzzled his shoulder. 'It's very vain, I know,' she said. 'I am, I suppose.'

'He's' – how did he know it was a he? – 'painted your left breast larger than the right. It isn't.'

'I hadn't noticed.' She took away her arm. 'You've spoiled it,' she said. 'Fuck you.'

He turned round. She was moving away and turning her face. 'I didn't mean to. I'm sorry.' He tried to hold her, but there was no response. 'I didn't mean to,' he said again but he knew there was no recovery. He dropped his arms. He had a real aptitude for relationships.

'It doesn't matter. It was childish anyway.' Her eyes were full. He wanted to hold her again but he knew intuitively that he shouldn't.

'Look, ignore me.' He fell into a rumpled corduroy

armchair. 'I have sensitivities where other people have piles. It's a fine picture.'

'It means a lot. A boyfriend painted it.'

'I rather gathered.'

'He died.'

'Ah – I'm sor – '

Then she smiled wickedly. 'Actually, I lied. He ran off with a friend of mine.'

'There. I knew he had a sight problem.'

'They're apparently very happy.'

'Selfish bastards.'

'But I still like the picture.'

'It's certainly a . . . a talking point.'

'I don't let many people come here,' she said, sitting down on the arm of the chair. 'So it isn't. I'm not an exhibitionist.'

He began to stroke her leg. 'The play was a little . . . avant garde for me – '

'American translation – rank rotten.'

'But I thought you were – '

'Wondrous, is what you thought.'

'Did I just say that? Wondrous, yes. Luminescent. The play? Sort of Beckett with added bleakness.' She smiled, stroking his hand stroking her. 'Why you had to stand twenty minutes motionless at the front of the stage I don't know, but it was visually very pleasant. Some metaphor about isolation? Society transfixing the individual's motivation? Stage fright?'

She leaned over and kissed him lightly on the lips. 'Tell me something?'

'Probably not.'

'Who will claim your body if you die?'

'Christ you're macabre.'

'Who?'

'It'll hardly concern me . . .'

'Who?'

'I don't know. Technically I don't have a next of kin.

51

An ex-wife who hates me, ditto a couple of cousins and an aunt. So the state I suppose. A pauper's grave for me, dearie.'

'I'll bury you. Catholic or Protestant?'

'Neither. Don't think the gesture isn't appreciated, but frankly I intend to be around for some little while to come.'

'Can you use a hand gun?'

'Sometimes, Lee,' he said, trying to slide his right hand up her jersey, 'your conversational cartwheels astound me.'

'Answer the question.' Her left hand stopped his just as it reached her bare breast.

'I once won a very handsome china pot at the carnival, with three darts in the bull.'

'You want a gun, which you can't use, to take on some people you won't tell me about but who are evidently dangerous. You are in a strange city, the bad guys' backyard, and you have about as much street savvy as an antipodean anteater, so I figure, there ought to be someone about to bury you.'

He tickled her stomach and as she brought her hand down to grab his he quickly changed his point of attack and clutched, successfully, her breast.

'Some words of advice. The best place to keep a Beretta is probably not in the flour jar. Even if it is wrapped in polythene. If you're under serious duress it's not a completely convincing line that you've just got to pop out and bake a cake before the mayhem starts. Where do you keep the bullets, for Christ's sake, in the icebox?' The gun was growing warm in his grip.

'Someone gave me it. He was worried about me living here. I only took it to please him. I couldn't stand the idea, so I dumped it in the place where I'd never come across it. I mean, can you imagine me baking a cake?'

'Only with hashish.' He was drawing beads on the floral lampshade.

'Don't get the wrong idea, Doherty. I only deal a little. To friends, members of the cast. Small-time. A bit of coke, some dope. You know, user-friendly kind of narcotics.'

'Well, that's all right then. Stashed in the sugar jar I suppose.'

'Don't be ridiculous.'

'I should have known – '

'Wouldn't have it in the place.'

'Sugar?'

'Of course.'

'Terrible on the metabolism.'

'Exactly.' She got up and stretched languorously, her jumper riding up to show her flat belly. 'Would you like a line? I could do you one that would keep an African elephant's proboscis numb for a month.'

'Why not? I'm beyond prosecution for minor misdemeanours and felonies.'

'Look' – he noticed for the first time a tiny scar, almost a laugh line, just below her right eye – 'if you're not going to tell me what you're involved in, don't tease me.' She went out into the kitchen and he heard her rummaging. He felt a kind of calm that he hadn't had since the whole thing began, which was palpably ridiculous. But it was there. Something to do with limited imagination, or affection? Or was there any difference? He looked at the gun. A 9mm Beretta. He pulled out the clip. Fifteen shots. It would take one up the spout too. Nice gun. Little recoil, anti-jamming mechanism. He had fired one in El Salvador, at a gun range frequented by pistoleros of Arena, who almost certainly spent their evenings knocking on the door of leftists. Why they needed shooting practice had defeated him. Two inches from the head you didn't need to aim.

She came back in carrying her weaponry, a small

chrome-cased razor, a shaving mirror and, in her right hand, a paper bag, a poke he used to call it, a coke poke, holding, it looked like, at least half a pound of the stuff. 'Jesus,' he whispered, 'are you planning to disaffect the Chinese army?'

She sat cross-legged on the floor and casually spilled a heap of the crystals on to the mirror, then began chattering at the pile with the razor, drawing up a line, cutting at that, then drawing up another. 'It's at times like this you envy Durante his nose,' he said.

'Who?'

'Never mind.' He pulled a hundred-dollar bill from his pocket, putting the gun down between the cushions on the settee. 'After you,' he said. She rolled up the note, held it in her right hand and with her left kept her hair out of her eyes then, on her knees, bent over the mirror. Her inhalations seemed to last forever. He slipped off the settee and kneeled behind her, starting to roll her jersey up her back. 'Quit it,' she said none too convincingly, '. . . watch the stuff.' But she lifted her arms and as the jersey passed over her head he kissed her spine between her shoulder blades. Then he gently turned her round and pushed her backwards down to the floor. She lay there, looking quizzical, her breath coming quickly and on the almost translucent skin of her breasts he could pick out a minute tracery of veins. He picked up the note, unrolled it and smoothed it and then scooped up a bill of cocaine. 'I've always wanted to do this,' he said, dribbling the fine powder in a trail from the valley of her breasts down her stomach and into her belly button.

'Pervert,' she said, starting to giggle uncontrollably.

'Shush, woman, still. Or you'll be hoovering the carpet with your nostrils for months.' Then he rolled up the note and started down the trail, while she shivered, in suppressed hysteria or passion he couldn't tell.

When he had finished he rolled his tongue round her belly button, she moaned softly and this time he could

tell. Then she pulled him down to the floor next to her
and began unbuttoning the fly of his jeans. His head felt
. . . precise, was the word. Well, it would do. Now, she
had her hands under his buttocks and was pulling down
his trousers. He thought, arcanely, I hope I changed my
pants, and then she leaned across him, a breast skittering
over his engorging cock, and buried her face in the mirror
on the floor. 'Close,' he said 'in the circumstances.' And
then he realised what she was doing.

When her lips closed over him the shock was arctic. 'If
there's a name for this it ought to be an eskimo,' he
managed to say.

Her head shook round him. 'Blow-hole job,' she
mumbled.

He called it his Domesday Book, a pictorial record of the
disappearing country and its people. Moving round the
land, outside it, seeing Britain bobbing on the horizon, or
shrouded in mist and rain, gave him a curious view of it.
It was his country, apart. He heard news on the radio, of
death, politics, traffic jams, happening a mile or two
across the waves and, for the first time in his life, he felt
interested but estranged. It was a pleasant feeling. Somehow he had no identity. He only existed in his own
estimation. Going ashore he felt as if he were materialis-
ing again, into the form that he hated and that if he stayed
on the land too long the set would become too firm. So
he went to sea again.

Often he thought that he must be having some kind of
breakdown. The book had no purpose, other than satisfying him. That was enough. It would never be published,
it existed only in his mind and in the thousands of
negatives and prints, of faces, of groups, of landmarks,
factories, rock formations, flowers, football crowds, cars:
it was completely personal and idiosyncratic, pretentious

probably and self-indulgent, and he thought it said every-thing about him.

At times he had felt that he had lost the power of language, he would go weeks without talking to anyone, and his only voice was the static of the World Service – he had tried Radio 4 but had given up on the self-satisfaction – but he loved the way the World Service spoke English to the world, to strangers, like him. Modulated, careful, for the hard of thinking. He had listened to the World Service in more troublespots than he could bear to recall. Somehow, the measured, slow tones of the voices were almost enough to persuade him that the present reality, the shells, the whine of bullets and the shrieks of the sufferers, was an illusion: that in a world as sensible and rational as the one portrayed by the calming sentences lapping like a tide from the tiny radio, such things could not be happening. They were, though. Always.

When he came ashore, always in places he had never visited, he could be exactly the person of his imagination. He talked to few people, and then usually only to ask if they minded him photographing them, and in the eve-nings, before going back to the boat, he would sit in anonymous pubs, absorbing the conversations, occasion-ally firing off a few discreet shots. Imprisoning a few souls.

There was no pattern to his progress. He listened to forecasts, whims, reported events on radio, the rhythm of place names and then set out. Sometimes he anchored for weeks, often he sailed for days. He lived outside time. But gradually he began to change physically. He became leaner, his hair lengthened, previously unused muscles toughened as he wrestled with ropes and sheets and winches and the bucking helm in bad weather, his colour became dark and always he seemed to have the taste of salt water in his mouth. His hands were deep brown, lightened only by chaps and cuts. He amended his diet to his circumstances: simply prepared food that he could manage in the small galley. Rice, fish, which he could catch or, more often, pick up as windfalls on quays, in ports where trawlers unloaded, stews of vegetables, bread, almost no meat.

When he needed money, and the major costs were books and drink, he accessed his account which, rather to his surprise, continued to grow modestly. He guessed that death and disaster were still modish. Sex mattered very little, although there seemed to be more than he needed. Perhaps the image of the mysterious, rootless visitor was attractive? Perhaps it came because he appeared to care about it so little? He had no artifice, except the temporal of his own invention which he could change mid-sentence, he had no location, no self-esteem to risk, no sexual manners to observe. It was a game without consequences. And because he was the recorder he could go up to women in the most odd places and circumstances, without intent, other than to take pictures, or to capture memory fragments for his text, and often, when he certainly had no conscious intention, he would be receiving signals. He was good-looking, he knew matter-of-factly, tall, narrow-hipped – that was probably important because he had read somewhere that the bottom was the most important facet of attraction to women – and he was worldly. He could be eloquent and impassioned. And passionate. And he gave pleasure, selfishly, because it was more important than taking, perhaps because he was atoning in some way. Or maybe his life had become an act in which he had to perform well? He didn't analyse it.

'Don't, Doc,' Lee advised. She dug him in the ribs. 'I'm not sure about boffing in all that water. I'd either get queasy or need a leak. Does the ship rock? I couldn't handle that. I get sea sick on the Brooklyn Bridge.'

'Not ship. It's a boat. Thirty-five foot.'

'What's it called?'

'She. *The Golden Handshake*.'

'Seriously?'

'No. But I knew a much-travelled editor who called his boat that. The boats got more grand with each successive sacking. She's called I–58.'

She snorted. 'Not *Saucy Sue* or *Gin Palace*. The I–fucking–58. That sounds like some kind of medicament for herpes relief. At the risk of being thought moronic, why, for Christ's sake?'

'It was the name of the Japanese submarine which sank the *Indianapolis*.' And then in a sort of sing-song: 'The boat that delivered the bomb, which flew in the Enola Gay, which dropped for forty-three seconds, which went off at 1900 feet above the Shima Hospital and blew up the world that Jack built . . . I was going to call her *Little Boy*, the code name of the atomic bomb, but fellow mariners might have suspected me of being a paedophile.'

'Have you ever considered that you might have a grave and crippling mental problem? No wonder they call you Crippen. You are one morbid son of a bitch.'

'You asked. It's distinctive; nice, if you don't think about the origin. I don't subscribe to all that shit about boats having personalities. Twee names, or else dreadful puns – like the *Mary Dear* – or sexual stuff. You don't give your house a name, or your car, unless you're a thoroughly pretentious prick. So . . . Anyway, I bought her about six or seven years ago. She was a hulk, had been lying abandoned in a yard on the west coast of Scotland for years. I got her very cheaply and spent a summer doing her up.'

'Then sailed off into the sunset.'

'It was pissing down. But then it always is there.'

She raised herself on her left elbow, the patchwork bed cover slipping down away from her breasts. She looked, he thought, achingly beautiful. 'God,' she said sombrely, 'I need a good analyst. I think I may be falling for you.'

'Rapture of the deep, they call it. Common enough. No known cure. Except a good kick up the arse.'

She took his chin in her hands, looked steadily at him for a few seconds and then breathed: 'Fuck you.'

'So soon? At my time of life it takes a little longer to recover than your average seventeen-year-old.'

'Let me tell you, none of my seventeen-year-olds have been average. There was one, I recall, who could do a hundred push-ups while reciting from *King Lear*.'

'How sharper than a serpent's tooth it is,' he said, 'to have a thankless child.'

'But exciting.'

'Indubitably.'

'That was from *Lear*.'

'The first bit,' he said. 'It's only line I know. Apart from when Gloucester says "let me kiss that hand" and the old lad says "Let me wipe it first, it smells mortal." You can imagine the state of these Elizabethan toilets.'

'. . . it smells of mortality.'

'Really? Puts a whole new context to the play.'

She shook her head despairingly. 'About mortality. This time, if you want, we can do it without the previous precaution.'

'Precaution,' he said. And then it occurred to him. 'Immediately afterwards I have to go back to the hotel, there's a precaution I've overlooked.'

He paid cash, slapping the large denomination bills down on the counter with relish. The assistant looked askance, partly because of the novelty of hard cash, but certainly also not quite able to figure out why parting with over a thousand dollars should so tickle the Limey.

'And I also need the address of a fast, reliable, professional darkroom.'

The young man – he wore steel-rimmed glasses and the kind of hairstyle affected by minor characters in superhero comics – fished in a drawer and pulled out a card.

'The best' he said.

'And discreet?'

Mystification left the assistant. He smiled knowingly. 'Oh, completely. You don't have to worry on that score. Completely discreet. Nothing at all that they won't have seen.'

Doherty smiled back. 'Nudge, nudge,' he said, enjoying the man's erroneous certainty.

'Pardon, Sir?'

Doherty tapped the side of his nose. 'Say no more . . . not even have a nice day.' And he grabbed the packages, winked and strode to the door, considering whether he should, as a last flourish, give a Chaplinesque sideways heelclick, but deciding that, much as he wanted to, it would probably be better for discretion if he didn't.

A wintry sun watered down. As he walked back to the hotel he berated himself. He really should have thought about it earlier. He put his omission down to jet lag and lurch of the heart. From now, he counselled himself, more attention to the gravity, fear and foreboding than the more uplifting feelings his body had been experiencing.

His room, untidy, was clearly unentered. No obvious disturbances, giveaway aromas. The dilatoriness of the hotel staff would help. He should have set up some, what would you call them?, tell-tales. These were the little glass markers, he remembered, screwed across cracks in Glasgow tenements to detect movement, further subsidence: a fissure in the glass calling for immediate evacuation. Or as immediate as incompetence could muster.

What he should have done was to fix hairs across doors, powder surfaces, measure the relation of objects to each other – the kind of thing your average agent does as second nature. But now, of course, he thought, he would be welcoming entry.

He put the packages down on the bed and tore at the wrappings. Obviously, he thought, he was being watched. Surveillance they always called it over here. Would the watchers talk to the shop assistant? Probably not. Anyway, what would that reveal? That a photographer bought some new gear, probably to take some lewd shots of the young thing he's tucked up with. Innocent. Well, carnal, deviant perhaps, but innocent. He stopped breaking open the boxes and mused for a moment that his libido had been rediscovered. 'Doesn't it always occur at the most awkward of times?' he said out loud.

He carefully pulled the autofocus Nikon from its box, tore off the loose covering – 'doing this a lot, aren't you?' – and slotted in the bayonet fix of the 21mm wide-angle lens – 'does everything have to remind you of congress?' – and then he switched on the main light and the two bedside lamps and took a meter reading. The light was very dull, the shutter-speed reading was an eighth of a second with the lens fully open. He'd have to uprate the film to get a decent speed. He spun the ASA dial to 1600 and altered the shutter setting to a hundred and twenty-fifth of a second. That would do. Then he tore open a grey shiny plastic bag and took out the coiled cable release, thirty feet of it, and screwed it to the camera. Finally he dug the motor drive from the debris on the bed, screwed it to the camera, and set the exposures to three.

Precautions. Expensive, but then he wasn't really paying. And that made the excitement all the more exhilarating. He thought of the provenance of the money and he wondered vaguely if he weren't some accessory after the fact to robbery, coercion: he almost certainly was, but beside the other felonies he would be charged with, it would be akin to committing a public nuisance. He put the camera assembly on the bed, opened the door and went into the hall, pulling the door behind him until it almost locked. Then he stepped in and out of the room a dozen times, checking his footfalls on the carpet until he was satisfied. Until he was absolutely sure of the area of floor even the smallest, the lightest step must hit. He took a towel from the bathroom and put it down on the spot, then stepped in and out of the room a couple of times on to it: he couldn't avoid landing on it.

He closed the door behind him and went to the bed and carefully folded out the Nikon box until it was a flat rectangle measuring about two and a half feet by two feet and pushed it under the towel. He placed the camera on the bedside table, pointing at the door and played out the cable release, slipping the bulb trigger under the cardboard. He repeated his entrances through the door, stepping unavoidably on the towel and, each time, and just as unavoidably, firing the camera. The cardboard was spreading the pressure and even the lightest of footfalls on the perimeter fired the sensitive trigger. The shutter going off was audible, but he could cover that. The point was, and he felt a surge of gusto in him, that the contraption worked. And just the success of it made him feel more confident. There was no guarantee that any of his watchers would illicitly enter the room, although it seemed more than likely, and there was no guarantee that with their presumed experience of such clandestine gigs they wouldn't discover the device. It was basic. But there was nothing to lose. So he set about camouflaging it. He took up the carpet, fished out the pocketknife with the marlin spike he always carried, and bevelled a small recess in the hardboard which covered the floorboards, laid in the cable release bulb and covered it with the cardboard. Then he laid the towel on top, played out the cable along the floor and up behind the table and down the carpet again. He repeated his covert entry procedure, the shutter fired invariably but, more importantly, the mechanism under the carpet was undetectable, either to the eye or to foot touch. He loaded a roll of T-max into the Nikon and carefully positioned the camera, hunkering down to squint through the viewfinder. The elongated doorway ballooned in his eyes. Perfect. Carefully he pushed a newspaper under the black body and pushed it back, tilting the mirror on the table so that the top of the camera and the shutter were hidden behind it. The cable fell away down the back undetectably.

Then he set a detritus of coins, notes, tickets, his passport, a subway guide, a few rolls of film, round it, so that the whole arrangement on the table looked carelessly discarded. Finally, he turned on the radio to a soft rock station, cocked the motor drive and repeated his entrance procedure, careful to step only on the active square on the way in. He felt jubilation. The camera had fired inaudibly against the background rockbabble. He set the exposure setting to six shots, primed his precaution, tiptoed round the firing platform, took the 'do not disturb sign' from the inside of the door, hung it on the outside doorknob and clicked the lock shut behind him. Then he punched the air and left the hotel.

He was now behaving like a tourist. He slept late with Lee, reassured himself about the future of the world with her when they awoke, usually in wall-rattling cadences, and then they breakfasted and went out. He loved the joke, dragging these men of violence – if they were being followed and he had to assume they were – to places of culture and spirituality; churches, art galleries – he loved the Museum of Modern Art – the New York Library. And across on the ferry to Staten Island where an aspic, 1940s America seemed to exist, with boardwalks, Little League baseball, Old Glory on masts at the bottom of gardens, soda fountains, rocking chairs and an almost complete absence of blacks. In a bar they discovered a waitress who was born a few streets away from him and when they reeled out four hours later, clinging to each other as much for support as affection, they hadn't paid for one drink.

Getting drunk wasn't the most sensible of actions . . . but . . . no, he reconsidered, it was entirely the most sensible of actions. And they walked for miles each day, dragging his unseen followers, he devoutly hoped, cursing through yet another day on the sidewalk.

In the evenings they would eat in a restaurant she knew or had heard of, or they would just pick one at random from the *Village Voice* or *The New York Times* and enjoy everything from Lebanese to Turkish, Indian or even Afghan cuisine. It gave him perverse pleasure to spend large amounts of their money on outlandish meals. Always they would wash the food down with several bottles of wine, the most expensive, and he took satisfaction in cooling a burning, spiced tongue in great gulps of treasured vintages.

'You're a philistine, Doc,' she told him one evening over the second bottle of Krug and a new fairly stained white tablecloth, after a day out which had taken in Picasso, the World Trade Centre and a New York tee-shirt which he had bought at the top, ripped from its polythene, scrumpled into a ball and pitched over the suicide barrier to watch it flutter to the gridded streets below.

'My sympathies are certainly in that direction,' he said, slurping another few ounces of champagne into her glass, most of which foamed over the rim into a golden puddle on the cloth. 'You probably didn't know – and even if you did I'm going to tell you anyway because that's the sort of domineering sod – '

'Nonsense,' she interrupted, 'I've been on top at least as much as you.'

He wagged his finger at her. 'Can't you ever keep your mind off it?'

She thought for a moment and shook her head. 'You bring out the disgusting in me . . . I'm pleased to say,' she answered, grabbing his finger, pulling it and his hand below the table and attempting to intrude it up her short skirt.

'Philistine is Arabic, don't ask me to spell it, for

Palestinian. I remember trying to explain the derogatory nuance to a fedayeen once on a cold night in a mountain hideout in the south of Lebanon.'

'Name dropper . . . What did he say?'

'You mean, after "eat this AK-47 shithead?" . . . he courteously explained how his people were scholars, poets, architects, mariners, while mine were running about in woad – although I'm not sure the Picts wore woad – trying to reinvent fire with a couple of wet roots. He had red hair. Interesting that. I got my own back. He boasted what a crack sniper he was and next day I challenged him to hit a passing bird. He took careful aim. Fired. Missed. I smirked and grabbed the Kalashnikov, waited for the next passing hawk and took it at fifty feet, better than James Mason in that film where he puts a bullet through a hole in a coin and they won't believe him because there's no mark. Or was it John Wayne? Anyway James or John showed 'em. So did I. Mind you, it was pure fluke. Coupled with me slipping the catch over to automatic and splattering the bird and multiply puncturing the ozone layer with an entire magazine.'

Then, almost as an afterthought: 'Oh, fuck it . . . I'm in love with you.'

'Graciously put, Doherty. You make it sound like a terminal affliction,' she said, smiling.

'For which of us I'm not sure.'

After a day out on the streets they usually went to a club – at The Bitter End he saw Bob Dylan's signature on a wall in the toilet, tipsily considered how he might chip it out and then decided that it was phoney anyway – or to a bar, and stayed to the early hours. Then back to her place. How many days did it continue, the moratorium on fear? Two, three? Each morning he went back to the hotel, checking to see if the trap had sprung and when he saw that it hadn't he unscrewed the cable release, took off the sign on the door and demanded of the management that the room was cleaned. When it was, he resprung the trap and went out.

The contact came when they were sitting in a 42nd Street bar opining grandly, and without the slightest practical experience, about the ideal constituents of a martini. The barman tapped Doherty on the arm, just as he was explaining that after swirling the vermouth with one drop of angostura it must be discarded. 'The phone. For you.'

'Can't be,' he replied.

'Doherty. A Brit.'

Doherty pointed at his chest and agreed. 'For me.'

The barman pointed to the receiver lying at the end of the bar.

It was the same voice, the Irishman, without any transatlantic delay on the telephone line. He was here.

'It could only have been you,' Doherty said.

'Now,' said the familiarly amused voice, 'you have to interrupt your idyll and get down to business. Your final instructions will be given tomorrow. At twelve noon be in Graftons. It's a cinema near to Broadway and 57th which shows skin flicks – '

'The pornography of violence,' Doherty said half-heartedly.

'Ten or twelve rows from the back. Contact will be made.'

'How will I see your rolled up copy of *The Times* in the dark?'

Doherty heard a dry laugh. 'A sense of humour is a comfort, I always think . . . Don't worry, we'll know you.'

'And when you don't turn up and I leave and the place blows up I'm wanted on both sides of the Pond.'

'Unnecessary, Doherty. Don't you think you aren't already? Haven't you heard about international co-operation to defeat the terrorist? Haven't you listened to the leader's rousing speeches on the matter, these ten years

or more?' Incongruously, Doherty's eyes strayed to the
high ceiling where a huge fan turned slowly, succeeding
only in disturbing the upper, smoky atmosphere. 'Nothing
will happen to the cinema, we'd hardly want to alienate
support over here, would we?'

The barman had switched on the TV and now he stood,
arms folded, his waist against the bar, staring up at the
screen, where in smudged colour and to a roaring background, tiny baseball figures swatted, slid and tumbled.
'All of this . . .' said Doherty '. . . the cost, the effort . . .
the stakes must be enormously high.'

'The highest,' said the voice, hissing now, venomous,
'remember that. And be there at noon tomorrow. Graftons. Broadway and 57th. If you get lost you better not
ask a policeman, just follow the men in greasy macs.' And
for two or three seconds the Irishman began to laugh,
gratingly, almost hysterically, and Doherty tasted mania,
before he cut himself off and Doherty heard the buzzing
in his ear.

They watched him leave the hotel. One man nodded
across the street to the other then, when Doherty had
almost turned the corner, began to walk after him. The
second watcher continued to sit at the window of the
diner, sipping his black coffee and letting his eyes
occasionally run over the sports results in the paper, for
verisimilitude.

The first man followed as Doherty ran down into the
subway, through the barrier, pushing a dollar token into
the slot, and on to the platform where he waited until
Doherty got on the train. Then he retraced the path and
gave the same surreptitious nod as he came back to his
position along from the hotel. The second man carefully
folded his paper, took out a leather billfold and dropped
a five dollar note on top of his check. 'Thanks,' he said to

the rheumy-eyed waitress. 'Welcome,' she said and he went out into the street and over to the hotel.

He saw the sign on the bedroom door, knocked hard on the panel just to make sure and then, in less than half a minute he had slipped the Yale lock and was inside. He was wearing surgical gloves which, no matter how much talcum he put on his hands before, always caused them to itch uncontrollably for hours afterwards. Could he claim for industrial injury? he wondered incongruously to himself. Inside he gave only a cursory glance to the room, noting the general untidiness, the radio turned to some raving FM station and then he made straight for the bathroom. He opened a cheap and cigarette-charred melamine cupboard on the wall and grinned in satisfaction. Then he went into his jacket pocket, took out a plastic bag which, because of the gloves, he had difficulty opening, and then a pair of nose tweezers. Carefully he picked a dozen or more hairs from the plastic hairbrush and dropped them into the bag. Then for a couple of moments he struggled to close the seal on it before he slipped the bag back into his pocket.

When he left the room the whole operation had taken less than four minutes and when he pulled the door behind him he gave a grin of satisfaction. His incursion had been undetectable. He peeled off the gloves, slipped them into a trouser pocket and started to walk back along the hallway, conscious that he could already feel his hands begin to tingle.

Doherty had recced the dingy cinema in the evening, watching for more than an hour the dismal slick of humanity washing in and out. Over the main door a neon sign offered 'All manner of perversions, 24-hours-a-day'. And all for two dollars fifty. He was constantly approached by hustlers, pushing drugs – crack, coke – or women. He tried to keep moving but he kept bobbing up against them. The cinema's emergency exit gave out into an alley littered with phials, needles, blackened silver paper, condoms, discarded fast food, upended trash cans. At the end of the alley an unscaleable wall covered with gang slogans meant that the only escape route from inside led right back on to the main street, emerging ten yards from the main door, so that surreptitious flight was impossible. Doherty felt discouragement in the bone. And he began to feel afraid again.

In the morning he had wakened at seven, quietly got up and wandered the neighbourhood for almost three hours. He sat in a coffee shop watching the workers, the winos, the unemployed, prepare for their days. He felt like grabbing dozy, ambling walkers and shouting at them, 'Have you got any idea what's happening?' like some crazed missionary of the sidewalk. He read a paper and found he couldn't recall a single item. Somewhere on his walk he bought a pot plant from a stall and wandered around with it, vaguely considering talking to it like some English Royal and generally adding to the ambience of street lunacy. When he got back Lee, walking around with a towel round her waist and her hair wet and tousled, said, 'Well, you haven't been jogging then . . . I couldn't sleep after you got up . . . I was worried.' And he knew that she had thought that he had gone. He held her tightly and felt himself shivering against her and she sensed that it was worse than that.

'I just have to go out,' he said.

'I know. And you may be gone some time.'

'No. I'll be back for lunch. There's nothing to worry about.'

She looked up at him. 'No? Liar.'

He broke away and went into the kitchen and she said, 'I know what you're after,' and when he was gone she found she was right.

*

The weight of the gun in his inside pocket was comforting. But for the first time in his life he thought, 'This could be my last day on earth.' It felt not so much scaring as disconcerting, frustrating. He was moving towards an inevitability that he was powerless to influence. He had spent years in a state of powerlessness, deliberately so, making himself, he had thought, the most marginal survivor on the planet. Maybe that's why they had chosen him? That was ridiculous. But why had they? What were his qualifications otherwise? No burning sympathy with the cause, although he believed that a united Ireland was the only solution, however bloody in the execution. Execution? Exactly. He had covered the war almost from its inception, he had known senior men on either side, Loyalist and Republican, many of whom were now dead. Or were there, he thought, three sides – the British army completing the triangle of bitterness? He had photographed Bloody Sunday. He had photographed Warrenpoint. He had taken pictures of IRA men in hoods with Armalites on their hips, he had taken shots of young soldiers in similar poses, the difference only in the balaclavas that blocked out the Provos' faces.

Then in 1980 he had been arrested and charged under the Prevention of Terrorism Act with withholding information. A bomb had gone off in London, killing a senior politician and when he came back into the country he was detained, he thought under a hysterical, catch-all quest for information; his film had been confiscated and he was asked, compelled, to answer questions about his entire movements in Belfast – where he had been staying, who he had been seeing.

'First let me talk to a lawyer, it's my right,' he had said. For serial murderers, rapists, arsonists yes, but not for you. Not to talk is an offence, you see. What he was certainly not going to say was that he had been talking to senior IRA men, that he could of course identify them, that yes, in the months that he had talked to them, they had admitted to crimes: what would his life be worth then?

But it wasn't that entirely. It was something pompous and difficult about the public having a right to know what was going on. There were no observers in this war, he was told, only participants. So, was all this now something to do with all that? That seemed ridiculous. But what then? Why?

He paid his money to a girl with dyed blonde hair who chewed and smoked simultaneously and he wanted to say that honestly, he wasn't like that. The cinema smelled like the inside of someone's wet dream. Thankfully the place was quiet. Hideously fascinated, seeking to distract his anxiety, he watched men of improbable length and girth do acts of ever more bizarre contortion to women of unfeasible acquiescence. And occasionally animals.

He kept his hand inside his jacket on the gun and remembered Mae West's double entendre. He waited. By quarter past twelve, as a donkey exited screen left having failed to satisfy some drugged nymphet, he knew his man wasn't coming. Rather, going to arrive. His eyes were well-acclimatised to the dark, if not the endless congress in the bright, and he could see no likely watcher. There were grunts and groans and rustles all around. But not his man.

And then, when he determined that he definitely wasn't going to show, he heard a seat fall and creak behind, he shifted the gun to under his left armpit and pointed it to the back of his chair and started to shuffle round in his chair when the voice said: 'Don't. Don't look. Anyway, I'm wearing a mask.'

'Then,' said Doherty calmly, 'you are the only person among those in this fucking place – and those entertaining it – with such modesty. Tell me, what is it? Margaret Thatcher? Donald Duck?'

He heard the light laugh. 'In another place we might get to like each other,' it said.

'No, I think not . . . just get on.' The gun was wet with sweat. He thought, I hope it doesn't go off prematurely. And then he started to smile grimly at the unconscious association.

Doherty felt a soft tap on his shoulder. 'Inside this envelope you'll find a key to a left luggage locker, together with an address and a map of where you'll be meeting this evening.'

Doherty took the envelope with his free left hand. 'Meeting?'

'The locker,' the voice continued, ignoring the question, 'contains a bag. You'll take that bag to the meeting and you'll be given another in return which you'll put back in the safety deposit box. And then you'll throw away the key.'

'That simple.'

'That simple indeed.'

'What if I run off with the money?'

'What money?'

'The money in the bag that they give me in exchange for the drugs I give them.'

Again the laugh. 'You're not terminally stupid . . . we're watching. And not just you. You know, you should be more circumspect with your affections. Drawing in others. I make myself clear?'

Doherty felt his finger tighten on the trigger, almost a dynamic of its own. 'I have a nine millimetre pistol pointing fairly precisely at your groin. Mind you, precision at this range isn't all that vital is it? For me that is. I should think the bullet would tear through this chair and your middle and leave an exit footprint from your arse about the size of an elephant's foot and still have enough momentum to blow the cock off any wanker up to five rows back. What would you think?'

In the pause between them Doherty was incongruously aware of the orgasmic groans from the screen. Ludicrously, the song line 'Happiness is a warm gun' came into his head. 'Your point is . . .?' the man said.

'You get the point exactly. Touch anyone close to me, connected to me, anyone I have ever said hello to in the street and I will find you. Somehow. And I will kill you, after having made you suffer a great deal of pain.'

He heard a movement in the seat behind and he wondered if the other man would simply end it all now with a bullet. But as the moment extended the man said: 'I go on for ever, Doherty. There are many behind me. I'm only a representative and you can't threaten or kill a movement.' And then: 'There should be no need for any violence . . . and if you really do have a gun, don't take it this evening. They may search you and decide that a gun is an earnest of bad intent.'

Doherty's tension eased. 'Who am I seeing? You have to give me at least an outline of the sketch if I'm to play a convincing part. If they ask me questions.'

'They are likely to be innocent foot soldiers like you. I'm sure they are as distrustful of us as we are of them.'

'If I'm going to do this and if I'm going in unarmed, risking getting tied to the wheel of a black hearse with an oxyacetylene torch at my privates, I want enough knowledge to have a reasonable chance of warding off the gelding.'

Two rows in front an old man got up and laboriously moved along the row. He was illuminated in the light of the screen. From behind the voice: 'There is,' – a pause – 'a convergence of interest between us. We can supply a substantial demand at a reasonable rate. Through our allies we can deliver to the doorstep all the high-grade merchandise they require.'

'You're remarkably prissy. You're talking about drugs. Cocaine, heroin for all I know. Class A drugs. Crack. Pushers at the schoolgates. Teenage addicts. Pimps and prostitutes. Gang wars in the ghettoes . . . a real moral crusade.'

'Please, Doherty, spare me the lecture. Do you want me to go on about ends justifying means, eight hundred

years of oppression? The right to national self-determina-
tion? We need the wherewithal to finally end the oppression. We can discuss the ethics of it over a glass of porter
after the Brits have gone. History is marked by alliances
of convenience for a greater good. Grow up.'

Doherty watched a close-up of a gigantic, erect penis
coming towards him: he felt like ducking. 'So with your
fellow Marxists and Maoists south of here . . . in Bolivia,
Peru? . . . Sendero Luminosa perhaps? . . . you trade
drugs for cash. With . . .?'

'Possibly . . .' the voice said, '. . . eventually.'

'You're selling the stuff to people here. To what's
euphemistically known as organised crime. The Mafia.
Stop me if I'm going wrong. And then they cut the stuff
and with their sophisticated conduits, their infrastructure
built on generations of bribery, traducement and corrup-
tion they sell it on the streets. And if the stuff corrodes
the fabric of capitalism, foments disorder, so much the
better. It's that chemical element in dialectical material-
ism that Marx never dreamed of. And with the proceeds
you and your comrades can buy guns – ground-to-air
weapons and fucking tanks for all I know.' From the
silence he knew he wasn't far away from the truth. 'That's
the historic alliance of convenience for a greater
good . . .!'

'Crudely and partially put.'

'But accurate.'

'Well,' said the whispering voice behind him, 'just look
. . . I never knew a woman could. And how on earth did
they get the camera down there to record it?'

Doherty took a bus downtown, delighting in the halting
progress, the changing landscape of people and the sense
of the island narrowing. He had left the cinema five
minutes after the other, observing the time limit. Then he

had torn open the envelope and memorised the instructions. The Port Authority building for the locker and then a bar in SoHo for the rendezvous. He felt better about that, they surely wouldn't nut him in public. Drag him into the toilet and severely mutilate him perhaps . . . But at least he didn't have to go to some abandoned wharf where a limousine would pull up quietly and flash its lights and men with shoulders that required them to go through doors sideways would climb out, bulging with menace. All he had to do was stand at the bar and he would be recognised. When he had asked how, his man had laughed. 'You'll see.'

When he opened the locker, Doherty saw. The bag was an Aer Lingus shoulder affair, in emerald green with lime lettering. Very inconspicuous. It weighed, he guessed, about fifteen pounds. He decided a taxi back uptown would be safer. If safe was clutching white-knuckled in the back of a big battered automobile while a resting Argentinian grand prix driver kept in practice gunning the bouncing car to its maximum, slewing it across the streets looking for holes in the traffic flow and burning ounces of rubber slithering up to lights.

He had decided to kill the time by going back to the hotel and lounging on the bed watching TV. He paid the driver, trembling more from the ride than in appreciation of his cargo. The driver, in the usual manner of the species, looked at the amount of tip, curled his lip and roared off.

Doherty called for his key from reception and climbed the two floors. The weight on his shoulder felt ominous. He got to the door and felt reassured to see the notice still in place and the hum of music from inside. He unlocked the Yale and stepped inside, doing his hopscotch routine to avoid the pressure pad, then chucked the shoulder bag on the bed. He felt desperately in need of a drink but had to make do with putting his mouth under the tap. He looked at himself in the mirror. For a man in your last day on earth, he told himself, he wasn't looking too bad. A bit of weight loss, 'not unattractive if I might say', and a shagginess to the hair at the temples, 'all the better to cushion the bullets'.

Then he was conscious of a sour taste in his mouth. Fear? Maybe, although it was becoming something of a narcotic. He cleaned his teeth, gargled, considered briefly his chances of escaping either with the drugs or the money . . . escaping at all. Grinned at himself in the mirror. 'I'd like to remember you this way,' he said, 'framed.' And then, his memory tripped and he decided that he might as well check the camera. He went into the bedroom, sat on the bed, moving the airline bag, and began to retrieve it from its bivouac.

He extricated the camera and looked down at the film counter and the motor drive, gripped the Nikon body until his nails whitened, and then checked again. Six exposures recorded. Right, he said to himself, right! And he got up, biting the knuckle of the first finger of the right hand, and began to walk round the room. The heavy gun bumping against his rib cage 'was the counterpoint of reality against his euphoria. Check again he told himself. Certain. Six shots. Think rationally, pessimistically. A Puerto Rican chambermaid, unable to read the host language, walked in and is now captured on the Kodak. Forget the quite clear evidence of neglect in the room, that not even the dust has been rearranged. But, come on, Doherty, he counselled, on the money that serving staff earn would you burnish the furniture or remake the bed for the sake of your self-estimation? As a Calvinist, yes, not with dozens more bedrooms to remake and the rent to pay. The likeliest explanation was that someone had come in, seen that the bedroom was in rough order and left. Triggering the camera in the process. But . . .?

He started to scatter through the camouflage on the bedside table until he found the card he was looking for, then rewound the camera, dropped out the roll of film and pocketed it. Then he pulled the airline bag off the counterpane, kicked it under the bed and closed the door behind him.

'I understand that four hours is the fastest service,' he was telling the assistant who sat on a typist's chair behind the counter. She was in her mid-twenties with a short suicide cut, through which black roots showed. She chewed on a pencil, which he found vaguely erotic, and occasionally scratched at her body through her jersey, a black training top with the darkroom legend, Downtown, running suggestively in an arc from her left breast to her belly button. In the circumstances Doherty found her fabulously desirable. 'I know that's the fastest it can possibly be done. But you see, I have an appointment in four hours and I'm leaving town so what I need is contacts in two hours. Enlarged contacts. For which I will pay,' he went into his trouser pocket dramatically and pulled out a wad of notes, 'one hundred dollars extra to the darkroom and,' he peeled off a twenty dollar bill, 'fifty dollars to the arranger.' He slapped his hand down on the counter with the bill under it and smiled at the girl. 'To be going on with. And for the peroxide,' he said and took his hand away.

'Mister,' she chewed, 'you have a persuasive way about you.'

'I hoped I had.'

She tossed the roll of film in her hand. 'These must be hot shots.'

'I'm hoping so. The processing instructions are on this note.' He handed her a slip of paper. 'Make sure it's followed exactly. Exactly.'

'Absolutely. Come back in a coupla hours. I'm fascinated.'

'Fascinated, indeed' he said and winked as he left.

*

He returned by cab – another rubber-burning journey – to the hotel and packed his bags, then went downstairs and paid his bill to the end of the week. 'I'll probably be staying on,' he said to the surly man in the cubicle with a grammatically improbable name on the card in front of him on the desk, 'but I thought I'd better pay you now while I've still got something left.' The man grunted uninterestedly.

For the next hour, in a fever of euphoria, expectation and doubt, he zig-zagged across the city, hopping on to buses, in and out of stores – in one he bought some expensive French underwear for Lee and an extravagant and voluminous greatcoat for himself – killing time. Then he made his way back to the darkroom. The woman shook her head at him. 'Bailey you ain't,' she said.

He felt his stomach lurch. 'They haven't come out?'

'Something has come out. Question is what.'

'Please,' he said as calmly as he could, 'show me.'

'The sheet's still in the fix.'

'How long?'

She rocked her head, considering. 'Five minutes or so.'

'Show me.'

'Your risk,' she said and disappeared, coming back seconds later with the contact sheet, running with chemical. 'You're going to be disappointed.'

He grabbed the wet sheet and slapped it on the glass counter, squeegeeing off the fix with the heel of his palm, the acrid smell in his nostrils. 'A glass,' he said staring down at the sheet, holding out his right hand, into which she dropped the enlarging eyepiece.

Six frames. He put the glass on the first and huddled over the print. A figure. Unidentifiable. The second looked as if it could be a man but the door was open to the bedroom and the figure was too badly silhouetted. On the third, even through the sheen of fixer, there was no doubt. A man, face to camera. Pin sharp. 'Perfect,' he said, 'fucking perfect,' and he banged his fist on the glass, looked up and said. 'Absolute joyful perfection.'

'All I can say,' answered the girl, 'is some people got strange artistic standards.'

He looked at the other frames. Two blurred; in the third, because of the angle of the camera to him, the man's profile was obscured by his shoulder. 'How much,' he said, 'to drop everything else and print me half a dozen blow-ups of this?' His finger jabbed the frame, 'in full-face shots.' He spun two more twenties on to the counter.

She shook her head and ran her fingers through her short hair so that at the crown strands stood up electrically. 'How about fifty bucks and a large drink?'

'Done,' he said.

'There's a bar two blocks down. Emile's. Wait in there and I'll bring the prints when they're done.'

'Don't let them wash too long,' he said. 'Longevity is not essential. They only have to outlast me. Which may not be too long. Bring the negs. And,' he said as he opened the door to go out, 'no record of the transaction in the books.'

'Shtum,' she said, holding a finger to her lips.

The bar glittered in illumination of the inevitable silent television screen. The barman was one of those impossibly good-looking, probably gay, certainly thespian young men, with centre-parting and Bertrand Russell locks, who serve tables in smart bars in all western capitals. Doherty thought he might talk to him, thought better of it, ordered a bottle of champagne, unopened, two glasses, demanded an ice bucket and found a booth where he could watch for anyone coming in. Then he called for a Bud to lubricate his cogitation. He reviewed his situation between gasps as the achingly cold beer hit his tongue. Wanted on one continent, at large on another and moving dangerously towards the conclusion of a deal which would very likely see him either dead or doubly wanted. He could see no way to extricate himself. Oh, well, he said to himself in an ironic toast, if there is no way to alter the situation one can at least profit from it. If life in future – if there was one – was to be on the run, then at least he should ensure that he could live out whatever time he had comfortably. Physically, if not mentally. There had to be some kind of guarantee of that. Immediately he knew what he would do.

As he was draining the cold beer and giving the last shiver he caught sight of the girl coming through the door. She wore a black flight jacket and patched Levis and she had a packet under her arm. He began to peel the gold foil from the champagne bottle as she approached.

She sat down opposite him and her knee brushed his. 'Well,' she said, slapping the packet down. 'The goods. Don't complain if they fade in a month.'

He uncorked the bottle, a whisp of gas rose like gunsmoke, and he poured two glasses. 'I'm Stuart, with a U,' he said, giving the first name that came into his head, an old friend, who had set off one bright Scottish morning in a kilt to blow up General Franco and had ended up sentenced to death: he couldn't rid himself of allusions.

'First or second?' she said. 'Name.'

'First. And yours.'

'Janey.'

'Well, Janey,' he passed her a glass, 'here's to . . . photography.' He took a quick gulp and then picked up the packet and tore it open.

She said, as she picked up the cold champagne: 'I don't suppose you want to say why you're paying a large amount of money and entertaining a woman you've never met before with what looks like a very expensive champagne to produce some pictures of what looks like a very furtive guy in a room somewhere. Are you some kind of detective?'

He clinked his glass with hers. 'Exactly,' he said and he

put the index finger of his other hand to his lips. 'Shtum, as you said.'

'Look,' she put down her glass. 'I probably shouldn't have got involved in any of this.'

He sensed that she was about to go – women were always about to go on him – so he grabbed her hand, her left, and he felt rather than saw a ring on her wedding finger. 'I swear to you that you have done nothing illegal. It's all about industrial secrets . . . I can't go into it. It was a set-up to see if that guy would show. He did. Nothing illegal will happen. My client will tell the opposition that they've been rumbled and some deal will be struck, the details of which will never be made known to the likes of me. My client will pay me handsomely – and cover my lavish expenses,' he motioned with his head towards the bottle in the bucket, 'my stock will go up on the circuit and everyone will be happy. Except my mate in here,' he tapped the packet, 'who'll never work again in this town.'

She smiled. 'I knew you had an almost honest face . . . which made me wary. They're always my downfall.'

He pulled the pictures out of the packet and spread them on the table in front of him. 'Let me look at you.' The quality of the enlargements was poor: the film had been hugely pushed, the negatives had been thin and the magnification was immense. The face was grainy, but definitely recognisable. The man was about forty, with a fleshy face but a surprisingly long, thin nose, steel-rimmed spectacles and a receding hair line. He made an unlikely-looking terrorist, Doherty thought.

He topped up her glass. 'I've finished work for the day,' she said. She had an out-of-town accent. Mid-Western?

'You're married,' he said pointing to the ring.

She looked down at the hand holding her glass. 'No,' she said 'It's inherited. Just a device. To put off horny photographers.'

'It doesn't work though?'

'It doesn't work.'

He tried to steal a casual glance at his watch, not wishing to seem churlish but anxious about timing. 'I have an appointment this evening. And I'm kind of involved.'

'I know that kind of involvement,' she said wistfully, 'it's very serious.' She drained the glass. She was going again. He reached into his pocket for the money. 'No,' she said 'please. Don't.'

'At least let me buy you a meal. Tomorrow. Later this week. You've been more help than you know.'

'That would be nice. Call me.'

'Not at work. Give me your home number.' He took his glass off the coloured coaster – why were Americans fanatical about coasters on tables? It was as if glass would fuse to Formica – and spun it across the table. She rummaged inside her jacket and produced an eyebrow pencil and began to write. She said softly, 'On the back of a cartoon coaster – '

' – in the blue TV screen light,' he cut in. 'You're too young for that kind of music.'

'I was a hippy in a previous incarnation.' She put the coaster on top of the pictures. 'Call me.'

And he thought 'Why do you always make your life complicated, Doherty?'

Bars do not a prison make, but it felt like it, he thought, looking round another one. How many had he been in today? This one, off Bleecker Street, was fuggy, the smell of dope was cutting the tobacco smoke and, looking round the thankfully crowded place it was evident that Kerouac was the set course for the clientele. How many woolly jumpers could rub up against each other without spontaneous combustion erupting? He devoutly hoped that the *de rigueur* sunglasses would not obscure visions if two Mafiosi gave him a double tap to the temple. If there was one thing he wanted, next to survival, it was posthumous revenge.

He was drinking a Wild Turkey, which was exactly what he felt. The airline bag was at his feet, with the strap running under his shoe in case any of this crowd could detect chemical ecstasy through polythene, paint and cheap canvas. He had dumped the gun at the hotel, slipping it under the mattress – he hadn't been in a mood of great originality – and opened the bag. There had been, he counted, twelve packets, in opaque polythene, and holding one in his hand he reckoned it weighed about a pound – although whether Imperial or US he wouldn't wager. What was the street value of that cocaine? It was certainly more expensive in Britain than here. How many grammes to a pound? More to the point, how many years to the pound in prison? He desperately needed to go to the toilet, but he wasn't going to lose his protected place at the bar. And anyway, if they were here watching him and he went it would be simple to remove the goods, and the top of his head with a silenced short, in the powder room, or whatever they were calling bogs these days in America. He crossed his legs.

A woman next to him, talking to an Ivy Leaguer with embellished tie braces, stumbled and bumped into him. 'Pardon me,' she said. She was about thirty, in a camel coat, probably something upwardly mobile in banking he thought sourly, conducting an illicit affair with the Ivy League colleague in braces.

He thought again about his reaction to all of this. He hadn't felt the corrosive fear that other people seemed to get in danger. Probably some dead cells in the part of the brain that governs self-preservation. What he felt was exactly what he had felt under fire, high, boundlessly exhilarated. Not calm and certainly not unafraid, but fuelled, in control, enjoying himself. Insane.

'Excuse me,' the woman next to him said. 'Excuse me,' she said again, 'do you have a light . . . Doherty?'

'Shit,' he said vehemently.

'It's an emancipated profession these days,' she said, smiling only with the mouth. And then: 'Don't you know it's rude to gawp at a woman with your mouth open.'

'I wasn't expecting this.'

'Clearly not.'

'How did you know me?'

'Come on. You've got Brit written all over you. And then, there's the bag.'

'Yes.'

'You were wise not to carry anything, umm, unfriendly.'

'How did you know?'

'You surely didn't think it was your physical magnetism that brought us together a minute ago.'

'You checked.' She nodded. 'Tell me,' he said, 'do they have schools for it?' Then he leaned closer and whispered: 'You missed the Derringer in the sock.'

She pulled her head back. 'My friend is going to go to the toilet with you to check you th – '

'Like fuck he is. We stay here with the nice people.' Over the woman's shoulder Doherty could see the man thinking about making a move. He was handsome in a dumb way. Broad shoulders, probably did weights first thing in the morning in his boxer shorts while the coffee bubbled on the stove. 'I'm a go-between in all this. The gear's in the bag. I don't know what the deal is, but I certainly don't intend to be the shit in the sandwich. I give you your stuff, you give me mine. No recriminations. And tell your friend to chill out, he's getting very red about the old school tie.'

She turned and whispered something to the man, who visibly relaxed. 'Okay,' she said to Doherty, 'let's exchange gifts.'

'Where's yours?'

'In a car, fifty yards down the street.'

'Let's go then.'

As they walked towards the car Doherty said, 'What we do is you open the car, give me the key, check out my produce, then hand over yours. I give you the car key, you drive off and we have the reunion once a year, same place.'

She nodded, her partner grunted. They reached the car, the man opened the door, got inside, put the key in the ignition, turned half a turn and pressed the button to roll down the window. Then he handed out the key. Doherty took it and handed over the shoulder bag. Now he was frightened. He began to shiver, praying it wasn't detectable, and looked around in what he hoped appeared a precautionary and not anxious way. He saw the man open the bag, take out a penknife, dig into one packet, taste the scoop on the sharp blade, then go through the same procedure again with another packet. Then again.

'Hurry the fuck up,' Doherty hissed.

The man ignored him. 'It's his head as well,' the woman said. The traffic howled past. After cutting into two more packets he was satisfied.

'Now show me the colour of yours,' Doherty said. The man reached into the back seat, produced an identical Aer Lingus bag, unzipped it and held it up. It was stuffed with bills, hundred dollar bills, in bound bundles. 'Take out two . . . no the second one from the bottom . . . and flick through them so I can see the filling.' Doherty watched him slowly riffle through the wads. Solid money, he thought. 'Okay, hand it over.' The bag came through the window, Doherty grabbed it and then chucked the car key back.

The woman got in. 'Until next time,' she said.

'Just a one night stand for me,' he said and he waited on the pavement until the tail lights of the large black car melded into the traffic, then he went off in search of a taxi.

*

He drove, like everything else he did, as if he were being tested. She was conscious of the artifice. She vaguely wondered whether he also acted in bed. He probably did. Don't we all, she thought. Anyway, it had all gone smoothly, so much easier than she had imagined it could. A great wash of relief had gone through her and she was winding down now. Once they delivered the bag all she wanted to do was to get home, make a large Martini, wallow in the bath with potions and unguents she had swept off the supermarket shelf, until her skin was as wrinkled and furrowed as a ploughed field, dress langorously in silks, dab perfume propitiously all over, then listen to music. Something stirring, for the shaken. Shostakovich. Maybe even Mahler. Beethoven. Then maybe a line or two, and a call. And eventually sex. Drawing out the pleasure until the whole day roared in her memory.

She looked at the back seat. The bag rolled on the car's suspension. She could feel it glowing, not just in its lurid colours. She wanted to ask David if that was his real name, which was impermissible. Then she started to giggle and put her hand over her mouth to staunch the bubbling, uncontrollable laughter.

'Pardon?' he said.

'Nothing,' she said. 'I was just musing.' And then: 'It went well. I think we might have helped in establishing an important liaison.'

'Don't think' he said. 'Others might object.'

'Sorry,' she said. 'It's just relief. I'll calm down in a while. I haven't done this much before.' Never she meant.

'Yeah,' he said.

'I suppose it's a kind of blooding.'

'Probably.'

He reached for a tape, still concentrating on the road, and slotted it into the stereo. Springsteen. Music to grow muscles to, she thought. Then she turned and looked at him, wondering what he thought, if he did. He eased the big car to a halt at the lights, gently, as if a glass of water was balancing on the bonnet, playing the part of the professional. The street was quiet. New York could look enormously pretty, in a promiscuous sort of way.

She stretched her legs, thinking about the bath, and the rest to come, turned her head and noticed the motorbike waiting alongside for the green light. And then, in the last millisecond of her life, the gun in the hand.

Before the bike driver had fired off the first shot in the clip, his passenger, in Adidas training shoes and tight leggings which would not snag on any obstruction, was off the pillion and running round to the other side of the car. As he raised his Hechler Koch, the first shot from his partner splintered the glass on the passenger's side and hit the woman on the bridge of the nose, passing through the brain membrane and spinning wildly, before it exited, still at a killing pace in a spray of bloody matter which blinded the driver, who had turned to speak.

If he blinked, it was his last sentient motion. His leg kicked for a few seconds afterwards, after the eighteen shots churned through him, ricochetted round the car, burying into seats, pinging harmlessly off the internal metal, and as his atomised brain dripped back from the roof of the car.

The motorcycle passenger, his helmet and visor lightly pitted from shards of glass, opened the rear door on the driver's side, reached in to the bag which was now freshly, psychedelically coloured and pulled it out. The opened body behind the wheel gave a final leg kick and the man with the automatic, his voice muffled by the scarf and the helmet, said: 'A real trouper, that Frankie Vaughan.'

Then he climbed onto the back of the bike and they roared off, both laughing so uproariously that the Yamaha shivered as it went.

Doherty put the airline bag on the floor between his feet in the back of the cab and pulled a plastic carrier bag from an inside pocket of his coat. It was dark in the back. Doherty made sure that he was out of the driver's line of sight in the rearview mirror and then he began to transfer the money from the Aer Lingus bag into the carrier bag. Then he wrote a note on a page he tore from a notebook and slipped it into the airline bag. He pulled his left arm out of his coat and put his hand through the wire handles of the carrier, wriggling it up his arm so that the handles cut into his shoulder, then he slipped his coat back on. The operation took seconds and then Doherty slid along the seat so that he could see the driver's eyes in the mirror. They concentrated on the road and the competitive cars.

When they got to the building Doherty told the driver to wait for him. 'Uh-uh, not without you show me some cash.' There was eighteen dollars on the meter. He gave him a twenty, promised him a twenty dollar tip and dashed into the building, with the airline bag over his shoulder and the carrier bag inside his coat held tight against his body by his elbow. Do this at a run, he told himself.

He found the locker key, looked around quickly then opened the lock and pushed the bag into the locker. Then he walked briskly from the building, breaking into a trot as he got through the doors. The taxi driver was still there, window rolled down, reading a newspaper written in some middle European language. Doherty slid inside, said 'Go' loudly, and realised his voice was trembling. The driver leisurely folded his paper while Doherty resisted the urge to scream, then put the car into gear and moved off.

Would you know if you were being followed? Not by professionals, he thought. He looked round constantly but could see no consistent pattern of cars in the traffic behind. In a movie he would tell the driver, 'I'm being followed, lose that car,' and the high-speed chase would begin with over-dubbed skids and breathy engines. But since he had been in New York he hadn't found a taxi driver who could speak English in anything other than street names, so that option was out, even it weren't too conspicuous.

It wasn't that he was going to hold on to the money, as the note made clear, but he had to have some assurance that their end of the deal, enough money to set him up for the future, would come through, and safely. They surely couldn't expect anything else. Prudence is a Scottish characteristic, he told himself, if not in your case. But it's time you took some control of your destiny, Doherty. He wondered about that. Maybe he had, and it was to be a short and brutal one.

He paid off the cab at the hotel and walked quickly inside, searching the shadows. Rather than take the lift he ran up the stairs, turned the key in the bedroom lock, kicked the door open and ducked back out of sight. Then he began to snigger at the ludicrousness of the action: the walls were made of paper and putty and even a small calibre round would pass through like butter. He took a deep breath and plunged into the room. It was empty. He slammed the door behind him, threw off the coat and the bag of money, got down on his knees and retrieved the gun from under the mattress. He tucked it into the waistband of his trousers, first ensuring that the safety catch was on – he had little enough to worry about and didn't want it further foreshortened. Then he opened his leather shoulder grip, packed in the plastic bag, threw on his coat, picked up the two pieces of luggage and went out into the hall.

The porter in the hallway nodded to him as he left, the first recognition in a week, and he went off in search of another taxi.

Twelve blocks away the police were starting to put up a line and push the sightseers away from the car. The forensic team had arrived and were unpacking their equipment: one of them, a young man in his late twenties with sandy hair already going in places, was making chalk rings around the few external bullet holes in the body work. The car doors were still closed, with the bodies slumped together, although blood sprayed in the torrent of bullets mottled the dark outside paintwork on the driver's side below the missing window. Both corpses were facially unrecognisable, as if the heads had been minced. Shards of the craniums had pierced and lodged in the plastic roofing of the car and, remarkably, the front windscreen was undamaged although from the outside the view, as Lieutenant Marian Matthews remarked, it looked 'like a Jackson Pollock . . . from a limited pallette, red and grey basically'.

Matthews had long got over cursing his father for his predilection for John Wayne, and the old man's naming of him after The Dook. And his father, in turn, had almost forgiven him for his education, the law degree, and then law enforcement. The boy would have to suffer his conscience that after five generations Matthew's Dairy would die with him. But the boy suffered only from a life-long aversion to milk. Well, for as long as he could remember, and he certainly didn't intend to ask his mother about the early months.

As he looked into the car he recalled that six hours into his shift he had only had cups of black coffee to sustain him. He turned to Detective John Delaney, a twenty-year-old man, and said 'Del, let's step away from the scene for a few minutes and let the wizards do their work. Grab a coffee and a bite to eat. A hamburger would be choice, although I may go light on the catsup.'

Delaney said: 'Lead on, College.'

It took Doherty more than half an hour to get a cab – there was clearly some obstruction further down, police cars, sirens cawing and lights flashing, weaved past him as he walked. What he needed to do, he thought, as soon as he could get there, was to grab Lee and go for cover. Cover? That was amusing, he had enough greenery to bury them successfully for years. What they would do was find somewhere, upstate perhaps, to wait for a response. In his note – had the bag been recovered by now? – he had said that if they were willing to deal, a small ad should be placed in the personal section of *The New York Times* saying 'The medicine's ready, Doc.' And giving a contact number.

He walked on, the heavy shoulder bag cutting into his flesh. What if he was mugged now? They would never believe that story. He stayed near the edge of the pavement and felt the reassuring weight in his waistband. Eventually a cab stopped, he gave directions and climbed in. The driver was black, he noticed a textbook on jurisprudence on the bench seat next to the man.

'Interesting?' Doherty said, motioning to the book as the cab took off.

'No sir! Dense. Exceedingly dense.'

'Studying law?' he said, obviously.

'Yeah. I do this in the evenings. Used to be a cop before.' Doherty stiffened. 'Gave up after the third kid. Wife couldn't stand the life. Y'know, the hours. Never knowing when I was coming back.'

'If you were coming back.'

The man laughed: 'Don't know about that. She see too many movies . . . and, mind you, she kept looking wistfully at the insurance policies.' He swung hard right to avoid a slow-moving car. 'Liked the life, though. Kind of miss the excitement. But don't knock school. It can get pretty hot sitting in class next to a nuggety eighteen-year-old with an itch in her pants. Hell, yeah.'

They passed another police car going in the opposite direction. 'A lot of activity tonight,' Doherty said, continuing the conversation.

'Shooting, I heard on the radio. A driver called it in. Too many guns in this town.'

'Amen,' said Doherty, feeling the weight at his waist.

'Right,' said the driver, pulling over, 'here we are.'

Lieutenant Matthews drained his second black coffee. Delaney was wiping his plate with the end of a bun. 'Well,' said Matthews, 'what do you figure? Drugs, gangland slaying?'

'For sure,' said Delaney, between chews. 'Jealous husbands usually wait to catch them at it.'

'And they don't usually jump off motorcycles at traffic lights with automatic weapons in their back pockets and blaze away.'

'Eye witness says two of them. Helmets, leathers. Driver offs the woman with a pistol, then puts the bike on its ramp while the pillion passenger is opening up on the man, probably with an Uzi I should say from the description. Then the first one, after ensuring that his bike ain't gonna get damaged in the fracas' – he pronounced in frackass – 'empties the rest of his mag into the dame's head. What's left of it.'

Matthews – 'College' – tried to catch the waitress' eye for another coffee, failed, said, 'Fuck it,' and then 'The mortician's gonna have a helluva job prettifying those two. Not a lot of raw material – '

'A lot of raw material,' pointed out Delaney, 'none of it much use.'

'One thing troubles me.'

'Don't tell me . . . the kids' orthodonty bills.'

'That too. But John and Jane Doe were very well dressed. You notice? Not your usual gangland threads. Class. Brooks Brothers suit. Her coat must have cost five hundred bucks. Doesn't figure. Doesn't fit the pattern.'

Delaney, who was in his mid-forties, twelve years older

than College, with a Fifties flat-top which looked incon-
guous on top of his lined, cavernous face, said: 'So they
got the rags at a garage sale?'

College said: 'I'll bet you the price of this meal that
we've nothing on either of them.' And then: 'Come on.
Back to the scene to give my legendary powers of detection full reign.'

'Yeah?' said Delaney. 'So it's another unsolved.'

'Looks that way,' said College, picking up the check.

Doherty watched the tail lights of the taxi disappear. He
waited in the lobby of Lee's building, staring up the street
for any sign of a tail. It was quiet. Lee wouldn't be home
for a couple of hours, after the show. She had given him
a key and while he waited he would throw some things of
hers into a bag so that they could leave immediately she
got in. He didn't want to frighten her, but he certainly
couldn't persuade her that the haste was because he was
dragging her off on a surprise break. Probably he would
have to tell her the truth, or most of it. But away from
here.

He looked out again. Still no sign of anyone following,
he thought, and decided he would go up.

Afterwards he would believe that the sense of foreboding
began as he walked along the corridor. But certainly,
as he turned the key in the lock and felt the first wave of
heat as he opened the door, his stomach began to clutch.
He switched on the lights inside the door. 'Lee!' he called.
And he put down the bags and from some disturbed
sense, pulled out the gun. The heat was unbearable, like
a sauna. He had begun to sweat. Under his coat, his
jacket and the shirt he could feel moisture running down
his stomach. Clutching the gun with both hands he moved
into the living room. It was empty. Condensation ran
down the uncurtained window. A table lamp lay on its
side. He caught the nude picture of her out of the corner

of his eye. The oven was on, so was the range. The heating, he guessed was also turned up full. He couldn't begin to think why for the coruscating panic which seized his head. Perspiration in rivulets ran into his eyes, he blinked, he tasted salt in his mouth. And bile.

Cautiously he moved towards the bedroom door. He could hear his heart racing. He used the gun to gently prod open the bedroom door and saw it shake in his hands. He heard the buzzing noise of a fan heater and the temperature turned up a notch again. He wiped his eyes quickly with one hand and then re-gripped the pistol. The light was off but now he could see, in the light from the street lamps and the neon, that she lay on her back on the bed. Naked. Just before he threw up he noticed that she had been disembowelled. And that the gash to the side of her throat was so deep and wide that her head lay floppily, like a puppet's.

College was not at his best on less than three hours sleep, punctuated by the screams of a teething baby. The scene of the crime had yielded little: spent ammunition by the bushel, fingerprints aplenty and a lengthy statement by the only apparent witness, an old lady out walking her dog, together with pooper-scooper. Two unidentified men – presumably men – had calmly pulled up beside the black Buick, unidentifiable in leathers and dark helmets, made a double hit and roared off, probably before the lights got to green. A highly professional killing. But of whom? By whom?

The dawn was streaking the sky when he got to bed and when he got up, the baby – he still hadn't got used to calling her Therese – was still bawling. Sandy looked at him reproachfully as he stumbled into the kitchen and made coffee. She was trying to feed the baby, between howls.

'Double homicide,' he offered as pacification.

'I suppose it's useless to ask when you might be home.'

'Fraid so,' he said, watching the percolator bubble. 'Probably a gang thing . . . but the Chief is going to be sorely pissed. It's all right them wasting each other in their own backyards but when they do it on the streets of Manhattan, alarming the citizenry, causing traffic jams, exposing his record to scrutiny, heads get shaken in their shoulders. You know,' he went on, pouring coffee into a Brer Rabbit mug, long since having given up the struggle for his own, separate identity, 'I got seduced by all those Edward G. Robinson movies. Those big, grand ones where the cops called each other peace officers, saintly sounding. Loadda fucking crap.'

'Sshh. Don't swear in front of Therese.'

'Sorry,' he said, swigging from the mug, 'I forgot babies of four months were fluent in profanity.'

'Don't, Matt, please.' He continued staring at the bubbling coffee. 'You could have gone into a law practice' she said.

'Sandy,' he said, more violently than he intended, 'not now. Not again.'

Delaney looked no better than he felt when he got to the precinct. 'Sorry to keep you,' he said, 'but the five-mile swim took a mite longer than usual.'

'Particularly after the run.'

'Exactly,' said College. The room was comparatively quiet, no crazies struggling on the lino, a dose of prostitutes in the corner, a couple of black guys with their hands behind their backs, cuffed, but that was it basically. 'Okay,' he said, sitting down and draping his jacket over the back of the metal chair, 'what have we got? Apart from two unidentified Caucasians chilling-out in the morgue?'

'Car was rented, he gave a fake licence, pace . . .'

'Pace the victims were up to no fuckin' good.'

95

'Yep.' Delaney had a penchant for loud ties, College thought, definite sign of an inferiority complex. 'Coupled with the fact that he had an unregistered .38 in his well-cut suit pocket and she had one of those dinky little silver .22s that well-bred ladies carry in their handbags next to their condoms. And no IDs on either.'

'Prints?'

'John and Jane's all over the car, obviously. Several others. We're trying to eliminate those of the people at the hire company. We haven't got a match yet of their prints in records.'

'And that's it?'

'Pretty much. Blood grouping, tissue type, ballistics etcetera.'

'Etcetera.' College yawned. God, he thought, his kids would grow up with a stranger in the house. 'Del, at times like this I ask myself what Holmes would have done now.'

'Lootenant, if you're telling me you've taken up the violin I'm putting in for a posting.'

'And I suppose the opium solution is out as well, Sergeant?'

'On duty, certainly. But maybe you and me can get together later with a coupla scanty-clads!'

'So we have to rely on tried and trusted methods of detection then?'

'Like blind luck?'

College sighed. One of the prostitutes, tall, addled, with a flared skirt which barely covered her pudenda, and didn't when she swung her arms, which she was doing now, at poor family-man Lopez, was screaming 'Fuuuuckyooouyoouubaaastid.' It is,' he said, 'going to be one long day.'

The prospect lengthened considerably when Delaney slapped the *Daily News* on his desk, in the middle of a call to Sandy. In lettering large enough for a spy satellite to focus on, the headline said DRUG WARS. Next to a huge, flashlit grainy picture of the shot-up car and the two bodies. 'Sandy,' he said, 'I have to go now, I'll call you later when I know when I'm getting off.' And then to Delaney, 'So these fuckwits know it all?' stabbing a finger at the page. 'This is really going to help the Chief's equilibrium.'

He read out '. . . police are working on the theory that last night's slayings were drug-related . . .' ''Cause it's the only theory we got.' '. . . raising fears of gang warfare spreading out into the streets of Manhattan.'

He threw the paper down. 'Where did this crap come from Delaney?'

'From the usual place,' answered Delaney, pointing with his middle figure to his backside.

'More good news.'

'Yeah?' College was continuing to stare at the discarded paper.

'I owe you a meal. There are no records of John and Jane's fingerprints in the files. Persons of unblemished character, seems.'

'I'll bet,' said College, finally sweeping the paper off his desk. 'When are we getting the autopsy result?'

'Coupla hours.'

College picked up his desk phone and punched in an internal number. 'Basinger? It's Matthews. Our two most recent guests in the cold place, no previous, is that right? Yeah?' Delaney watched him nod into the phone. 'Well,' he said before hanging up, 'make my day.'

'Well?' said Delaney.

'They've found a partial print on the car key which matches neither of the deceased nor any of the Hertz staff.'

'So why the long face?'

'Two reasons. First, there's no match in records. And second, it doesn't make sense. The engine was still running when the squad car arrived so the perps can't have touched it. And second second, it still doesn't make any sense because even if they did, these were pros and they had to have been wearing gloves. So – '

'So it's probably a print from the guy that hired the car before.'

'Why is life a conspiracy against me?' said College, picking up the phone again.

At 5.32p.m., as he did at the end of every working day, John Dollan put the cap on his fountain pen, tidied his desk once more, rose and walked to the window, drawing the blinds over the city. Then he put on his barathea coat, closed the office door behind him, tutting for the nth time about the state of his secretary's desk, went into the hall and tapped lightly on the facing door with the gold-lettered plaque which said Emmett Dollan. Then he opened the door, looked at his son across the wide glass desk, asked him if he was ready and waited for the boy to finish his telephone call. Boy? The boy would be thirty this year. And he would shortly be a grandfather.

Dollan senior was tall, lean, with a passing resemblance to a younger John Kenneth Galbraith, someone had once told him. He was sixty-five and still a long way off retiring. A swim in the morning, tennis at weekends and on summer evenings had kept his vigour and he had kept his enthusiasm for the job. Company law, he remarked to anyone who enquired, is endlessly fascinating, endlessly changing, a constant challenge for a restless mind.

Emmett pushed a file of papers into his briefcase and closed the gold clasp. 'Interlogik,' he said, 'there's a meeting first thing.'

Dollan nodded. 'Right?' he asked. His son nodded, then switched off the room lights and they walked slowly along the corridor to the lift.

'Traffic's bound to be bad,' said Dollan.

'Dad. You say that every evening at this precise point.'

'Do I. I'm sorry. I'll remember that tomorrow. At this precise point.' Emmett laughed.

As they went down in the lift Dollan said: 'Your mother will be asking about Helen and the baby. Any little titbit to satisfy her?'

'No, Dad. Same as ever. Same kicking. Tell her no further bulletins will be issued until the important one.'

'No,' Dollan said, 'I don't think I'll tell her that.'

The lift reached the basement and the door opened. The two men walked towards the black Cadillac in the reserved space, their footsteps echoed and Dollan thought, as he did every day at this time, about the smell of fumes in this garage. Ten paces from the Cadillac Dollan noticed two men walking towards them at a right angle. 'Mr Dollan?' the leading man called. 'Yes,' said the two Dollans simultaneously, then stopped, looked at each other and smiled. The leading man drew back his coat and pulled up a sawn-off shotgun, the second man dropped into a firing position holding a pistol. The first blast reverberated round the garage. It caught John Dollan in the upper chest and neck, punching out a raw hole, knocking him over on to his back and spraying his son with blood. Emmett Dollan had instinctively started to recoil when the shotgun went off again. The second blast hit him, primarily, in the left breast, shredding it, pellets piercing the heart, the aorta, lacerating the stomach. He spun round with the force of the hit and ended up face down in the oil stains. The second killer, unnecessarily, walked over to both bodies and shot them twice in the head.

'Lootenant,' Detective Angel Perkins called, 'report of a double shooting. Wall Street. Coupla lawyers.'

'Jesus Christ,' said College, 'what is going on here? They're going in twos all of a sudden. Mind you,' he turned to Delaney, 'no news is entirely bad. Lawyers you say, Perkins?' he shouted to the detective who was still on the phone.

Forty-five minutes later Matthews and Delaney were looking down at the two corpses. Sergeant Michael Abernethy, a big black in his mid-thirties who had been an aspiring light-heavyweight until his hands gave up and he joined the force, was speaking. 'No apparent motive, Lootenant. Father and son, both lawyers, specialising in expensive company litigation. Wealthy. Both live on the island. It happened about 5.35. The attendant says he was nearly deafened. He saw two men – '

'Don't tell me,' said Delaney, 'on a motorbike.'

'Motorbike?' said Abernethy, turning, giving off a whiff of garlic from his breath. 'No. Why?'

'Doesn't matter, Sergeant. Go on.'

'Two men, in a Ford, lit out. Attendant didn't get a close look. Didn't get the car's number. Thinks it was green. Security here is pretty lax.'

'Probably didn't think they needed it. Who's gonna hit a couple of lawyers off for a pre-prandial Martini, or whatever?'

'Aggrieved client,' said the sergeant.

'Yeah?' College shook his head. 'Like Exxon, IBM, maybe? So, what did they hit them with, apart from the shotgun?'

'.32 probably.'

'Any cartridges?'

'Nah,' said the sergeant.

'You know,' said College, 'Dollan's name's familiar. Let's get back to Castle Doom and check.'

'Well,' said Delaney, 'at least the *Daily News* can't link this to a drugs war.'

'Sometimes,' said the lieutenant, 'you can be extremely callow.'

*

The file on Dollan was not substantial. It requested reference to the Federal Bureau of Investigation for further information and stressed that, if apprehended on any felony whatever, however inconsequential, or if any officer should have cause to observe or question John Dollan, on any subject, the Bureau should immediately be informed. College whistled through his teeth. Apart from that there was one sheet. Dollan had stood bail for one Joseph Patrick McCartten, alleged Irish Republican Army quartermaster, former sniper, whom the British had wanted to extradite. And the file noted that he was also chairman of the Northern Ireland Action Committee.

'Poppa Dollan,' said College to Delaney who was laboriously typing a report – somehow cops could never manage typing, either through some synapsial block or because of the meathook fingers – 'was an IRA sympathiser.'

'Him and half the NYPD,' said Delaney.

'Puts an angle on the hit, maybe.'

'What you thinking?'

'I dunno. Just some connection. Arms dealing maybe? Fund raising? Perhaps the other side offed them because he was too successful? Wanted to terminate the money supply? Well,' he said, 'I guess now I make my duty call to the Feds, like it says here.' And he picked up the phone.

When College arrived for his shift next day, Saturday, he flicked through the overnight reports first, as he always did. He hadn't slept well again. Sandy had refused to speak to him and curled herself in a venomous ball away from him in the bed, all because she smelled beer on his breath. 'One drink, Sandy,' he had said. 'Okay two.' He had to wind down at the end of the day. Yeah, she had said, and what about her, how did she get to wind down with two kids and no husband around to wind down with?

Rather than retaliate he had grabbed a six-pack and slumped in front of the TV, watching an old movie and drinking desultorily until he thought she was asleep. Then he had crept into bed, whispered to her, felt her flinch, then he had turned over and was asleep almost immediately, dreaming of the sea. It had been a pirate movie.

'Another homicide,' he said to himself. Delaney was hanging up his coat. College caught the tie, great gashes of red, yellow and brown. He shook his head. 'Young woman,' he said.

'Pardon?' said Delaney.

'Slasher victim. Young woman, Lee Garrison, about twenty-three cut into takeaway pieces. Bit actress. Hey, that's funny!' he smiled toothily at Delaney. His eyes felt raw. 'Beat cops broke in on the insistence of friends when she didn't turn up for the play she was in. Found considerable amounts of cocaine secreted around the apartment. Obviously dealing. Jesus,' he looked at Delaney, trying to avoid sun blindness on the tie. 'Five murders in twenty-four hours, New York's statistical average. So how come Delaney, if it isn't a conspiracy, they all fall in my patch?'

'The *News* will probably ask that.'

'Follow glory where ye may.'

'What?'

'Sometimes things like that just pop into my mind and I have to get them out.'

'A sort of mental random static, you got.'

'It's probably harmless.'

'Well,' said Delaney, hitching his holster harness and sitting down, 'just in case, I'll buy you that meal I owe you tonight.'

And College thought of Sandy with foreboding.

Delaney took the call from Basinger while College was talking to Captain Lorenzo. Rather, while Lorenzo was chewing him out. The privileges of seniority, thought

College, ritually ass-kicking the next in line. The Captain had no more idea of what to do than he did, but his ignorance carried greater authority. The Chief was incandescent. Blood was running in the streets. Politicians were fulminating. The news media were heaping kerosene on the whole affair. College came out of the Captain's room, kicked the coffee machine, poured another cup of the stuff, then, back at his desk, saw Delaney's note.

'Basinger,' he said when he got through to Albany, where all the print records were stored, for some unaccountable reason, known only perhaps to a couple of bureaucrats in the department. 'It's Matthews.'

'Lootenant,' and he heard the man scrabbling for something, 'interesting news. The corpse – '

'Which particular corpse, or do I get to choose?'

'Oh, sorry. Garrison.'

'Yeah.'

'Thought you'd be interested. You remember that partial print we got offuv the car key in the Buick shootings? Well, it matches prints we got inside Garrison's apartment.'

'Shit,' said College. He put his hand over the mouthpiece and whistled. 'Hey, thanks, well done.'

'Yeah, well we're still no nearer to identifying it.'

'Keep workin' on it.' And then, 'Hey, Basinger, you don't have a rather tall and foxy daughter do you.'

'No, why?'

'Oh, nothin. Just my luck.'

He shouted 'Delaney,' at the top of his voice at the mill of people in the room, 'get your butt over here boy.'

'He's interviewing some geek,' Perkins said, round his green cigar.

'Perkins,' he said, 'at last we have some drugs and a connection.'

'Is that good or bad, Lootenant?'

*

Guiseppe Moroni made a tradition of Sunday brunch. Some friends, members of the family round for drinks, barbecued fish and steaks, some pasta prepared by Antonella, outside round the pool if the weather was fine. Or in the conservatory, surrounded by his precious orchids, and his beloved friends and family. He always wore a white dinner jacket. He cut a splendid figure he thought, moving among his guests filling glasses, playing with the children. Still had a stomach he could squeeze into pants he bought ten years ago, on account of the swimming and the tennis, three days a week at least. He had taken care of himself. Still caught the occasional ooh-la-la glances from the ladies. He wasn't ageing badly.

The day was bright and fine, with a watery sun. He smiled to himself. He would put up a prize, a thousand dollars, for a race among the men. Two lengths. The pool was heated, it wouldn't cause any heart attacks. He unpeeled the foil on another bottle of champagne, uncorked it and moved among his friends topping up glasses. He told Antonella to bring as many towels as she could find, and made the challenge. There were good natured groans and then half a dozen of the younger men started to strip down to their underpants. There were shouts and whistles as the varied underclothes appeared. There was a penchant for lurid boxer shorts, Moroni noted, what ever happened to Italians and briefs? Then six men, shivering in the crisp air, took up diving positions, waiting for him to give a sign. He raised his arm and looked about him.

The conservatory was first to go. The explosion erupted outwards, shattering the massive panes, spraying millions of razor-sharp slivers up and out, shredding the plants and sucking greenery up into the vacuum. The second explosion went off in a metal garbage can next to the barbecue. Thirty pounds of Semtex, nails and rivets killed Moroni instantly, and his cousin Mario and his wife Luciana; and spread out in a lethal metal hail, tearing through flesh, canvas, floral cotton; embedding in concrete, fizzing into the water. One bolt, white hot, passed through the stomach of one of the poised divers, causing him to jacknife and plunge into the whipped water, before the bolt buried itself three inches into a larch tree, smouldering.

After the reverberations of the explosions there was a second of pure silence when nothing whatever in the air or the environment stirred, and then the moans started, of the dying and the surviving.

The first ambulanceman on the scene, Kenny Currie, a lolloping big lad with tight black trousers and crepe-soled shoes, came out on to the blood-spattered patio, looked down into the pool which had turned pink, noted the floating vegetation and bobbling bits of flesh, and said quietly: 'Jeez. It looks like a bath of Pimms.'

Although it was his day off, the Captain called him in anyway. 'What do you want me to do, Sandy, resign? Don't answer that!' he said as he left. She started to cry, which made him feel worse. He took the subway, which made him feel even worse, and when he got to the station the Captain said 'Nice of you to drop in, Matthews.'

'Captain,' he said, 'I'm not responsible. Don't take it out on me.'

Delaney was there and a man College didn't know. Dressed like an investment banker. Longish, brilliantined hair, late thirties, gold signet ring. 'This is Agent Owen Williams,' the Captain said and College thought he saw a faint wrinkle of distaste cross the man's face. 'He's being attached to the investigation and he may have some information.'

'Go,' said College.

'First of all, the latest killings – '

'Whoa,' said College. 'Which latest?'

'I didn't say on the phone? A coupla hours ago Guiseppe Moroni, capo of one of New York's finest Italian families, together, at last count, with eight others, ended up as the bolognese in a lunch-time cook-out at his place. Two high-explosive charges, and several buckets of nails, bolts and rivets, took the capo, his friends, family and acolytes instantaneously to the dark place.'

'Allah al Akbar,' said Delaney. 'Ain't he just.'

'Now,' continued Williams, 'what we are sure of is that this is not fratricide in the family, or families. Our infiltration is pretty good.'

'So, what the fuck is going on?' said College.

'Word is that the two dudes in the Buick were Moroni's foot soldiers, on some kind of scam, we don't know what, and were terminated. By whom we don't know. But the family, for some reason, figures that lawyer Dollan has some connection, and retaliates. We think that the fatal party today was, in part, a celebration, a thank you to the guys who did it. That two of the deceased or maimed did the hit.'

'There's an ineluctable conclusion to this.'

'Precisely,' the agent nodded.

'That whoever then set off the whizzbangs in Capo's backyard was . . . IRA.'

'As you said, ineluctable. It's going to take days, but I'd bet that when we get all of the forensic the device is going to prove to be a classic, textbook IRA bomb, probably remotely triggered . . . probably even be able to ask the boys across the water to tell us with some certainty who's likely to have put it together.' College looked at Williams. How I'd describe him is oleaginous, he thought. And, I bet his pillowcases are permanently stained.

'This isn't making any sense,' Delaney said.

'Motivationally.'

'No,' agreed College.

'To me neither,' said Agent Williams.

'A question,' said College.

'If I can answer,' said Williams.

'You can. Will you, though? Dollan. Tell me about him. And the Northern Ireland Aid Committee. On the file it says you guys have got them on check.'

Williams shrugged and held up his hands. 'Pretty straightforward. We've never been able to get conclusive proof but it's certainly a front organisation for the IRA, raising money for arms. On the face of it it's a benevolent organisation. Dollan and his well-connected chums, lawyers, a couple of judges, the odd senator, senior cops, sons of ould Ireland, pull together to raise millions of dollars a year. The network stretches into every Irish enclave, from collections in bars, to fund-raising events. The big guys make sizeable donations, and then the money goes out of the country, through a Swiss account or two, and then on to the arms market or into Colonel Gaddafi's back pocket. All in the name of patriotism. But we've never been able to prove anything criminal.

'The son, Emmett, was persona non grata in the UK. Kept popping up at demonstrations, commemorations and jamborees, spouting off about the Brits. So they excluded him from the country. The Dollans were so close to the top Sinn Fein people you couldn't get a skin between them. You know, Sinn Fein are the IRA without the Armalites anyway.'

'Shit,' said the Captain, 'the papers are going to have a field day.'

'So, what's the plan?' Delaney asked 'Stand on the sidelines watching them blow each other to bits, cheering?'

'It's tempting,' said Agent Williams, 'but your government says no. It's apparently bad for our international reputation, all this tit-for-tat. Probably worried about the tourist trade.'

'As Delaney said earlier,' College came in, leaning back in the chair with his hands behind his head, 'motivationally this doesn't make a load of sense. With most of their money coming out of here, and with a high sympathy factor, it doesn't make for good strategical planning for the IRA to risk that by bringing the war to our streets. There's another thing. The killing of Lee Garrison. She's a small-time actress, fairly major drug dealer from the evidence, died a couple of days ago at the hand of what looks like a psycho. Prints at the scene match a print from the scene of the killing of Moroni's people, if that's who they were. Which was an extremely cool and professional job. So, explain and comment! I don't believe a pro, ice-water in the veins, executes the perfect job, leaves a print on the car key and then, freaks, or for kicks, tears apart a pretty actress who majors in dope.'

'Stranger things, Lootenant . . . stranger things.'

'I know, Williams. I'm just not happy about it, is what I'm saying. Disturbs my neat templates of criminal behaviour. Pros don't panic.'

'Not even under the influence of a pretty girl?'

College shrugged. 'I know, I'm looking for perfect, rational explanations.'

'What about the forensic?' the Captain asked.

'It's not all in yet. What look like alien hairs under her nails. Semen too. Not under her nails. Usual places.'

'Sex attack?' asked the agent.

'Could be but, nah, somehow I don't think so. See, the trouble is that we're having difficulty putting precise times to anything because the killer had all the heating going so it was like a furnace, affected the body temperature and all. But, we've got the fingerprints in the apartment and I'm getting a DNA test, the genetic fingerprint thing, done on the hairs and the semen.'

'Good,' said Williams.

'Why?' said the Captain.

College spread his hands. 'Why not? Might tell us something.'

'How reliable is it?' the Captain continued.

Williams answered. 'Sometimes it's inconclusive. The

test is only about five years old and sometimes it goes wrong. But when it's specific it's totally individual-specific. It was invented by some professor in Oxford, England, and it seems that everyone's DNA constituents are unique, like fingerprint patterns. This professor, Jeffreys, he said, "Suppose we could test a million people every second. How long would it take to find one exactly the same? The answer is that the universe itself would die before we found one the same."'

Delaney whistled.

'We're working with the British Home Office,' Williams continued, 'trying to set up a genetic fingerprint database.'

'So, where to from here?' asked College.

'Well, the leads, the indicators such as they are, point across the Atlantic. Irish emanations. A call to the British Special Branch can't do any harm,' volunteered Williams.

'Certainly can't,' agreed College.

Doherty sat in the all-night Burger King nursing a succession of coffees which cooled in his hands. He had bought a hamburger eventually to stop staff pestering him to eat. It lay untouched. His stomach still heaved. Everywhere he looked, on the window wet with condensation, on the jackets and coats of other itinerants, on the large price board over the fast food serving counter, he could see her. Torn open. The bed where they had made love hours before sodden and dark with her blood. And her eyes – still open, the face turned towards his – were pleading. He knew that was ridiculous, that he was simply reading his own guilt into it. But it was true. If he had never met her she would be alive. He was responsible for her death by caring for her, loving her. If he had maintained his vow of uninvolvement she would be here.

In her bedroom, after he had stopped shaking and the hysterical crying had abated to a blubbering burble, he had kneeled down beside the bed, her blood seeping through from the carpet to his knees, and held her hand. He remembered the terrible smell and he began to shiver again and choke on vomit. Then he had made another vow, to find the man in the picture, to track him down and then tell him why he was going to die. Slowly. It wasn't atonement. It was simply vengeance. For him. Thinking about it, going about it, would keep him sane. Or at least functioning. It would keep him alive. And if he could get to others of them he would kill them too. Until . . . until? It didn't matter. He had said – and he had to be given a name, to make it more personal – that they went on for ever. Well, he had to go on, for long enough. He put his hand inside his coat and felt the butt of the gun. It was cool now.

The six pictures of that face were fanned out on the table in front of him. He told himself that he was being conspicuous sitting here for hours, gazing at pictures, and as he had begun to come out of the shock he knew that he had to move, seek cover. How quickly would the police identify him? Pretty quickly, he knew. The whole thing had been a set-up. They, the Provos, his man, would probably call the police anonymously and give his identity.

At first, when he saw her there, he had thought that his running off with the money had caused it. But even he could tell that she had been dead for some time.

Try as he might, he couldn't stop thinking about how it must have been. The final terror. Did he, they, let themselves into the flat? Had they raped her? He thought of the scene and he began to cry, soundlessly, staring down at the cold meal going out of focus in his eyes, pushing vainly at the tears running freely down his cheeks. Conspicuous he thought. And then, 'All they'll take me for is just another maudlin drunk.' Perhaps true. Why did they have to . . . to tear her apart? He shuddered.

After he had released her hand he had closed the eyes that kept looking at him reproachfully. And then he had taken all the cocaine he could find, in some effort to dignify her death. Were there other stashes? Would the police put it down to some drug-induced frenzy, a pusher killed by her client? Hey, close the book on that one, Mac! He reached into his coat pocket and felt the packet. Crystals, he could feel, were already ooze-deep in the lining. He dug into the packet and clasped a large pinch of coke which he surreptitiously stuffed into his mouth, swallowing quickly in a wash of cold coffee. He had to stay active for the next few hours, which were crucial, until he could find a place to lie low and work out a strategy. And then, looking down at the face on the table in front of him, he thought of the only place he could go.

He wiped his face on the paper napkin, gathered up the pictures into the packet, pulled his luggage from under the table and set out.

It was 7.30a.m. Doherty shivered in his coat and his mouth felt numb. His heart was racing but his mind felt high and clear: the terrors had receded to the periphery. He was standing in a phone booth, his luggage anchored between his feet. The early morning rush to work had just started and as he began dialling the number he noticed the feet passing and the surprising number of young women, dressed for power-wresting, with track shoes on their feet. He clutched the bent card and finished punching the numbers into the phone.

The phone rang in that curious long American drawl. He imagined her with someone, or oblivious in the shower, out, out of town. He closed his eyes in silent prayer.

'Hu . . . hello.' The voice was sleepy.

'Look, sorry,' he stumbled, 'sorry to disturb you so early . . . it's – ' Shit! he had forgotten the name he had given, ' – it's not David Bailey here.'

'Hi,' she said, sounding warmer.

'I'm a couple of blocks away from you. It's a long story. But there's something I need to talk to you about. What do you say I grab a handful of croissants or something, come round and explain?'

'Sure,' she said guilelessly, 'that would be real nice.' And he felt shame at the subterfuge. 'Give me twenty minutes to shower and dress.'

He bought croissants, orange juice, milk and the morning papers at a Polish delicatessen on the corner of her block in Brooklyn. He stopped outside the shop and quickly scanned *The New York Times* and the *Daily News*. He ignored the front page splash in the *News* – DRUG WARS – and flicked through for any mention of Lee's body or of him. Then he went back through it again, combing each page. And then *The Times*. Nothing. He felt relief wash over him and then disgust at the selfish feeling. He binned the papers, picked up his luggage. The cocaine was pulsing in rolling electric waves through his body.

She was wearing black trousers and a severe white shirt, buttoned tight up to the neck. He avoided properly looking at her body. Her hair was damp and springy where she had evidently tried to finger-dry it.

She said: 'Hi,' again. And then: 'You look kitted out for an occupation. Come in.' She showed him into the only room. It had natural light and little else. A bed, a double, hurriedly made, a beaten-up tweed sofa, stained floorboards and a couple of armchairs. And, in a corner, under a barred, smeared window which looked out hazily onto a fire escape, a sink and cooker.

'It's my minimalist phase,' she said apologetically.

'You should see where I live at home,' he said, instantly realising that he would probably never see the boat again. 'I checked out of my hotel,' he went on, explaining the baggage. 'I was half-thinking about going upstate . . . I thought I'd give you a call first . . . before work . . . what time do you start?'

'Not until one today. One to ten.' Then she said, quietly, not looking at him directly: 'What happened to the involvement?'

He saw the bloody tableau again. He said just: 'It ended.'

'Ah,' she said, putting her meaning to his visit. Thinking, she threw you out.

He looked at the walls. She had taped and pinned up pictures – originals, some from books, a few of which looked uneasily familiar – over almost the entire wall area. Hundreds of pictures. She noticed him looking. 'Stolen mostly, I'm afraid. From the darkroom. I make extra prints of shots I really like. Some classics ripped from magazines, even library books. So, don't ever go to New York public libraries looking for photographic books, particularly Bruce Davidson, Erwitt, Eugene Smith. Chances are I'll have been there and filletted them.'

'You take pictures?'

'It's a long story. Like yours. You wouldn't be interested.'

He threw his bags onto the sofa and handed her the brown paper bag of groceries. We have the time, he thought. 'I would,' he said, 'and will you heat or will I?'

She smiled. It was an anxious, eager-to-please smile, as if she didn't often get attention. He found that surprising. 'Take off your coat, why don't you?' she said.

'Yes. Later,' he said. And then: 'By the way, where is the shower.'

She rolled her eyes up. 'Oh . . . shared. On the landing,' and she lit the gas oven and poured water into the kettle.

Then she started to talk, mostly to the locked window, shy and embarrassed about speaking about herself. She fidgeted endlessly with her damp hair. 'Actually it's only a short story. I'm not that old. Brought up in the mid-West, college in Kansas, for God's sake, for some reason

113

I can't remember . . . well, there was a boy involved . . .
history major. I guess I got the hunger for photography
reading about the Depression, looking at the pictures, the
dustbowl stuff, Ansell Adams . . .

'I decided I was going to be a photographer. Arrogant,
huh? Eventually I came to New York. And I had to get a
job. I didn't have a proper portfolio. A darkroom seemed
a good place. The pay's awful, you wouldn't believe what
a dump like this can cost, but I've learned a lot.' She
turned to face him, folding her arms under her breasts,
which he tried not to notice . . . remembering. 'Had to
hawk the camera, though.' She paused. 'And your hard
luck story?'

'The kettle's boiling,' he said.

'Evasive.'

'No. I just need a caffeine buzz . . . too little sleep.' My
God, he thought, that's the last thing I need. Haifetz
could play high aching solos on the tendons and nerves in
my head. 'Pour the coffee.' He cleared the bags from the
sofa and, presumptuously, no time for side, sat down. 'If
you put out the croissants, sit down, I'll explain . . .
everything . . . I can.'

She started to spoon coffee into two mugs and then
opened the oven, burning her fingers on an inside tray.
'Shit,' she said, sucking them. He got up, told her to sit
down and used the tail of his coat to lever out the tray.
Then he retrieved two plates from the washboard – 'No
butter, sorry!' she said – and slid two croissants on to each
plate, poured the water into the cups and handed her
breakfast. Then he took his and sat down on the sofa
beside her.

'I recognise a couple of the pictures,' he said, biting
into a croissant. It tasted like iron filings so he put the
croissant back on the plate and then the plate on the
floor. 'Mine.'

'No shit!' she said putting down her plate and cup and
jumping up. 'Which?'

He pointed. 'That spread next to the McCullin homage. Lebanon. Sabra camp. The mother with the child. And the wedding.' He paused. 'Actually I lied to you about my name the other day. It's not – Stuart.'

She traced her finger in the air until she found the spot on the wall. 'Doherty. J. H. Doherty,' she said, turning to look at him. 'Wonderful pictures . . . what ever happened to you?'

He smiled wryly. Indeed. 'Now, that is too long a story.'

'God,' she ran her fingers through her hair again, 'and I made that stupid crack about Bailey. Dumb. I'm sorry.'

'Look, sit down again. I have something to tell you which is difficult. I don't want to alarm you.'

'Don't tell me, you want to take nude shots of me,' she was laughing and shaking her head in disbelief. 'God, I can't believe this.'

'Please, sit down.' She joined him, clenching her hands between her knees as if they might be out of control. 'Look,' he went on, 'I have to stay here for a couple of days – '

'No problem, really, no problem.' She was smiling down at her hands.

'You don't understand,' he said, standing to take off his coat, keeping his elbow tight over the gun, 'I have to. And you have to stay here with me, incommunicado.' She looked round at him, fear and bewilderment beginning to suffuse her face. 'You aren't in any danger. I haven't done anything. At least I haven't done what they, the police are going to believe. And that's bad. Very, very bad. I just have to figure a way to get out of here. I can't check into a hotel or wander the streets. I need a safe place. I'm sorry it's yours. Really I am.' She was biting a knuckle and her eyes were screwed up, watering. He could see the bewilderment, the mounting panic. 'I really need you to believe me. I really haven't hurt anyone despite what you'll read and hear – '

'Please,' she said, starting to cry now, putting her hands over her ears, 'I don't want to know.'

'I haven't hurt anyone. I won't hurt you, I promise. I wish I had another choice, rather than involving you. You'll never be able to accept this. But,' he drained the coffee, 'I have to get out of here and find someone. Find a way. I'm using you, I'm sorry.'

She looked up at his photographs on her wall, then at him. She took a deep breath so that she could say the words clearly. 'I can't believe that anyone who took those pictures would deliberately hurt anyone.' Her look was imploring, tears ran down her cheeks. 'I have to believe that. I wish I could trust you,' she said, 'but I can't trust anyone.' He wanted to touch her in reassurance. But he couldn't.

Delaney was eating an ice-cream. College shook his head. A grown man, haircut like that, juvenile taste in ties. Now sucking on a cone. And in winter! College's sense of order was deeply offended.

'Any more tit for tats?' he asked.

'Quiet so far,' answered Delaney. 'What did London say?'

'Talked to some goddamn Chief Inspector Grant, Anti-Terrorist Branch. Scotland Yard. Laid it all out for him. Shootings, the bombs, forensic, DNA, the Irish connection etcetera, etcetera. And he says, "Now that is very interesting," in that snotty, blasé way they have. Like they were observing fresh elephant turds.' College mimicked a British accent: ' "Get back to you on that one." '

'Old boy?'

'No old boy. Maybe the odd toodle-pip!' He thought back to the conversation. 'Jeez. These Brits. You know, they practically arm the Russians, give them the keys to the secrets cupboard and then tidy up after them, and they can still act superior, in a voice like they got a jaw full of novocaine.'

Delaney had finished his ice-cream and was licking his fingers. 'Was that good, Del?' College inquired.

'Top hole,' replied Delaney.

'Don't ever grow up on me.'

'Willco.'

'Enough,' said College. 'I've wired them what we got. Prints, plates . . . Grant promised to get back to me today.'

'Wizard,' said Delaney.

'I warned you.'

'Rather,' said Delaney and College lobbed a two-pound file at him which thumped into his chest and fell apart in a flutter to the floor.

Mid-way through the shift the Captain summoned College. More accurately, he called, 'You get your butt in here, Lootenant. Pronto.'

College got his butt in pronto.

'The boys in rubber have pulled a stiff outta the East River,' he said without even offering a seat. 'ID says Sean McDaid. Irish. Bust outta the Maze Prison, Northern Ireland two years ago. Cousins have been looking for him since. Senior bomb-maker in the IRA.'

'Well,' College put his hands into his pockets. 'At least it saves going through those embarrassing extradition procedures,' he said.

'The point is, Lootenant,' the Captain tended to go even redder in the face when he was truly angry, 'that we appear to have a fucking war on our hands here. Why, we don't know. Where it goes next we don't know. How to put the lid on it we don't know.

'Have you seen the papers? Huge pictures of bits of body floating across the front pages. And they've gotten hold of the Ireland angle from somewhere. Ulster, USA the *News* is calling it.'

'Are you thinking this McDaid was the bomb maker? That the family got him.'

'Can't be sure. He certainly hadn't been in the water long.' College noticed the thick, matted hair on the back of the Captain's left hand which seemed to creep over his watchstrap and wedding ring. 'Shot once through the mouth . . . Where is Williams?' the Captain added irritably.

'He was around earlier. Probably getting instructions from the Bureau about what he can and can't tell us.'

'Matt,' said the Captain mollifyingly, 'what the hell are we going to do about this mess?'

College held up his hands. 'Honest, Captain, I don't know. Keep plugging. Following the book. Maybe this latest killing will be the end of it. Maybe McDaid's prints will check out with those earlier ones. Maybe he's the man and it will all be tied up. If not, maybe if we can find the guy who sparked all of this. The catalyst. Maybe that would end it. I dunno. Maybe we should talk to the Italians and counsel them to modify their behaviour.'

'A lot of maybes there, Matt. Try talking to the families, try talking to a landslip!'

College felt like the older man now, purveying a piece of hope. He appreciated that the Captain was under direct pressure from the Chief. 'Thing is. This guy. We know everything and nothing about him. We have his prints, physical and genetic, we have his entire and distinct biological profile which makes him a unique human being in history, we know intimately how he's made up but we still can't identify him. And until we can put an identity to him, all of that information is just so much crap.'

The Captain sighed. 'Got to be Irish.'

College agreed. 'Certainly by descent.'

'A recent arrival?'

College shrugged. 'Maybe, maybe not. But we can't pull every Irishman in this city who's recently come in. We don't even know what kind of passport he's got. He could be second, third generation.' He paused. 'To be frank, Captain, excepting divine intervention, it looks like, like I said, we just have to keep plugging away, waiting for a break.'

'Let's pray for McDaid being the answer.'

'Amen to that.'

Even his closest colleagues would never claim that Chief Inspector Jonathan Grant had his saintlier moments. He was an aloof, hard copper, with a particular distaste for all things Irish, even racehorses, for which he normally had a penchant. But he provided the break College, who was feeling depressed after learning that the murdered McDaid's prints didn't match the suspect's, had been waiting for.

'Chief Inspector Grant, Anti-Terrorist Branch, Scotland Yard,' the voice on the phone announced.

'Howya doing?' said College, realising that he was sounding like an archetypal New Yorker. Archetypal Brit accents got him that way.

'Well, actually, I'm sending across some information for you about our man.'

'Our man?' said College.

'Our man, yes. The prints you sent and the genetic plates match those of a suspect we're after for a pub bombing nearly three weeks ago in West London.

'You don't say,' College said, continuing the New Yorker role.

'Chummy,' – College rolled his eyes at the expression – 'is called Jerry Doherty. We got a fingerprint fragment of his on a glass in the pub, after days and days of painstaking work. He lives – lived on a boat. Strange cove. We matched the pub print with those all over his boat. Took

119

away hairs from there too. According to the DNA tests there can be no doubt that Doherty's hairs from the boat and those you found at the murder scene are the same. Absolutely, unequivocally, the same. Our man and your man are the same man.'

College put his hand over the mouthpiece and said, 'Delaney, we've got chummy.'

Delaney said, 'What?'

'Chief Inspector,' College went on, 'what else have you got on Doherty?'

'It's all coming across to you, Lifftenant. Doherty is a photographer, or was, who got a bit too close to the conflict. Sympathetic to the other side. Spent a lot of time there and presumably went native, or something like that. Knows all their top people. According to our information he was largely used as a conduit, infecting the news media, I'm sure you know the kind of thing. He was arrested and charged under the Prevention of Terrorism Act. That's where we got his dabs and mug shot. The charges were eventually dropped. It was a political decision. We were absolutely sure he was guilty. Subsequent events have proved us right.'

'Chief Inspector,' College said down the trans-Atlantic wire, 'over here when we drop charges we have to get rid of the forensic. Aren't you meant to dump the prints and pictures when the guy walks?'

'Come, come, Lifftenant,' said Grant. College could feel him smiling.

College laughed. 'Good on the Yard. Just like I thought. Well, now we can put a face to the profile. Just one thing, though, Chief Inspector, which troubles me. Doherty doesn't sound like your standard pro. And he's pretty careless with his hands. What do you make of that?'

'Who knows? Perhaps he's being used as a tool by the Provisionals, I don't know. As for the print we got on the glass. Well, not many people drink in pubs with their gloves on. Rather conspicuous. And he couldn't really have expected us to recover a print from the wreckage, it was something of a forensic miracle.'

Quite divine, College thought. 'Chief Inspector, I'm very grateful to you. The NYPD is very grateful to you. If you should get by here drop in and I'll buy you several large ones.'

'And you here, Lifftenant.'

'Captain,' said College, spinning a print onto the desk, 'here is our man. The link goes from London, where chummy – that's Britspeak – let off a bomb in a bar, leaving his print on a fragment of glass, to the boat he lived on, where Scotland Yard retrieved loads of his hairs. The DNA matches the hairs recovered from under the dope girl's nails. The prints from the bar bombing match the prints in the girl's flat and from the car key in the Buick hit. Indisputably. There's absolutely no doubt that we're dealing with the same man, from the London bomb to the hit on the legman and woman to the dop dealer. Irrefutable evidence.' College was glowing.

The Captain picked up the photograph, looked at the man. The usual grim mug shot. He was in his mid-thirties – actually thirty-seven, according to the wired sheet – lean, longish hair, good-looking, eyes that scored you. He said softly: 'Get out of that, Doherty.'

'It wouldn't do any harm to issue this picture to the press with a bit of background. Put the heat on. Might flush him out.'

'Sure,' said the Captain. 'Feed him to the gentlemen of the press.'

College picked up the print and went out.

Matthews was quietly savouring Delaney's twenty-dollar meal. He had insisted on Chinese, partly because Delaney claimed it gave him dyspepsia, partly because it was more expensive than Frank's, although College said that the reason was because it was closer. 'Liar,' Delaney had answered. 'Some example. Taking advantage of a junior officer.'

'Less for you to waste on the ponies,' said College, not at all perturbed. College was feeling expansive: he dropped the rib, licked the barbecue sauce from his fingers and said, 'Right, detective, tell me how you figure it?'

Delaney slumped back in the booth and stared into his glass of beer warily. College had insisted that instead of Bud they had to 'go ethnic'. 'Will it cost me?' Delaney asked. 'Imported froth from Singapore. Anyway, guys like you with all that white meat between your ears are meant to do the figuring for us humble drones minding the store.'

'Tut-tut, Shocking mixed metaphor, Delaney.'

'No need to being my ethnic background into it,' said Delaney, burping.

'Mixed, you stupid – '

'Mick?'

'Right,' said College. 'Give me a Mick's metaphor then.'

'He who plants the potatoes reaps the whirlwind,' Delaney said.

'How you can get drunk on two beers, Delaney, staggers me.'

'Certainly staggers me!' The man in the leery tie replied, raising his glass. 'It's on account of us bog-Irish having smaller brains than you WASPs. Bigger night-sticks, though. Chin-chin.'

'Not again,' said College.

'Funny that, my wife's always saying that, too.'

'Christ, I believe you are drunk.'

'On two little Chinese beers, Lootenant? Drunk? Not at all.' He waved an index finger. 'Just a little squiffy.'

'Sergeant,' said College, 'can a senior officer respect-fully request that you turn in the stage-Britishisms?'

'Since you asked nicely . . . you charming blighter.'

College rolled his eyes and waited until Delaney had swallowed the beer. 'So, how do you figure it?'

'In my own time since, after all, I'm the one who's paying for it.'

'Goddamn you Del . . .'

'Right.' He tapped his head. 'Something about Doherty or the stuff the Brits sent us sucks. Where's he been the last few years for instance? They don't seem to know or they ain't telling. Has he been abroad . . . on active service?' He sucked on a tooth. 'The IRA's the most experienced, professional, dedicated guerrilla army in the world. They've been at it more than twenty years, since when you, College, were a humble grade school student. So, if Doherty's one of the top men, hardened and experienced over the last few years, how come the Brits aren't giving us the whole sketch about him, the whole intelligence file? And how come, if he's so fuckin' good and so fuckin' dangerous he's leaving his spoor all over the place like he's begging us to pull him? It's my hunch that the IRA's just using him because he's important for some reason on this business. Useful. Maybe even dispensable.'

'I go along with that. And this whole thing has got to have something to do with drugs, right? Viz, the Garrison killing, or maybe,' said College 'that's just what they want us to think?' He looked around for a waiter. 'The hell with it. According to the autopsy Garrison was a casual user, nothing heavy. So, it's drugs for me.'

'You have a tendency to over-intellectualise, Looten-ant. Fuck the motivation, Doherty has set off a range-war in Manhattan. For which we will get the bastard.'

'Well-argued, if a little ungrammatically. Why do you think he killed her?'

'Who knows? Maybe he just freaked. Too much press-ure. Too much marching powder, sex – shit they found semen in places where normal people grow wax.'

'Maybe she resisted him and he went crazy. Maybe he wants us to think that? Maybe she knew too much? Maybe he wanted to leave a message for others?'

College picked up his beer. 'Had to be about drugs. A deal between the Provos and our New York families. Volunteer Doherty was the go-between and he double-crossed his masters. Something like that. Panicked. Maybe Garrison was connected to the Italians,' he went on, feeling less certain, 'and she had fingered him?'

'So the IRA will be looking for him.'

'As will Sicily's finest.'

'And us. A curious alliance. But I'll buy it all.'

College looked at his beer for a moment, smiled, and then drained the glass. 'You will?' he said. 'You are.'

'Still lots of loose ends.'

'Sure. But aren't there always?'

'He's sloppy.'

'Which is why we'll get him. Or someone will.' College looked at Delaney. 'After that wearing burst of mental activity Del, and to show you what a decent cove I truly am, the next round is on me.'

'Gee, wow, Lootenant. And what's the catch?'

She phoned the darkroom and said that she had to go out of town for a few days. A sick relative. Doherty wondered if she might lose her job. He tried to justify what he was doing, with little success. Here you are, he thought, scaring some unfortunate, probably lonely, girl out of her mind. All she did to get herself into it was to be kind. He told himself that he, too, was an innocent victim, that he would not hurt her, that the end justified the means – but what was the end? Death. His, he was sure, but, he prayed, not before he had found and destroyed . . . it was

strange, he couldn't give him a name. Somehow that was
too personal. He had to think of him as some sort of
malign force, without scruple, a crazed idealogue. He
couldn't permit himself to think of him as an ordinary
man, with family, friends. What kind of man could kill or
have killed a lively, intelligent, beautiful – then the horror
of the charnel room came back. He shuddered. Even if
he hadn't physically done it himself, he was the cause.

'Are you ill?' she said.

'What?' He looked over at her. She had stopped crying
and had clearly been watching him for some time. 'No.
Tired. Shattered.' It was true, he was. But the person he
had been, whoever that had been, was irrecoverably gone.

'You should lie down.'

'Not yet. I have to think.'

'About . . . about escaping.'

'That too.'

'You can trust me. Honestly.' He could see the sin-
cerity, or at least the effort, in her eyes.

'I probably should . . . but I can't.'

She was sitting on the floor with her knees drawn up to
her chest and her hands clasped, supplicatorily. 'What
was it?' she said hesitantly.

'That I'm supposed to have done?' She nodded, looking
away. 'It would only frighten you.'

'That,' she said, 'only makes it worse.'

'Killed a woman,' he said harshly, wanting now to scare
her, ashamed. It worked. He saw her flinch involuntarily
and then bite her lip. 'It's not true. I – I loved her,' he
said and to his embarrassment tears began to run down
his face. 'I think I must be in shock,' apologetically. 'I
found her.'

'You should go to the police.'

That was the stimulus he needed to staunch the self-
pity. 'No. No, I shouldn't. I should find who did kill her.
I know who killed her, or who arranged it. Not the same.

125

The pictures. The pictures that you processed,' that involved you, he thought, 'that was him.'

'How did you get them? Who is he?'

He was relaxing again. He thought, if I tell you about all of this you will be in danger. It will prejudice your life. 'That's all. The rest is for me.' And then it occurred to him how he might be able to find out who the man in his hotel room, his grainy foe, was.

His practical experience of disguise was more than twenty years out of date, blackening his face and tying on a bandanna as a 'Guiser' at Halloween in Glasgow: a blacked-up face was not quite appropriate for this immediate environment, he thought. He had put on an old baseball cap which he adjusted and pulled the brim down to his nose, then he turned up the collar of his greatcoat. You look, he told himself, exactly like someone who is making a great effort to be noticed. But it would have to do.

'I'm sorry,' he told her, 'but I'm going to have to tie and gag you. I won't be gone long.'

She shrunk back in the corner, not saying a word. He found a pair of woollen tights and a belt and lashed her hands and feet together, then threw a leather loop round the leg of the cooker. He felt despicable, but there was no point in apologising any more: it had to be done. Then he put a wad of tissues across her mouth and tied a scarf round. He looked down at her. Tears were rolling down her cheeks and she looked absolutely terror-stricken. 'Getting upset will just make it more uncomfortable,' he said. 'I'll be back in less than fifteen minutes.' He unplugged the phone and then left, listening for a couple of minutes outside the door for signs of movement inside. There were none.

He bought newspapers, milk and, on whim, a bottle of Californian champagne and a bottle of French brandy in the store, then six large manila envelopes with card backing, and, coming out, he walked two blocks to the post office where he bought ten dollars' worth of stamps. A drizzle was blowing into his face as he walked back to the apartment block and he turned his face even further down into his collar and cuddled the purchases in a paper bag to his chest under the dampening tweed. The gun dug into his pelvis.

When he let himself into the apartment it was obvious that she hadn't attempted to move. He opened his coat, put down the bag and began to untie her, taking the gag off first. He was kneeling beside her and when he had finished untying her he caught her gaze, which was fixed on his midriff. He looked down. The handle of the gun was clearly visible. 'She wasn't shot,' he said, 'they cut her apart, mutilated her. The gun isn't mine. I'm not sure I even know how to use it.' Not quite true, he thought, just throw the catch, get in close and keep pulling the trigger. Normally works.

'How long is this going to go on?'

'I don't know,' he said. 'No more than a day or two.' There was a great weight of tiredness now. He was coming down from the rare place, buzzing was starting in his ears and his mouth was parched. He would take more of the cocaine, but not in front of her. That would frighten her even more. He smiled ruefully. There she was, having been trussed up and tied, her life invaded by some man who, she probably believed, was on the run for slitting up a girl not unlike her, and he was concerned about heightening her alarm.

He got up, found two cups in the sink, washed out the dark coffee rings, then uncorked the bottle of champagne. 'There's nothing to toast,' he said, 'but it might wash the sour taste away.' He handed her a cup and noticed that her teeth chittered on the rim as she tried to drink. So he started to talk about himself, about growing up, about photography, about newspapers and magazines he had

127

worked for, anything to make partially human the monster she saw in him.

He talked solidly for more than an hour, while the champagne lasted, more words than he had spoken in years. And when he talked about places, about wars, he spoke only of the people, the ironies, the decencies, the gallows humour, the warm, lucid places in the nightmares. At one point she said: 'What I liked about your work was a sort of, I'd call it feminine quality. I didn't realise you weren't a woman until I saw a profile of you somewhere. You only used your initials and I thought that was as a kind of cover for being a woman.'

He had never considered anything about himself in the least feminine. He told her his Christian names – she managed a half smile and he guessed, also, that she knew them – and of the succession of playground fights over the taunts. 'My father was a zealot, a tin hut evangelist, who saw the hand of God on everything. Me, I only saw that on the belt he used to chastise me for my Godlessness. I think he only chose the names – my mother never had a choice in her life – to ensure that I would have to grow up defending myself.'

'Is this,' she looked around, 'defending yourself?'

'Yes,' he said, and the memory came back, 'it is.'

Then he read the papers as she made coffee and saw that Lee's body had been found, a manhunt started. He couldn't bear to read the details or look at the picture of the room. When he turned to the front page of the *News* a garage picture of the death of the two lawyers, father and son, both prominent Republicans, stirred some deep languishing unease in him. He read the report and the conclusion that the shootings were revenge deaths and then the page he had turned past the previous day came swimming back. Suddenly he knew intuitively that the two people shot on the red light, riddled with bullets in the Buick, were the two he had dealt with, exchanged airline bags with – that he had triggered the killings. He reached for his coat and the pocket, the brandy bottle and the manila envelopes.

He wrote three letters, two of them short, the third a long account of everything that had happened to him. That one he sealed with one print of the man and the negatives and wrote on the outside 'To be opened in the event of my death' and he signed it. Then he folded the envelope and put it inside another and addressed it to Janey. He scrawled an accompanying note: 'Sorry to be melodramatic. Open this if you hear of my death. Or if you haven't heard from me within three months. There are instructions inside in the letter.' If she followed his instructions to the letter, his account would wind up with *The New York Times*. He still had a pathetic belief in the integrity of the press, in the power for good. He had considered sending the letter to his bank manager but he assumed now that the police would certainly be on to him and would have investigated his account and the traceable windfall (and would probably have removed it) and that they would instruct the bank to hand over any correspondence from him. He had also considered a British newspaper but there was still time for that, he hoped. Anyway, he owed Janey an explanation, if only posthumously. And she could always choose to flush it down the pan.

The two short letters were to journalists he could trust. The first, Julian Morlay, was a veteran Northern Ireland hand with unparalleled contacts in the Province. He asked Morlay – 'a life depends on it' he put rather grandly, Morlay was a rather smug individual – to find the identity of the Provo in the picture through Northern Ireland Special Branch (the paranoid bastards open files complete with pictures on every Catholic baby, he thought), an IRA contact or anyone else he thought appropriate. Given that there were more conspirators to the square inch than blades of grass, he was sure someone would come up with the name. He stressed to Morlay his innocence. Not entirely true, he conceded, but on the scale of crime he was involved in, his drug deal wasn't worthy of registering.

Then he wrote to David Crenshaw, a brilliant, idiosyncratic, curmudgeonly radical journalist who had a first class Oxbridge science degree and unerring faculties for detecting a story, usually to the chagrin of the government, and always when it was wreathed in secrecy. He specialised in the murky deeds of the unaccountable servants of State and he had become a sort of letterbox for dissidents inside the apparatus of government who vigorously objected, either out of principle or self-interest. Crenshaw was particularly interested in what he called the 'technology and tactics of oppression' and Doherty reckoned that with his network on both sides of the line in Ulster and his less conventional approach than Morlay's, he might come up with something the older man couldn't nose out. Besides, he was an incorrigible warrior and the scent of a juicy story would have him salivating: he also had a small boy's emotional responses and Doherty could see him beam, polish his glasses and rub his hands over the intrigue.

He finished addressing the envelopes, plastered them with stamps and sat back. Janey was lying on the bed reading. Shit, he suddenly remembered, he had forgotten to plug the phone back in. He got up, stretched and walked over to the phone point, feeling her watching, perhaps calculating whether she could get out of the door before he could grab her, or let out a scream of help. Which wouldn't get her anywhere in New York, where they hop purposefully over gang rapes, chasing frisbees. 'Are you hungry?' she said. He wasn't, his metabolism was still racing from the drug while his appetite was being lapped.

'Not really.' She was looking better, he thought, the strained, white look had gone, the pulsing at the temple. The same, however, cannot be said of you, catching his face in the small mirror over the sink. Bloodshot eyes, stained underneath, coated tongue, his eyeballs smarted and his throat hurt. And he couldn't remember the last time he had shaved. Another twenty-four hours and derelicts will be giving you dimes on the sidewalks, Doherty.

So he walked over to his leather shoulder bag, bought on someone's advance in a souk in Jordan another life ago, pulled the zip and started rummaging for his toilet bag, burying his hands through the layers of money. Then his fingers struck the camera, which he pulled out. Janey, he noticed, was oblivious to his movements. 'For you,' he said on whim, holding out the camera. 'Legally bought and paid for' – he had some doubt whether that was technically true, given the provenance of the money – 'it's an autofocus, but I'm sure you could bear that. And don't refuse, because when I go I'm leaving it and what you want to do with it, whether you want to chuck it through a window or not, is up to you.' Perhaps, he thought, giving you the camera will convince you that you really are going to outlive this.

She took it, saying nothing, just turning the camera over in her hands, spinning the ring and dials. 'Promise me,' he said, 'that you won't hawk this one.'

'I promise,' she said. 'And thank you.'

'When I go there's no need to tell the police about it. No point. They'd probably impound it out of sheer mean-spiritedness. It's legally bought. Truly.'

'You expect me to go to the police?'

'I've held you against your will. Why wouldn't you?'

'I see,' she said.

'The Nikon's not a bribe.'

'If the circumstances were different I would be more grateful.'

'If the circumstances were different we wouldn't have met. Just use it. Work on your portfolio.' He scrabbled in the bag again and came out with the remaining film which he tossed onto the bed beside her. She broke open one of the boxes and took out a canister, loaded the film into the camera and wound it to the start.

'A favour?' she asked.

'I'll try.'

'Before you go, would you take a picture of me?'

He saw that she was blushing, which was certainly progress from the whey-faced terror of this morning. 'Sure,' he said, 'there's plenty of time to pass.'

He slept fitfully. As soon as he submerged, tendrils of dreams would entwine him, pulling him down and eventually he would struggle free, waking in sweat and, occasionally, tears. But he could never remember the dreams. Janey lay beside him, fully dressed. He hadn't tied her: he couldn't bring himself to do that again. She woke when he did, asking him what was wrong. 'Nothing,' he said mechanically each time, 'go back to sleep.'

Earlier, he had posted the letters, walking out with her in the heavy rain. And now he wondered vaguely where, in the notoriously inefficient US mail system, they might be. Janey had promised she would make no attempt to alert anyone, if she could come out with him. Suddenly the consequence of being inside, being in captivity, frightened her, and, he thought foolishly at the time, he had agreed. Walking, he had kept his hand inside his jacket on the stock of the gun, more for reassurance, faithfully acting the scene, because he knew that he wouldn't use it on her. They had bought vegetables and spices and wine, some musky Italian vintage, and he had cooked his standard Doherty Madras which had him, alternately, sweating and shivering, although how much was due to the cocaine and how much to the chillies he wasn't sure.

After the meal he picked up the camera and took shots of her over the remnants – wine glasses, bottles, discarded dishes and plates with scraps of food still clinging. Very Cartier-Bresson. As he handled the camera he realised that he had no picture of Lee, apart from the one he would carry with him for ever.

Then he had taken more shots, long exposures in artificial light, on the bed, with her arms clasped round her knees, the unshaded bedside lamp casting long, harsh shadows. After those, and using tissue and toilet paper, he rigged up a diffusing screen and took a series of portraits, most really close in, cropped, strong pictures full of character. Through the lens he could see the steel of her determination, the will in the willow. Her face was not classically beautiful but she had an integrity, an inner certainty, a spirituality or whatever it was, that radiated in the viewfinder. Or maybe it was just the way he saw her.

They finished the wine and he noticed her fret, playing with her hair again. After a few minutes she said, hesitantly, staring at a far darkened corner, 'Would you take some . . . nude?'

'I'm much better on the head shots,' he said, thinking it a bad idea. 'The lower bits confuse me.'

'Sorry,' she said, embarrassed.

'No.' He realised he was waving his arms, slightly drunk. Probably on relief. 'I will. It's just that I'm not . . . to be honest, I never have.'

'Neither have I,' she said, giggling, putting her hand over her mouth to suppress the ripples.

'Two virgins.'

He looked away as she stripped. 'These are going to have to be very long exposures, so you're going to have to stay extraordinarily still . . . but you know that. They'll have an ethereal quality, I suppose,' he said. 'Or maybe I could get some lamps around and do a kind of Bill Brandt treatment.'

'Please, no,' she said, and he heard the rustles of falling material 'I'm self-conscious enough about my bottom.'

133

He looked at her. Without clothes she was insubstantial, almost diaphanous in the light, only the dark circles of her nipples and the shadow area of her pelvis seemed tangible. 'No need to be,' he said.

It was after one of the dreams, as he fought out of the dark green, that he decided what to do. He didn't know how close the police were to identifying him but he had to assume that they were, or had done. Sum it up, Doherty. Prints all over Lee's flat, there was an Irish connection which would inevitably lead even the most persistently myopic cop to Scotland Yard and then to the bombing of the Two Brewers and his fingerprints, and his picture and the mass of speculation nestling, he was sure, in a Special Branch file: he hadn't believed the reassurances that when the Prevention of Terrorism charges against him were dropped his prints and picture were destroyed. And he had evidence of a sort for this prejudice. When IRA mainland campaigns had been launched and the level of security tightened, the boat had been broken into twice, nothing taken, locks carefully drilled out and replaced and if it hadn't been for the tacky varnish he would never have known. Then, just after the Brighton bombing, when he had been about to take a cross-channel ferry, he was tapped on the shoulder by a Branchman in the queue for the boat. And then questioned about where he was staying, by three of them, about what he was doing. He had refused to answer. After half an hour or so, while he swore and screamed about rights, demanded a telephone, then the toilet, then threatened to do it on the floor, one of them had slithered out of the interview room and, having undoubtedly phoned some superior in London, came back, nodded, and he was free again. It testified to their power that the ferry waited for him. The curious looks he got from his fellow passengers did nothing for his holiday spirit.

So, he had to assume that the airports, shipping terminals, points of exit, would be under heavy surveillance. Heavy manners. Anyone with a Jock accent and a height over five-ten – unlikely, he had to admit, in his stunted race – would be sent in mailable pieces back to New York. He couldn't afford to wait until the search scaled down. Which could take as long as the Federal deficit could stand it. He couldn't hole up in the apartment, the risk on the streets or in staying in hotels was ridiculous. So? So, exit by an alternative route. Simple. Conceptually sound, empirically flawed though. What alternative route? Through Baffin Island with seals? By hot air balloon over the Pole? Disguise perhaps, depilating the legs and posing as a Miss World contestant? Naw, they'd be expecting a Scotsman to don a skirt.

There were only two direct routes, sea and air. The risk of flying commercial routes was too great and there weren't any non-commercial by-ways that he could see. Which left the sea. He wasn't going to stow away on a South American tramp steamer, he couldn't risk the QE11 and there was no question of trying to work a passage. So, any alternative? An idea rolled up and he started to laugh at the suicidal gall of it. A single-handed crossing. Up and down the east coast there would be thousands of boats equipped for a trans-Atlantic passage – men, lunatics mostly – had gone across single-handed in everything from twenty-feet sloops to glorified canoes, granted at more propitious times of the year – it was just a question of acquiring one. It was that simple, really. The navigation and sailing were not beyond him – old men in leaking bathtubs and knotted handkerchiefs for sails had done it – and he had the money to buy all the food and charts and accoutrements he needed. All he needed was the will. The nerve, the requisite craziness.

He put his hands behind his head and constructed the voyage. He'd either nick or buy a thirty to forty footer, preferably with some sophisticated instruments and aids (it was a piece of piss to break into a boat, he thought, remembering his own experience), provision her, keep a sextant on the sun and stars – better still, a satnav pointing at passing satellites – and three weeks or so later hit Britain. He had the gun, he could blow the shit out of any sharks or dangerous marine life that got too close. Once he had got clear of US coastal waters he would probably be safe until he hit Britain. The authorities would not launch sea searches for a missing boat, and even if they could predict some nut sailing it due east, if he picked the right boat, the summer plaything of some rich Wall Street executive for instance, he would probably have days, weeks, before a theft was detected. Who can legislate for the lunatic? he thought, turning on his side and beginning to relish the idea.

But? Not but, he told himself, buts. It was the worst time of year – God, they got icebergs in the Atlantic in flaming June – in mid-winter, with the right footwear, you could probably walk across most of the way. It took time to get to know a boat and, even allowing for that, he wasn't psychologically or physically prepared for the disasters that would inevitably occur: he thought about cat-footing on a tumbling deck, trying to throw up a storm jib in the middle of a Force Ten (he was queasy at the thought), trying to lash up a repair to the self-steering gear, the forty-foot seas, the constant diet of tinned, congealed meat, life constantly at a thirty degree angle and not a pub within at least 1500 miles. He could take any privation but the absence of alcohol. He thought of 1984 and of Winston Smith and his rats and then of his own breaking point – probably the announcement of prohibition.

Besides, Doherty, he told himself, you have a phobia about drowning. Yes? as well as the flying, and teetotalism, the religion, and patriotism and the thousand natural prejudices your flesh is heir to, or author of? So, who needs the sea of troubles? It's one thing a bit of offshore cruising round Britain but at least there you can put the radio on the emergency frequency, set off a flare, turn right or left with a reasonable prospect of hitting land. Out there, with only a pilot whale and precipitation in sight, the only solid you were likely to hit – apart from the icebergs and cruise liners – was the seabed.

Enough of the romance, try the realism. So, he stretched, and told himself it had to be by air. Time was not a problem, neither was money. Earlier he had taken his booty to the toilet and roughly counted it. There was getting on for a hundred thousand dollars. It was too dangerous to fly from a US airport, clearly, but if he could get out, to Canada, or South America, no one would give a shit about where some gringo was going to or had been. He imagined the map of America in his head: near enough three thousand miles of border to the north and the same to the south. One little guy in that landscape of possibility. It shouldn't be difficult to slip across. Anyway, almost the entire US effort was deployed in keeping people out, wetbacks particularly, not in containing them. The most arrogant democracy in the history of the world does not perceive of its citizens, or its guests, trying to escape its seductions. And he had the passport. The other passport. Paranoia, he told himself as he began to slip into sleep, has its practicality.

Doherty thought: by Grand Central Station I sat down and thought of a way of disposing of the gun.

He was looking across from Pershing Square at the magnificently arched windows of Vanderbilt's memorial, marred only by the concrete vaults of the Pan Am building towering over it. The Vanderbilts have asked us out to tea, he hummed, we don't know how to get there, no, sirree. The station was on two levels. Originally this was designed so that the posh passengers on ground level did not have to mix with the milling, bewildered immigrants

who were marshalled in the basement before being processed for a new life: now trains ran in and out, turned on
turntables to be pointed back the way they came and
below the basement, in a warren of dark, rat-infested
service tunnels, financial emigrants from the American
dream, the dispossessed, the derelicts huddled from the
chills.

He walked across E42nd and into the station concourse,
glitzier than it had been when he first came to New York
a dozen or more years back, when it was full of off-track
betting booths, dingy shops, tatterdemalion guises and
get-ups. The Beretta was nuzzling for attention at his
groin. He walked to the Grand Staircase and down to the
lower level, hoping the outline of the gun wouldn't be
spotted: there were cops all over the terminal.

He smiled, thinking of his friend Stuart, who had set
out to blow up General Franco in a kilt, with a rucksack,
the hitch-hiking assassin. Getting near the Spanish border
he had taped the plastic round his waist and then collared
a lift in a failing car which wheezed to a halt, in the
burning midday sun, yards short of the border. Stuart had
to push it across and as he passed into Spain, sweat
lashing off him, the tape began to slip and the biggest,
most explosive, caber of an erection appeared to bulge
from behind his sporran. Doherty hoped that his wasn't
noticeable.

And he thought of Lee and the gun, pushing into the
dark, baking flat and of the terrible dead look she gave
him.

On the lower level he went into the cool tiled Oyster
Bar, slung his bags under a table and ordered a bottle of
white wine and a plate of oysters. What sort? the waiter
had asked. We serve twelve different kinds. The dearest,
said Doherty, gazing up to the vaulted ceiling.

He had considered carrying the gun with him. For an
hour or so he had worked out how he would secrete it in
a twenty-four pack of photographic film, carefully taking

off the cellophane, junking the film and cutting a hollow hideaway – a variation on the old hollow book gambit – in the packets. He would then glue the packets back together and re-seal the cellophane. It would probably work, in more dextrous hands. He had thought it would be the ideal way to smuggle a gun through. He knew that only about one in three pieces of hold luggage was x-rayed at airports, probably considerably less where he was going, but better still if he carried it as hand luggage: he could refuse to put the bag through the machine (it really did affect film although the authorities claimed it didn't) and ask for a hand search: no security guard was going to tear open an apparently pristine pack of film without an advance tip-off.

But the risk was too great. It was going to be hazardous enough trying to get out without having to worry about over-vigilant airport security. So, he'd leave it in a left luggage locker. His solutions, he considered, came chiefly from gangster movies of the Forties, many of which featured this grand old station – Carole Lombard, Bogey, Edward G, wreathed in smoke, train smoke as well as tobacco. Or maybe he'd pitch it from the train: he could see a low shot from the track as the train thundered past and then out of the window, spinning silvery in the bright sun, would come the gun, to land in the savannah. Then later that day a young boy, out with his dog Buster would find it and . . . ah, forget it, he told himself. Just wait until the mid-west and drop the damn thing.

The oysters and the Californian wine arived, uncorked. He poured a glass of wine and tackled his first oyster – was there an R in the month he wondered, or was it an N? – which was sprinkled with chipped ice, lemon juice and black pepper. It tasted like salty mucus. Pleb, he told himself.

He thought about Janey, about his leaving. He had considered asking her to come with him to the train, as human camouflage, buying two tickets, getting into the

carriage and dropping her off at the next station. He was
sure she would have agreed to doing it, but it would have
been wrong. Now she could claim he had coerced her into
helping him – walking through the barrier arm in arm
would have put an end to that. She had asked, 'Will I see
you again?' Of course, he had lied. Then he kissed her
lightly on the forehead and turned, hearing 'good luck'
from somewhere.

When he finished eating, feeling light-headed from the
wine, he retrieved the tab from under the plate, winced
at the price and left five ten dollar bills. Terrorism must
be made to pay, he thought. Then he went to collect his
ticket.

He was halfway across the concourse when the cop
stopped him. 'Hey,' the man said, tugging his arm.
Doherty felt the gun burning at his stomach, his head
began to cloud and he could feel his legs begin to buckle.
The cop, big, ruddy-faced, the peak of his cap almost flat
against his forehead, tugged his arm again. He was
motioning with his head behind Doherty. Doherty turned
his head slowly, envisaging rows of police in flak jackets
and firing positions. Across the marbled hall he saw at the
door of the restaurant the waiter, signalling down to the
bags at his feet, Doherty's bags.

'Thanks,' Doherty said to the cop, 'asleep.'

The cop let go of his arm and smiled, then turned and
moved off. The adrenalin hit Doherty's stomach and he
gagged on the seafood.

His cabin, first-class, was smoky, green bakelite. It
reminded him of art deco cafes and knickerbocker glories.
He stretched out on the berth and dozed. A little while
later he was tugged out of reverie by the train starting and
pulling aside the curtain he watched the dull station give
way to the dirty tenements of the city. He thought again
of black and white movies and pursuits along corridors,

and the one where the pact was made by two men to murder each other's wives – except that one was drunk and joking.

He sat up and began to unpack for the trip. When he had put his few clothes away in the lockers, he began to open the packages he had bought earlier. The new self-focusing camera, Olympus this time as it was less bulky than the Nikon, the motor drive and the stroboscopic synchronised flash which screwed on. He fitted the batteries to the camera, the drive and the flash unit and screwed them together. He switched on the flash and heard it hum into life, then he set the motordrive to six exposures and pressed the shutter release and, just as the salesman had promised, the flash went off half a dozen times in two seconds – near enough, he wasn't counting.

Doherty switched off the unit and pulled out the canister of pressurised air for blowing lenses clean. And then the can of Mace. He had remembered raiding Lee's handbag and the can she carried. Later, beside her body, going through her bag looking for something to treasure – a picture of her, or her parents, something in her handwriting – he had found the Mace again. Almost absent-mindedly he had put it in his pocket, something reassuring, talismanic, rather than useful.

He took both cans into the little toilet, ran hot water into the basin and carefully, in the steaming water, detached the labels from the canisters. Then he took the sticky Johnson label and stuck it to the Mace can and scrumpled the other label into the waste bin, before putting the disguised Mace can on the glass shelf to wait for the forgery to dry.

He didn't know if it was illegal to transport Mace, but he assumed it was. 'Just remember,' he told himself, 'don't mistake it for deodorant.'

*

Doherty unwound as the train slowly made its way across America. The top speed was around fifty miles an hour because the track was in such poor shape, central government being averse to such dangerously socialistic nostrums as public subsidy. When the engine finally arrived at Los Angeles, uneventfully, even boringly, he thought, having observed more of the flat prairieland of the mid-West than anyone since an early pioneer, he was grateful for the city.

He took a taxi to the Greyhound depot and bought a ticket for San Ysidro. In the demi-world of poor travellers, vagrants in the mall, he hung about for an hour, drinking Coors in a darkened lounge, while around outside panhandlers with outstretched palms moved through the terminus. Then he bought books, newspapers, but his notoriety, it appeared, had departed from the public mind. There was nothing in any of them about him. *The New York Times* had an elliptical article about peace descending again on the city, or rather, war was back where it belonged, in the ghettoes. But no mention of him. For a second he felt a sense of peevishness, then he wallowed in the anonymity.

The bus took the coast highway, with the ocean to the right through the filtered glass. Doherty watched the city disappear, then nuclear facilities pop up like sinister concrete polyps on the coastline and then, falling down the hill to the sea, San Diego, where the annual rainful would about fill a teacup. The sea was choppy, with a good surf, and Doherty thought about the Beach Boys, Jan and Dean, Deadman's Curve, and Richard Nixon, for some reason – it was probably thoughts of toxic waste or because the Western White House, as it was grandiosely called, was somewhere about here. And maybe so, too, was Yorba Linda, which sounded like a Spanish hooker, but was actually the birthplace of the excrescence.

Less than an hour later, while Doherty was reading baseball reports – in which he had a fascinated interest, it was like learning a new language – the bus pulled into a messy dun-coloured row of buildings and people began to pull luggage from racks and move to the front, jostling for precedence. Doherty took his place in line and filed off. He was in Mexico before he knew it. He walked through a hallway, following Mexicans from the bus, a few Americans, and clutching the passport which he waved around almost as if hoping to attract attention, he passed what might have been a checkpoint, walked twenty yards further and then asked a middle-aged Mexican man in jeans and a Mickey Mouse teeshirt if he was in Mexico. The man nodded and Doherty walked out to the taxi ranks and the Tijuanan evening.

'It's like Sanders of the River,' said College, 'damn quiet out there, Del. The natives ain't restless.'

'Relax,' said Delaney, 'there'll be another homicide along in a minute.'

The two men were waiting for the Captain and Agent Williams. College thought, if I had gone to a more fashionable school I could be a Fed now, fancy suits, cream shirts, twenty grand a year more, a good neighbourhood and maybe even a wife that liked me. Williams looked like the kind of guy with an exercise track in his basement, muesli and a shoeshine to start the day and a dog, probably one of those little foreign ones that squeak and shit all over the yard. Easier to clean up shit, he thought, than the garbage all over, dumped by those good old folks who loved the idea of having a cop on the block. Maybe he'd get a Rottweiler.

'Delaney,' he said, 'why is it that we never get the chance to get corrupted?'

'Speak for yourself, Matt.' Delaney was wearing a tie that would have graced a Forties cop movie, loud, flappy; all that was missing was the hand-painted Betty Grable motif.

'Come on.'

'Well, in my opinion it's because most of the people we deal with are dead. Therefore unable to bribe New York's-finest-but-wishing-that-they-wasn't.'

'Have you ever taken any backhanders, Del?'

'Is that a microphone I see in your pocket, Lootenant, or are you just pleased to see me?'

College got up from his chair and sat on the edge of the Captain's desk. 'When I was a beat cop I was offered a hundred a week by a strip joint owner – nah, it was a meat rack, really – who was getting heavy pressure, just to alleviate the weight, so to speak. If I had been a bit more experienced I would have slapped him in the mouth. If, however – ' he wagged his finger at his partner ' – I was as experienced as I am now I would have asked for one-two-five.'

'Something is troubling you, Matt. Tell the chaplain.' College was playing with a pen, his legs were up off the floor and slung across the Captain's chair.

'Just generally hacked-off. Nothing serious.'

'The reason,' said Delaney, brushing a hand over his flat-top, 'you didn't get into any serious scams is, your average cop doesn't trust a college boy to be dishonest. Thinks he's got some quaint notion of honour. So they wouldn't involve you in any of their business.'

'Great. So, I've got a college education to blame for my lack of financial success.'

'Nope,' said Delaney, 'your quaint notion of honour.'

College stood up and went to the window. 'There are nine million stories in the Naked City,' he said to the window. At the corner he could see two groups of youngsters, none of them older than nineteen, dealing crack, he assumed. 'Del,' he said over his shoulder, 'I'd like to be near an ocean somewhere.' He turned round and through the glass partition saw the Captain and Williams walking towards the office, through the desks, the detectives, the suspects, the general chaos of crime.

'Here we go.' Delaney stood up. College stood away from the desk, the Captain's territory.

Williams was wearing a double-breasted suit, herringbone, in arbitrageur's grey. Never trust a man in a double-breasted suit, College's old man had told him. The Captain was in shirt-sleeves, a dark stain under each arm. He sat down, the other man did the same. College found himself the only one standing, so he looked round and retrieved an iron and plastic chair and sat down.

'Williams has something to say.' The Captain's face looked like a storm and he seemed fixated on the black Braun digital alarm clock he kept on his desk, which shut up obediently for five minutes if you screamed at it. College felt a scream coming.

Williams unbuttoned his jacket, it fell open and he got up from the cane chair and settled on the edge of the Captain's desk, for all the world as if he were addressing a business meeting. Business of the clean kind, where you robbed marks without sticking a bazooka in their ribs. 'The news is good. Our intelligence sources tell us that peace has broken out between our two sets of warriors. High-level talks, apparently. A visit from two senior IRA guys, a meeting in an uptown hotel, four-star, of course, and some pact was hammered out. This happened about a week ago, and so far it's holding. We've just come from the Chief, and he's very pleased.'

'Williams,' said College, 'how come if you and your chums are on such knowing terms with the bad guys, you don't let us in on it. So's we can manacle a few . . . better, blow them away?'

Williams smiled. 'Lootenant, like you I just know what it's given to me to know and do what I'm told to do.'

'So?' said College.

'So, it looks like peace in our time.'

'What about Doherty? What on him?' College was getting more agitated – at times like this he could regret giving up smoking – and he got up and started to shuffle on his feet.

'Well, we had the airports, the terminals well-covered. But we're sure that he didn't go out through any of them.'

'Sure,' said Delaney. 'But you're sure he is out.'

'As sure as we can be.' Williams paused, looking at Matthews. College looked at Delaney, then at the Captain who was still grimly observing the minute hand.

'Captain,' said College, 'what the fuck is this shit? What is going on here.'

The Captain looked up and shook his head.

'We're sure from our sources that he's away,' said Williams. 'Out of our jurisdiction.'

'So how do you know?' said College, closing in on Williams. 'And where the fuck is he?'

'I can't tell you that,' Williams was relishing his privileged knowledge, 'but we do know, with virtual certainty, that he's back in Britain.'

College was going red in the face, his teeth were clenched, out of the corner of his eye he saw Delaney put up a cautionary palm. 'So if we know so much about him, why don't we grab the fucker and bring him back here to face Murder One on several counts, not to mention probable drug trafficking and a host of less serious charges, like conspiring to set off bombs on the Sabbath without a valid fucking permit?'

'The British authorities will get him,' said Williams. 'Then, at a higher level than ours, it will be decided, between our two countries, what's to be done.'

College put both hands on the desk, next to Williams, and lowered over the Captain. 'With all due respect, Sir,' he said with heavy irony, 'this sucks. If you ask me, this guy,' he made a nodding motion to Williams with his head, 'was only here to find out what we were doing. Which, as it went, wasn't goddam much. He certainly didn't help in any way. Now, after, what?, at least twenty violent deaths in this bout of carnage we find out that our man has magicked himself out of our jurisdiction. So, Captain, what do we do? Tell me that.'

The Captain looked up. 'Get on with other business.'

'You mean we tie a nice ribbon round the file and throw it into the archive.'

'We give all possible assistance, when requested, to the British authorities, to the Bureau and we get on with our business.' The Captain slapped his desk with a flattened palm, a terminating motion.

College stood back and turned to Delaney. 'What was it you were saying about college guys and the code of honour?'

College was getting drunk, slipping down bourbons as fast as they were poured. 'Tell me about it, Delaney,' he said.

Delaney shrugged. 'What's to tell? Our masters pulled the rug, for their own reasons. Grow up, Lootenant.'

College drained his glass and motioned to the barman for another. 'I always wanted to ask, Delaney, who chooses your ties?'

Delaney took his arm. 'You don't want to fight with me, Matt. I'm just the foot soldier . . . with the individual dress sense.'

College put his arm round him. 'Del. In your will, do me a favour, put in a bit about how I get to dress the corpse. You'll never get in up above with neckwear that would blind a fucking angel.'

'Buy me something tasteful for Christmas, Matt.'

'I'll get you one that you can turn upside down and shake and it snows down it.'

'Perfect.'

'We ought to get a couple specially made to commemorate this fiasco.' He was slurring his words, he knew, and his gestures were getting more theatrical, but he didn't care. 'How about two sets of castrated balls?'

'Remember what they told you in basic, don't take it to heart.'

College sat down on the bar stool and stared intently along the wooden counter at two women drinking frothy concoctions through long straws. He began to wink and started singing to himself, 'Sittin', drinkin', superficially thinkin'.'

'Matt!' Delaney said. 'You oughtta go home.'

'Spider and the Fly,' College sang. He began to do the handjive. 'Rolling Stones. Spider and the Fly is right.' He slammed both fists on the bar. 'I'll tell you what I think. There's been something wrong about this right from the start. I told you, it didn't add up. Some fuckin' amateur running about town setting up drug deals, blowing people away. Leaves clues all over the place like he's on a suicide mission. Then what happens? He spirits away like smoke and the brass shrug and say, *c'est la vie* or *morte*. The whole thing stinks.'

'Tell me how?'

College unclenched his fists, turned his hands palm up and shrugged. 'Fuck knows. It's all been a set-up. You know who are the losers? Firstly, the Italians. We got the president sitting up for the first time and Congress going apeshit, voting special funds, setting up task forces to crack down, we got all the newspapers mounting campaigns, special investigators, grand juries, arraignments, the jails are bulging with guys with swarthy complexions, randoms. No one gave a shit when it was a bunch of blacks and Puerto Ricans and Mexicans running round the ghettoes high on crack and spraying each other,' he made a gun with his right hand, 'with the utmost prejudice. But, you know, see the tentacles of organised crime stretch out, have a few bodies litter the streets of Manhattan and bombs going off in million-dollar neighbourhoods and that's different. That's serious. That's fucking with the power.

'Secondly, you've got the IRA. Twenty years you had

148

them supported from here by second, third, nth generation Irish. Millions of dollars a year, Congressmen in
their pockets. You had a judiciary which sure as hell
wasn't going to send back their boys to Britain to face
kangaroo courts, get thrown into internment camps. Now
you get a guy with an Irish accent pissing in the street and
he'll be on a plane quicker then you could knot that
gruesome necktie. And, know what?, if there was another
famine in Ireland now they couldn't raise a nickel in relief
between here and Nebraska. That tell you anything?' He
sat back on his stool. 'And then there's the girl with guts
all over the carpet.' He remembered her, the extinguished
beauty. 'But no one gives a damn about her.'

He drummed his fingers on the bar. 'So, Delaney, if
these are the losers, who're the winners? Hmm?' He
called for two beers from the bartender. 'No need to
answer that.'

Delaney waited for the outburst to blow out and
watched as College rolled the glass of beer between his
hands and looked over at a woman who was sitting with
her elbow on the table, her head turned away, talking to
a college friend who was staring straight back at
Matthews. He sang to himself: 'She was common, dirty,
looked about thirty.' Then winked again. The woman
smiled. He turned to his partner, put his arm round his
shoulder and kissed his flat-top. 'Where will it all end,
Del?' he said. Then he excused himself, picked up a glass
in each hand and weaved along the bar.

BELFAST

The notion was inconceivable, Doherty wanted for a
bombing. 'I knew you as well as anyone ever knew anyone
else,' Mary Cavanagh thought, 'and Marx would have
been proud of you, you wouldn't join anything that would
accept you.' Apart from a hatred of authority, she remembered, his only ideology had been a deadline, a dramatic
picture, besting the opposition. 'You bastard,' she said
quietly to herself.

It was getting dark now. She got up, poured some coal
onto the flickering fire and then started to close the
curtains. The stereo from next door was thumping bass
notes against the common wall, outside an army Saracen
was skelping along the street, lights out. They never idled,
even though they were in probably the safest part of the
Six Counties: no IRA unit would mine an occupied street
in the middle of the Falls, and rockets had an unfortunate
habit of bouncing off the armour and going wild. She
closed the curtains and turned back into the small room.
The spinster Cavanagh, she thought, keeping the house
going, waiting for a brother who would be at least thirty-
five before he got out, older than she was now. And the
prospect of parenthood receding faster than that Saracen
out there.

She walked through the living room of the house she
had lived in all of her life, still as it was the day the
ambulance took her mother away, but dustier than it ever
had been . . . I know, ma, she said to herself, a lazy
slattern. In the kitchen she put the kettle on, listened to
the quiet, punctuated by the sonic bass booms, and told
herself not to get maudlin. She thought of Doherty again.

150

It had been four, five? years since he left. She shivered. And nothing, not even a card from afar. When she had been going through the time, she had clung to that bitterly. Now? All the love bleeds away. Leaving? The spinster Cavanagh, the lazy slattern . . . and she smiled to herself. It was good to survive. And Doherty, how had he survived? Dangerously, it seemed.

The kettle began to boil. It makes no sense, she told herself. Not Doherty. And not the lads. Where was the strategy? A civilian target, a pub, not even frequented by soldiers. It had made no sense when she had gone back to the first reports and in the days that followed it hadn't got any clearer. The lads hadn't claimed responsibility for the bomb – she guessed it was a personal and unapproved venture by an Active Service Unit, probably after one of them was shortchanged in the bar – and were clearly embarrassed by it. The British press, after the usual hysteria about a new mainland bombing campaign and the witch hunt for Doherty, had all but forgotten it. Just another incident on the bloody trail.

She spooned coffee into a Long Kesh mug and poured on the boiling water. Catching sight of the whisky bottle in the open cupboard, she thought, why not? and poured a large tot into the black coffee. It inflamed the coffee, her stomach. Oh, Danny boy, she heard herself saying, these pipes are calling. Where are you? Gone, and I must bide. Are you in America? she wondered as she slurped the coffee, burning her tongue. She breathed in rapidly, panting, with her mouth open. And then she began to hum the Londonderry Air, going back into the living room and trying to close her ears to the beats on the wall.

She hadn't seen Danny for ten days or more, since the trouble in America blew up. Blew up was the right description. She had lost count of the score, who was ahead on the retaliatory killings, the shootings and explosions. It seemed to have stopped, but whether there was to be a lasting peace or just a wary truce she didn't know.

The media had gone to town. From the quality investigation specials, which had all the usual hallmarks of dictation by the security services, to TV news footage, documentaries – you could hardly move in the street without bumping into a film crew – parliamentary reports, analysis, conjecture and ranting, one conclusion was certain: the Provos had suffered their worst-ever propaganda disaster. That was an understatement. It was devastating, cataclysmic. Drug-peddling, dealing with the Mafia, it was ruinous. The Movement was riven. Paralysed. And not only were the Brit and Loyalist politicians fulminating, raving for blood – what was Tom King's term? Extirpation of the IRA? – the Catholic clergy, virtually unanimously, was preaching the extinction of the armed struggle. It was a grievous blow to the struggle. Perhaps terminal. Even the hard-line wing was dallying with a moratorium on the Armalite. And one thing was abundantly clear to her, the telex and fax tide from the Republican Press Centre carrying the Army Council's denials of trafficking and gangsterism hadn't altered perception one iota.

She switched on the television, turned down the sound, and sat in the old moquette armchair. A game show, full of people making outlandish gestures and showing yards of teeth, blinked at her. She sipped the coffee, relishing the sweet taste of the whisky on the back of her tongue. She had been drinking whisky, trying doggedly to acquire a taste for it, when she met Doherty. There she was with an English degree from Queen's, fancying herself a bohemian, ekeing out her dole money with part-time shop work, mixing with the failed poets and epic novelists of the city, or sliding into dives and drinking clubs off the Falls, chatting to the lads, reaffirming the cause in cigarette smoke and stout fumes. It was in the Auld Hoose, weeks before the Orangies bombed it, she first saw Doherty. He was alone, wearing a multi-pocketed, green, thigh-length jerkin, tall, longish hair, a fisherman's bag over his shoulder, standing at the bar drinking a large whisky and looking not so much conspicious as a candidate for an outrage. She noticed the eyes on him, to which he was oblivious. He seemed to be humming to himself and she guessed that the only reason he hadn't yet been taken out and stiffed was that no one could quite countenance the gall of the man. It was none of her business, she was waiting for John Reardon, with whom she had been making unsatisfactory love – more rutting really – in a succession of bedsits and student squats and, tonight, she guessed, she was in for another bout of unfulfilling copulation. She moved to the bar and stood about ten feet away from him. Yes, he was undoubtedly singing to himself. He glanced round, caught her eye, gave her a brief nod and passing grin, then returned to his glass and the worldless song. She looked at Tom the barman, he shrugged, poured her a Bushmills and moved away. She picked up the glass, took a sip, trying to suppress the grimace, and looked round the bar. Perhaps three or more of the men, she saw, had reputations. All of them seemed fixedly staring at the tall young man. It was none of her business. She picked up her glass, began to move away from the bar, had second thoughts and walked up to him. 'Mister, I don't know who you are and more to the point others in here don't know who you are. But they certainly know what they think you are. A Brit. If I were you I'd make a hasty exit now.'

His elbows were on the counter and he was staring into the glass mirror behind the bar. He turned slowly and straightened up, towering over her. 'Well that's certainly a novel chat-up line,' he said, smiling broadly.

She looked at him, sensing her face flare. 'Your arrogance and stupidity could be terminal, eejit. You look like a Branchman, an undercover Brit and with that Scotch accent it's a dead certainty.'

'Uh,uhh,' he said wagging a finger. 'Scotch,' pointing

to his glass. 'Scottish,' pointing to his tongue. 'My name's Doherty . . . pleased to meet you . . . umm?'

'Look,' she ignored his question, 'it's no concern of mine what happens to you, Doherty. Just don't say you weren't warned when the bag goes over your head.'

He was laughing at her. 'I'm waiting for someone. Someone you would have heard of . . . Jackie Little. And he might be a bit embarrassed if some of his young enthusiasts dealt summarily with me. Don't you think? And I'm sure if you stay chatting to me until he arrives, I'll be perfectly safe.'

She was wearing a black beret, with her tangled hair pushed up into it, and a black PVC three-quarter coat, a designer Provisional. 'I'm Mary . . . Cavanagh and I'm waiting for my boyfriend.' Why did she say boyfriend? But she was relaxing a little. 'What do you do, Doherty, if it's not the Special Branch? And do you have another name.'

'I wouldn't wait.' He had a wicked smile. 'Go for the punctual type, like me, Mary.' His eyes were green, she saw, and his grin was lop-sided and although he clearly hadn't shaved recently, nevertheless, he looked to her like a big, exuberant, confident schoolboy. 'I take pictures. I'm realistic enough to say that I take brilliant pictures. I have other names too. But you can call me Doherty.'

The whisky tasted fiery and brackish on her tongue. 'You're certainly not modest, Doherty.'

'Modesty's just braggadocio in disguise, don't you think, practised mainly by the English.'

'Nooo,' she said, considering, 'mainly by men.'

He put his head back and laughed and then drained his glass. 'Another for you, Mary,' he told her and ordered two doubles from Tom. He raised his glass, 'To absent friends. May they remain so.'

'Is Little a friend?' She couldn't imagine the O/C of the Belfast Brigade being the most compatible of company.

154

'Purely a professional acquaintanceship.'

'This isn't your first time in Belfast, then?'

'You mean, why do I walk into a known Provo pub on my own, so blithely, armed only with a battery of cameras and my own natural courage if I know the terrain? Because, Mary,' and he fixed her with his green eyes, 'because it is the only way. People have a primeval respect for pure lunacy. Besides, Little's doing this deliberately. It's one of his morbid jokes, like drilling the knees of skateboarders with squeaky wheels. Keep the press man waiting with his jaws clamped shut to stop the chattering and a hand over his arse, soften him up, make him more amenable to the line he wants purveyed.'

'And it's not working.'

'I wouldn't want a decent girl studying my underpants too closely. On the other hand . . . Anyway,' he went on, 'where is this boyfriend and why is he leaving you in a bar to be scooped up by any man with a particle of sense in his head?'

'But presumably,' she smiled sweetly, 'as you've already admitted to having none of it, I'm perfectly safe with you.'

He put down his glass and almost drew himself to attention to say, 'I loath safety. And time-wasting. Meet me later for a drink in the bar of the Europa. I'm a resident. About eleven thirty. I won't wait past twelve.' Then he had shaken her hand. 'I hope you'll come.' And she had gone. And she had come. And afterwards in his bed she had said 'You must think I'm – ' but he had put a finger over her lips. 'Think of yourself, Mary.' The problem was that she had never properly been able to.

She heard from Danny through a friend, a scribbled note – she knew better than to ask how it came through – which said only that he was well, she mustn't worry, he didn't know how long he would be but that he was thinking of her. No love, just yours, Danny. She wondered where he was, who he was with? Was it business or was he rollicking somewhere with some woman, girl, younger than her? She crumpled the note and put it in her pocket and tried not to think of the future.

She thought of Doherty again. He had been in her mind a lot. She had loved him, without heed to the danger, as he had advocated, and she had been wounded. She knew now that there was a part of him that love and loyalty could never reach. Or at least hers. There was something ruthless in his affections. He inhabited, he laid waste, without meaning to, but razing just the same. He had been married, he said, but that had been a mistake. A youthful foolishness. There was a child, but they had lost touch. Or he had not kept in touch. He spoke little about his family, an only child, parents both dead. One night when they lay in bed he told her about the death of his father. Perhaps it wasn't true but he said that the man had been a miner, that when he took off his shirt the chipped coal in his back looked like bruising, or blue buckshot, that he had quick hands which he used relentlessly, particularly on Doherty, and that before the boy had developed the weight and heart to get back at him, he had been killed. Prosaically. It had been a Friday and the boy was sent to find his father, before the money was all gone. He had found him in the usual place, Milne's, knocking back the half-and-halfs, swaying at the bar, hectoring about the wrath of the Lord, or about Glasgow Rangers. He stayed out of his father's reach, shaming him into leaving, watching the other men shuffle and look away. He was only twelve or thirteen, but the publican, realising what was happening, had not thrown him out. And his father had left, draining the last whisky defiantly and slamming the thick-bottomed glass on the counter. Doherty had kept ahead of him, outside of the arc of his swing and the man, red in the face, reeking of drink, had tried inducement, holding out a half crown in his left palm. He swung with his right as Doherty came in and the boy, expecting it, had ducked, sending his father stumbling, off the pavement and into the path of a car.

'He was the first person I saw die violently,' Doherty said, 'and, God forgive me, I felt a huge rush of elation and happiness . . . the coin went spinning into the street and I eventually found it lodged in an old tramline. It was more than we usually got out of him on a Friday.'

He had kept the coin, later having it drilled and mounted on a chain which he wore on his neck for years. She had touched him tenderly on his naked chest. 'Why did you do that?' she asked. He shivered, but he didn't answer.

Now she wondered if he had used her, not for sex, that was mutual, but to get a particular entrance to the Catholic community. Through their relationship he had become accepted, trusted enough for it to be known that he wouldn't betray. He had his own contacts with the lads, but what he didn't have was a passport to the day-to-day life of her streets. She provided that. They spent hours of each day walking, talking, visiting, he taking pictures, she smoothing the way. His photographic appetite was voracious: from street scenes, children, bingo sessions, marches and processions, funerals, shots in pubs and drinking clubs, of hurling, men gambling, army patrols, the hospital and, she remembered most of all, a stunning set of pictures, a pictorial essay really, about Clonard Monastery. He asked nothing, but she wondered what he took.

After about a month together he rented a one-bedroom flat near Queen's and he rigged up a makeshift darkroom in the toilet. She hung her stockings and underwear between the drying rolls of film, to his continual annoyance. Often he would print late into the night: she would hear his stifled oaths through the wall as she slid into sleep and in the morning the faces, the places from the day before would be shimmering under water in the bath, their sunken city.

He had taken hundreds of pictures of her which, after he had gone, she had locked in a suitcase in the attic and never looked at again. One day she might.

On a Sunday just before the start of the marching season he had asked her to take off her top, she had, and he positioned her on a hard-back chair with filtered sunlight falling on her from the high window. He had the camera on a tripod, with a long lens and a cable release, and he took dozens of pictures, marginally adjusting the positioning after three or four shots. She had felt shy, about her breasts, but after he had processed the pictures she saw that all of the images cut off just as the cleavage began, and she felt slighted. That night he didn't come to bed and when she got up in the morning he was slumped in the armchair, dozing. And when she looked up she saw what he had done. Over almost the length and height of one wall, at least six square feet, was a montage of her, face and shoulders, composed of the dozens of shots he had taken of areas of her face. The different pictures did not perfectly abut, but left a small margin of white wall all around, so that each could be considered individually or, standing back, the whole effect, which was almost spiritual, was like a massive exposure on church glass. She was overwhelmed and began to cry gently. Doherty held her, and for the only time said 'I love you.'

Well, she said to herself now, I suppose you thought the once would last for always.

Later, after they made love, and as he began to go under into sleep, she asked him why he hadn't taken the whole of her body. 'Wall's not big enough,' he slurred. When she pushed him he said: 'You have the most beautiful body I've ever seen. I want to remember it alive, in here,' face down on the pillow he tapped his temple with his left hand, 'not on paper.' She didn't understand.

And probably he didn't either. Fuck you, Doherty, she said bitterly, for leaving me in danger.

She finished washing the dishes and put the light out in the kitchen. The late evening was coming to an end on TV, the fire was all but out. She thought idly that women of her age took to cats for company, then switched out the light in the main room and went upstairs. She had taken off her jersey and was running the water in the bathroom when something distracted her. She turned off the tap and listened. A light tapping echoed from downstairs. Danny? she thought and picked up her jersey and went down into the living room. The tapping was coming from the back door. She left the kitchen light off and said quietly, 'Who's there?'

No answer.

Again. 'Who is it?'

Eventually. Reluctantly. 'Doherty,' he said and she felt her stomach churn and she began to shiver.

'God,' she said and then, 'go away, Go away.' But she put on the woollen jersey.

'Can't,' she heard him say. 'I've nowhere else. I need your help. Please, let me in.'

'No,' she said, 'you can't come back into my life.' And her mind was set against him but her hands were on the key and doorknob.

'Please . . . I beg you . . . if you ever cared.'

She turned the key violently and jerked open the door. 'You bastard,' she shouted at the dark shape, 'don't try emotional blackmail on me. Who the fuck do you think you are?' She couldn't make out the face.

'I'm in bad trouble. I had to come here . . . to try to sort it . . . I don't know if I can. But I need your help. Please. If you won't help I'm just going to sit down here and wait, for the Provos or the Peelers. You can turn me in. I don't particularly care.' He began to sit down on the couple of bags on the step. Her eyes were becoming accustomed to the dark and she was beginning to make him out. He looked exhausted and thinner than she remembered him, the lips were chapped and blistered, he looked even warier than before, but essentially unchanged. She stood back from the door, folded her arms, which he took as a sign to come in.

In the kitchen he stumbled, then dropped the bags, stood up and looked down at her. 'You haven't changed – '

'Yes,' she said bitterly, 'oh, yes I have . . . and don't think you can get to me by your smooth tongue.'

He smiled briefly. 'You won't let me down.'

'Like you did.'

'Like I did.' His skin was stretched taut over the bones of his face and now she could see he had a scruffy beard, flecked with grey. He noticed her look and rubbed a hand over it. 'Not very becoming I grant you.'

'Vanity or disguise, Doherty?'

'Neither. These last two or three weeks I haven't had much call to shave.'

She closed the door, locked it and said, 'You better come through and tell me about it.'

He sat in an armchair, hunched inside a dark jerkin, hands in pockets, his left leg hooked over a chair arm. 'How have you been, Mary?'

'Well, of late,' she answered, looking down at him. She had put on a table lamp and the light fell, yellowing, on to Doherty's face. 'And you aren't going to affect it.'

'I wanted to contact you . . . but the longer I left it the harder it became. Until – '

'Until you desperately needed me.'

'I was going to say until it got impossible. But yes, you're right. You're probably the only person who can help me. I'm wanted by the police – '

'Yes. You're well known hereabouts. I know. I read all about you. Bombing was hardly your style, Doherty.

Rather complicated. You could barely mix up developer as I remember.'

'Not just that. Murder. In America.'

She looked at him. There was something daunting in his eyes. Callousness? 'You graduated from the emotional killing, then?' He didn't respond. 'Yes, you've been something of a celebrity, national news, the papers – charting your trail of terror . . . I was going to make coffee,' she said, 'but it had better be the Bushmills.'

'You got to like it, then?' he said as she hunted the glass and the bottle.

When she came back in from the kitchen she had the bottle on a tray together with two Lourdes souvenir glasses. 'Well?' she said, after pouring the drinks and sitting opposite him on the settee. And he started to tell her what had happened since the morning when the post brought the Broad Black Brimmer, skirting the depth of his feeling for Lee, and then, finally, his intended manhunt for the face in the photograph. He talked for fifteen minutes and she noticed that when he talked of the girl his jaws muscles clenched and his eyes narrowed. She threw some lumps of coal on the smouldering fire and by the time he had finished it had flickered into life again.

She topped their glasses up and sat back in the chair. 'So what do you want from me? And why should I help you? I owe you nothing. I don't want you back in my life, even briefly. And,' she looked at him and paused for effect, 'I'm not even sure myself that I don't want something terrible to happen to you.'

He sipped the whisky, then dipped his finger in it and started to run it round the edge of the glass so that it sang, keened. 'Something terrible has happened.'

She fancied that he was on the point of tears. 'Is it revenge you want? Isn't that natural?'

'It is,' he answered. 'Oh, it is.'

'But it's crippling,' she realised. And then she said, 'What is it you want from me?'

161

He had stopped his one-note symphony on the glass. 'I don't know exactly. But I've been framed, set-up, I've become some awful, bloody catalyst for a war on the streets in America. I don't see any way I can get out of it all, any way that I can treat. It looks completely hopeless. I don't think that I particularly care any more. But I have to know why? Don't you see that?'

She was staring at him over the top of her glass. 'And?'

'I can't just walk up to them and ask, can I?' He was looking into her, trying to manipulate.

'You seriously expect me to?' She got up and began to poke the fire angrily, sparks roaring up the chimney. 'No, Doherty. You're mad.'

'Your brother,' she heard him say from behind. 'When they arrested me they kept on about him. About the shooting of a Para, an eighteen-year-old, about the same age as Brendan would have been then. He did it, Mary. I was in the next street, I heard the shots and I saw the lad die in a doorway and I saw the van drive off. He was hit in the neck cavity, just above the flak jacket and the blood was pumping everywhere. I took pictures of him as he died and his mates punched and kicked at me and tried to grab the film. It was Brendan. And I never told. About two hours later I was in a social club and he came in with three others and everyone started cheering and mobbing him. I knew then that he had done it.

'Later, when he was half-pissed, I asked him . . . how it had felt. Do you know what he said? He said "Greatest feeling in the world." There was this young lad, a nice lad, fond of his sister, a dab hand at Irish dancing, who had squeezed the Armalite trigger and extinguished the life of another young lad, probably a nice lad. And he told me about it and told me it felt good.'

He looked at her back, standing in front of the fire, poker now discarded and her arms wrapped around herself. 'They asked me about it and I said nothing. Because of you, Mary. I never told.'

162

Eventually she turned. Tears were running down her face. 'You really are a bastard, Doherty. Is there anything you won't use?' She sniffed and ran the back of her hand across her nose. 'They have him now, anyway. Life. Would another corpse make any difference to that?' In a far-off way she said: 'I'm only glad my mother wasn't alive then . . .' Then she drained her whisky glass in one and said: 'Don't trade with me, Doherty. You think I owe you. Well, perhaps we're even.' Her eyes flittered in the tears. 'Just after you left I found out I was pregnant. Even if I had known how to contact you I wouldn't. I had an abortion, Doherty, me, a good Catholic girl. Your child – ' she started to tremble ' – mine, may God forgive my eternal soul.' She bit a knuckle on her wedding finger. 'So let's just call it even.'

Doherty put his hands over his ears, turned and pulled his legs up to his chest. Exactly like an overgrown schoolboy, she thought.

Neither of them slept much, she lying in bed reviewing the past, what she would do now, he on the sofa, vainly trying to come to terms. He had tried to cut himself off from life and, somehow, in the doing, he had set off a train of events which had resulted in – how many deaths? He thought of the dead baby. He thought of Lee again and again, and he knew that he couldn't live with himself. How much longer, he thought?

He heard Mary moving, then the sound of running water and the creaking of the stairs. She came in wearing a towelling robe and stood staring at him, whether or not accusatorially he couldn't tell. Eventually she said: 'All right. I'll do what I can.'

He sat up, still wearing the jerkin. 'Thank you. I'm sorry – for everything. I didn't know. I can't tell you how sorry I am. For the pain I caused.'

She shrugged, a long way from the past. 'It doesn't matter. It's all gone now. Finally, let's put it to rest.'

He straightened on the sofa. 'I don't know why I left,' he said. 'I've thought about it constantly. All I can say is that I had to, it was time. I did love you, in the only way I can. It wasn't good enough. I don't know, perhaps you have to like and respect yourself before you can live with loving someone? I really don't know. But it does matter.'

'I'm tired,' she said. 'I can't think any more about it. I'll make breakfast.' She went into the kitchen and dreamily started to open cupboards.

'Mary,' she heard him call. 'I can't stay here. It's too dangerous for you. You could end up inside.'

Just another sentence, she thought, opening the fridge. 'Where else can you go?' she said. 'The neighbours around here don't talk, as you probably remember.'

'Maybe not to the authorities. But it's your friends in the balaclavas that bother me most.'

'Suit yourself,' she said, tearing open a packet of bacon. 'You haven't gone vegetarian or anything, have you?'

Over breakfast – bacon, toast and coffee you could stand a spoon in – he told her about leaving America. He had spent a couple of days in Tijuana, staying in a hotel along from a hospital for terminally ill cancer patients which promised, for a large consideration, a miraculous cure. He had walked about the city, only a breath away from the richest state in the richest country in the world, but it was indescribably poor. It made him depressed, brushing off beggars all day.

Then, taking buses for the most part, the impoverished-seeming gringo, had made his way to Mexico City, which was even more depressing than Tijuana. The air was like a band across his lungs, the noise was constant and debilitating. He had spent two nights in a reasonable hotel, languishing in the bath, shutting out the noise, sleeping. Then he had gone to the airport and boarded a plane for Paris.

'I slept most of the way across,' he said. 'To be honest, it was alcohol-induced. No one seemed much interested in me. In Mexico City they checked my hand-baggage, asked me if I had bought any antiquities and when I clearly hadn't that was it. On you go.'

From Paris he had taken an Aer Lingus flight to Dublin and then the train to Belfast. 'That's it,' he said. 'Here I am.'

She stared at him across the table, put her coffee cup down and brushed a crumb from the corner of her mouth. 'I still don't know why I'm doing this . . . when I thought I hated you for so long.' She leaned forward across the table. 'Listen to me, Doherty, when all of this is over I don't want to hear from you or see you again in my life.'

'You have my word,' he said. 'I would for you, you know,' he said. And she believed him.

'God help us both,' she whispered.

When she went to work Doherty stripped down to his underwear and climbed into her bed. He could smell her perfume on the pillow, her remembered warmth, he felt guilt but modified it by persuading himself that, as he was not naked in her bed, there was no invasion of her deepest privacy. He wondered about men she had slept with in this bed, between these sheets and felt an old ache. Lee's violated body came back and he started to shudder. He dragged his mind to the man, his prey, his face and he thought of the ways he would kill him until, shortly, sleep swallowed him up.

He woke, hearing a movement in the room. 'I'm sorry,' he said fuzzily, 'I needed the rest. It's been a long time since I slept in a bed that wasn't moving.'

'I want to get changed,' she said.

'Sure.' He sat up and rubbed his face, ran his fingers through his hair.

'You still do that,' she said.

'What?'

'Always, when you wake.' She made a raking motion with her hands.

'I'm sorry . . . you must be tired. What time is it?'

'Almost seven.'

'Is it dark yet?'

'It is. Why?'

'I have to go out, to make some calls.'

'There's a phone downstairs.'

'I know. But they monitor every call between here and the mainland. Some spotty youth in GCHQ listening on your every word. Or maybe it's a Japanese tape recorder. Whatever, they would trace it to here. So I'll use a telephone box.'

She folded her arms again. It was a mannerism he didn't remember. 'So you put the others, those at the other end, in danger?'

'I know that. But I have to.'

'Right,' she said finally. 'Then I'll leave you to dress.' And consult with your own God, she thought.

He got up, rummaged in the larger of his bags for a new pair of underpants, a jersey and a pair of jeans. Everything smelled of sweat and stale cigarette smoke. Then he pulled on yesterday's socks and a pair of training shoes, whitened and cracked from usage, had a quick splash in the bathroom, ran his fingers through his hair and damp beard, and went downstairs. Mary was in the kitchen, the kettle was on – it was almost a reflex, it seemed, each time her feet hit the linoleum.

'I have a friend,' she said, over her shoulder while washing out two cups in the sink, 'who is involved. That I can trust. He's away just now, probably figuring out with the others what to do about the trouble you've caused

over there. But I'm sure I can get a message to him, talk
to him.'

'There isn't much time. Each hour being around here
adds to the likelihood of being discovered. And when I
make these calls, however long it takes for them to find
out, they're going to know where I am, they're going to
step up surveillance. Mary?' He had walked into the
kitchen. 'I can't stay here tonight. They're going to look
up the files and see the connection and come trawling
round here.'

'Yes,' she said. 'I've thought of that.'

'I don't know how far they'll take it, but you'd be as
well to polish the place, just in case.'

'Where will you go?' She was staring at the kettle.

'I don't know. I can't get too far tonight. It's too risky
to move around too much anyway. I'll find a derry, or
sleep in the park. Or just keep out of sight.'

She put two cups on the draining board and reached up
to the cupboard for the coffee. 'I wouldn't go for a
derelict house,' she said, spooning coffee into the cups,
'the lads love leaving booby traps for the Brits in them.'
She poured the water into the cups. 'I have a cousin off
the Malone Road. She'll put you up for a couple of
nights.'

'No. Someone else involved, it's too dangerous. For
everyone.' He wanted to hold her in gratitude but if he
made a motion towards her, or if she sensed it, she
stiffened.

'She's sound,' she said. That was all, an end to it. And
he would have to go along with it because, for him, it was
better than anything else. In the open he would be
spotted, by one side or the other. Time and space were
closing in on him.

'Right,' he said.

*

He eventually found a working telephone box on the corner of Tralee Street. He waited ten minutes, his collar pulled up against the drizzle and discovery, until the girl inside had finished her animated conversation. He watched, intrigued, as she stabbed at the air with her index finger, screeched into the receiver and finally slammed down the phone and spun out. The box was smoky, smelling of urine and tobacco. He put a column of silver on the metal box which had previously held telephone directories, wondered if these were the pieces of silver which would betray his colleagues, and fished inside his jacket for his address book. He prayed that neither of them would be out, then he picked up the phone, which reeked of perfume, and pushed a handful of coins into the slots.

He dialled Crenshaw first, the phone answered on the fourth ring, there was a pause, and then the winding tones of an answering machine. 'Fuck,' he said before the bleep, and hung up. He flicked through his address book again, found Morlay's number, and spun the dial. The phone rang, the tone seemed to echo down the underwater cable, and then, when he thought of hanging up, a voice said, 'Julian Morlay.' There was chatter in the background, Morlay was probably having a dinner party. Doherty could imagine him, clutching a particularly extravagant vintage wine, probably dressed in a dinner jacket, or some cushioned number Noel Coward might have camped in.

'Julian' he said. 'I wrote to you. You must remember.'

There was a long silence, Doherty could feel the alarm growing in it, and then eventually Morlay, the permacool destroyed, said: 'I can't talk to you. Don't involve me. If you call me again I'll go to the police.' His voice was trembling in panic. Then, slowly, 'It's not what you imagine.' And then the phone cut off. Doherty tried calling again, and then again, but Morlay had clearly put the phone off the hook. He tried Crenshaw once more, abortively, and then went out into the darkness. It's not what you imagine, kept sounding in his head.

David Crenshaw worked from a refurbished building in Clerkenwell which had been bought in the middle of the Seventies by a Quaker trust, and then split up into offices, studios and workspaces for radical causes. The rent was modest, but Crenshaw, who was nothing if not deeply cynical about even the most right-on appearing of causes, knew that despite the low rents, the increase in property values since the purchase had more than insulated the trust against its apparent charity. Indeed there would be millions in capital gain if the building were ever sold. His office looked down across the rooftops to the Marx library and the Green, and if he looked perilously out of the window he could check his bike was still moored to the lamppost.

Crenshaw was in his early thirties, with a shock of brown hair caught in a rubber band and into a ponytail at the crown of his head. In parallel to getting a first at Oxford he had invented a robotic tracking device, with a video eye and fibre optic technology, which was designed to find breaks in cable or pipe in the tiniest and most hostile environments. He had patented the device, then he had sold the development rights to a British company in the silicon corridor, from whom he received regular, often substantial, royalties. But he also had a continual and nagging source of worry: it was his suspicion that the company had amended his invention to make it into a covert surveillance device, crawling it into crevices and spaces to eavesdrop. He had no evidence for this, and guilt prevented him deploying his dogged investigatory skills to find out. But after a London siege he had read reports of a new piece of British technology which had brought every word and even, it was hinted, pictures, of inside the place. Meanwhile, the cheques were very welcome.

Crenshaw would also have admitted to being a workaholic, if he hadn't found the description so objectionable, associated, as it was, with addiction, and drink, which he abjured. He found more than enough stimulation and excitement in his work. He switched on his computer, typed in his security codes, and checked his day's diary. Relatively free. A piece to complete for an American magazine about hackers getting into British defence establishment computers and lunch with a former senior civil servant, who had been one of his best contacts, a man of the best of motives who railed against the politicisation of the apparatus, and who now acted as a sort of back-stop on his information, trying to guide him through the minefield of false tales the secret services were wont to feed to him. It was a matter of pride that he had never been successfully set-up, he had always smelled the rat and he knew that if they succeeded just once in getting him to publish a false story he was through. So he was cautious about the provenance of his information, rigorous in his research, but quite promiscuous in publishing it.

He had been prosecuted twice under the old Official Secrets Act but so discredited had it become, so unwilling were juries to convict, that he had walked free both times. His opponents in the government, behind their hand, smeared him liberally, accusing him of endangering the lives, even occasioning the deaths, of secret agents. It was preposterous and he would sue if anything like that was ever said openly. Sometimes at night he wondered why they didn't just ensure he fell under a car, but he guessed that he hadn't yet become dangerous enough to them. Which spurred him on ever further.

In the last two weeks he had been thinking about Doherty, his curious letter and the picture.

He had first met the man, what?, getting on for ten

years ago. Doherty had taken his picture at a defence rally shortly after he had first been charged. They had got talking, had a couple of meals together courtesy of whichever Fleet Street rag Doherty charged it to, and discovered a mutual, and rather embarrassing, common interest in boats. Politically he didn't consider the man particularly well-formed, a vague socialist of the old Labour type, but human, decent, occasionally raucous and cantankerous, but witty. Crenshaw had not for one second suspected that Doherty was guilty of the bombing. And now he could be virtually certain.

It was preternaturally dark, the lines of the street were smudged and he could see the rains sweeping the hills. An Army helicopter scuttled across the darkening sky. In the distance he could hear thunder explosions, although in this place you could never be sure that was what the reverberations were. Reflexively he pulled down the brim of the tweed cap he had found on the hallstand, beside the cane fly-fishing rod, a musty overcoat and a gnarled knobkerrie, and waited, scratching at the growth on his face. Then the rain hit, in a sudden burst, straight down, bursting off the glass, drumming so loudly in his ears that it almost drowned the ringing telephone.

He picked it up. 'David. Thanks for ringing back.'

'A pleasure. Just had to rig up the scrambler.'

Doherty smiled, the man was gadgetry-mad, his house was a mass of sensors, pads, consoles, spaghetti wiring and software. Take him away from a computer for eight hours and he would have withdrawal symptoms – he'd be in bytes – Doherty thought, smiling to himself. He was also the oddest of contradictions, from his insistence on bicycle travel everywhere, to a phobia about microwave ovens.

'Have you anything?' Doherty said.

'Indeed, cousin.' And Doherty wondered if the scrambling had meant that the lad in Cheltenham had now torn the headphones from his ears screaming at the howling, or, alternatively, if the Japanese tape machine recording it was now quietly smouldering.

'Well?'

'Very interesting. Your friend is not what you thought' . . . not what you imagine . . . 'I was looking across the water and getting nowhere until I showed the picture to a contact, one of the Gower Street brigade, who blanched visibly and lied badly. Which, of course, put me directly on the track and led me to another contact, in a different branch of the same service, if you get my drift, who confirmed that oh, yes the subject was with Five. With a lot of undercover experience, guess where?' Crenshaw was relishing the fruits of his detection. 'I think my man from Curzon Street rather enjoyed the discomfiture he thought he might cause the other lot. Any help?'

Playing on the hatred between Five and Six, thought Doherty. Then: 'A name, David?'

'Yes . . .' he heard a shuffling of papers 'Rupert Montague, ex-Guards etcetera, no club that I can find, apparently a fanatical rose grower, lives in Maidenhead. He's in the book.'

The drumming rain on the glass reached a crescendo. 'David, you are brilliant.'

'Yes,' the voice in Doherty's ear agreed. 'Good luck.'

'Thanks.'

'Want to tell me what it's all about?'

'I'll write it all down and get it to you.'

'Big?' said Crenshaw.

'Monumental,' replied Doherty, hanging up.

Doherty had asked her to change dollars into sterling, ten thousand dollars, and he insisted that she do it through at least three banks, not to arouse suspicion. She now had over six thousand pounds in her handbag, in hundreds, more money than she had ever seen.

She hadn't heard from Doherty's for almost forty-eight hours. He wasn't at her cousin Theresa's. She wondered if he had been picked up by one side or the other, felt a guilty rush of hope that he might have been, which would take matters out of her hands, then realised that she would have heard – either on the news or the grapevine. Even when they were lovers he had rarely given her advance notice of his intentions, he had felt that he could float in and out of her life at whim, so why should he be considerate now, when there was nothing between them. Nothing? Anyway, she was glad he was away, wherever he was, because it had taken the pressure off, particularly for Theresa who had unquestioningly agreed to put him up, someone who was quite evidently a fugitive of some sort.

She thought that he had probably gone back to some old haunt from the past. Perhaps he had gone off for England? Or had he reactivated some old contact of his and was bedded down somewhere planning intrigue?

So why was she doing this, risking jail at the least, harbouring an enemy of her own side, if there was nothing between them? She looked round her office, the dun-coloured walls, the khaki furniture, the uncovered lamp – funereal chic she thought – with the bright, fiery posters in greens, yellows and reds commemorating dead men, urging men to make others dead. The ridiculous thing is that I don't know. Guilty of loyalty, perhaps? She sighed, got up and walked out on to the landing and into the kitchen. When the emotional going gets tough, reach for the kettle. Perhaps it was something to do with providing a conclusion to a part of her life which had remained irritatingly unfinished, she thought. Whatever he had done to her by his going, his disappearance, she had much to appreciate him for. A different way of seeing, certainly, and of looking at life. She realised that before him she had felt in a sort of emotional slipstream, pulled and twisted by family, events, her environment, lovers. Now she made her own course. He wasn't entirely responsible, but he had helped. Most of all, perhaps, his going had deprived her of choice, of any decision on the future of the relationship. It had simply ceased to be, on his behest, while she was still in motion. Now she would provide her own ending.

The jangle of the phone broke the reverie and she walked back to her desk.

'Mary Cavanagh,' she said.

'As always, responding to urgency, Mary,' Danny's soft voice said in her ear. 'Later? Eight? In Slaven's?' He was quite open about the venue, they were surely listening, but there was no possibility of the Brits infiltrating Slaven's. Or if they had, they had been there for years, ingrained in the stain and filth.

'It's serious, Danny. Very serious,' she said.

'I better be on time, then.'

Patsy Slaven's looked designed to repel a full-scale armoured assault: it was fenced in wire to interfere with the progress of bombs and rockets, with concrete bollards all around to keep away cars or derail a half-track, and steel gates with stewards who vetted everyone going in, and frisked the unfamiliar, who were few. Once inside, the decor of the place, the general squalor, made you think that the security precautions weren't designed to keep people out, but punters in. The publican, Patsy, who had been a major figure in the Fifties campaign, liked the decay – he called it ambience, from a description in a profile about the place in a Dublin magazine article – and worked hard at being a character. Most people found it tiresome, but Mary liked Patsy, who had been a friend of her father's. She remembered him coming round to the house, bringing her sweets and small toys, after he had got out of prison.

Patsy wasn't in tonight. His son Padraig, who had been a couple of classes ahead of her at school, served her a half pint of Guinness. She took it to a table in the furthest corner to the door, and examined the chair carefully before she sat down. She sipped the stout. Whatever else he neglected, Patsy looked after his Guinness. And she noticed that the glass that held it sparkled.

The bar was filling. She watched, men mostly, filter in through the stewards, some of whom nodded to her. Danny arrived ten minutes late, moving across the floor to her, eyes watching him, a wide smile on his face, dark curly hair, a comforting presence, she thought, which might seem ridiculous given his reputation. He leaned over the table and kissed the top of her head. He smelled of fresh soap. 'Missed you,' he said and dropped a paper bag in her lap. 'A refill?' he asked and when she said, 'Whisky, I think' he said, 'Ah, so it is serious,' and walked over to the bar. She watched him, a slightly rolling gait, authoritative, and, of course, he managed to be served immediately.

As he carried back two glasses of whisky and two halfs of stout she looked inside the bag. A white t-shirt, with a New York decal, and a plastic replica of the Empire State Building. She looked up at him as he put down the drinks. 'So,' she said. He raised his eyebrows conspiratorially.

He sat down and took a draught of the beer, licking the foam from his lips. 'It's good to be here,' he said.

'When did you get back?'

'Two or three days ago,' he said. And then: 'There were things to do, I couldn't get in touch. You know how it is.'

'I do.'

He smiled. The twinkle stuck in her head. 'I shouldn't really be here now. But you said it was crucial. And I take it this is not about us.'

175

She took his right hand, clenched it, then let it go, uneasy that the gesture should be seen. 'It's about someone I used to know. And it's about the trouble there's been.'

The pleasure left his face. 'Doherty.'

She nodded and looked down at her drinks. 'I knew him about five years ago – '

'Knew him?'

'Danny, please, don't make it any more difficult.' She noticed that he looked at her coldly. 'He was working here. He's a photographer. Was. I don't know. It doesn't matter now.' She took a gulp of the whisky and avoided his eyes. 'He's come back.'

'Where is he?' Danny said angrily, leaning across the table.

'I don't know,' she said, which was almost honest. 'Please, let me finish. He's come here to try to sort things out. He says he's been set up.' She tried to take his hand, but he moved it away. 'Danny, I believe him. He says he's been set up by . . . by – '

'Us.'

'He wants to sort it out, if it's possible.'

'It isn't.'

'I don't want to know anything about any of this, Danny. But I know what Doherty is, or isn't. He's not the type to get involved, he's not committed – to anybod . . . thing.'

'No?' he said, leaning across the table again. 'Well, whether it's for gain or glory, he's committed. To the Brits. He says we set him up. Really? We've men dead all over America. We're drug-dealing scum to anyone in the world who can read a newspaper. Even our own people despise us. The money's completely dried up, and the Army Council's decided when, not if, to call a ceasefire. Because of your uncommitted friend. And he thinks we set him up. Some set-up. Some own goal.' He sat back in the creaking chair. 'Grow up, Mary.'

176

Slowly he picked up his whisky glass and carefully drained it. 'There's no way out for him.'

'Danny.' She wanted to say, 'Don't be so cruel,' but instead, she said: 'He's sure the Provie's set him up . . . He has a picture. Of a man he says is involved.'

Danny leaned forward again. 'Sure.'

She felt her anger rise. 'Look. Whatever you think, I know that he's not working for the Brits. Someone close to him was killed by – '

'Not by us.'

'Danny, I thought you might help, because – '

'Because we've been lovers?'

Been? she thought. 'Yes, I suppose so.'

'You thought your present lover would help out a previous one . . . why on earth did you think that?'

She slammed her whisky glass down on the table. 'Probably because I thought you were a bigger and better man than you are. Probably because I want a solution too. I don't want him popping up in my life again, I don't want to be looking behind when I thought, at last, that there was something ahead of me. I was wrong.' She stood up, but he grabbed her arm and pushed her back into the seat.

'You realise,' he said, very calmly, 'that what you've done could have you end up on the wasteground with a hood over your head?'

'Let go of my arm, Danny . . . Or are you going to drag me out of here and do it yourself?'

He released her arm. 'Mary. Love. I'm not threatening you. I'm telling you what would happen if anyone else knew. What are you doing?'

She felt her face flushed. She took a deep breath. 'Look, I believe what he's told me. Listen to me. Go along with me. What if what he is saying is true? All of it. He has got a picture of one of them, someone who broke into his hotel room. I believe it, Danny. If he's been set up by the Brits this face can be identified. You've already said how bad things are. But if you could prove that the dirty tricks were theirs. Publicly prove it. What would that do to them?'

He smiled again. 'And what if this is all just a continuation of the game? If they . . . if he's using you to get to me and others.' He picked up the half-empty beer glass and banged it down on the table. The dark stout spluttered and foamed on to the table. 'Check mate.'

She put out her hand on his, holding the glass. It was wet and hot. 'He isn't. Talk to him. Convince yourself.'

He shook his head slowly, smiled and returned her hand touch. 'If I get stiffed by a Brit, Mary Cavanagh, I'll never forgive you.'

'He can give you the evidence. The testimony. It's the way out.'

He sighed, looked round the room. 'Okay. Fix it up.'

Mary squeezed his hand hopefully.

'I wish you wouldn't turn up like this, Doherty, scaring the shit out of me in the middle of the night.' She had opened the back door and he was now standing in the kitchen, looking and smelling damp and subterranean. 'Christ,' she said, 'you're like something out of a Hammer movie.'

'Fangs,' he said. 'I'm at the wrong house for ripe virgins then?'

'Coffee or stronger,' she asked.

'Stronger.' Then: 'I've sussed it out.'

'Which is the right house?'

'No. Who's behind it all.'

'Not the Provos.'

'You guessed?'

'Almost. I talked to someone. Go on.'

He took off his overcoat, dropping it on the linoleum floor while she pulled a couple of glasses from the sink, swilled them under the tap, unscrewed the top of the whisky bottle and poured two healthy ones. He grabbed a glass from her hand, mumbled 'Cheers,' took it down in one, wiped the residue from his beard, and held it out to her. She poured another. He leaned against the back door took a sip and said, 'Cheers. Slainte.'

'Well?'

'Well,' he said, 'when I was in New York I sent copies of the pictures to a couple of pals with polite requests to find out who the fuck this murdering bastard was. So I called them. One of them was so scared I could hear his teeth fracture. And he told me to get lost. He had obviously been nobbled. But he did let out that the whole crack wasn't what I had imagined. So, eventually I contracted my other pal who has traced this animal, quite conclusively, to the Secret Service. MI5. Gave me a name, his location, even his part-time interest.'

'It makes sense.'

'What?'

'I talked to my friend,' she said, clutching her dressing gown round her with one arm.

'And?'

'Apart from telling me that I would likely end up with my brains all down my dress . . . he said that they believed you were one of them. A Brit.' She took a calculated sip of the whisky and said: 'And you're not?'

He got up quickly and pushed his face a few inches away from hers. 'Of course not. Look at me. No. Not deliberately anyway. Believe me.' Then he kissed her forehead. He smelled, she thought now, of death, decomposition.

'I do,' she said wearily, 'but I don't know if Danny does. He thinks that maybe the game isn't over, that the final play is you reaching him and others, somehow.'

He let her go. 'I don't know. Maybe that is the game and he's right. I've been miles behind the play all the way through. I don't know if they're watching me now, if there's another trick to come. But I can't think why. I don't think so. The IRA is effectively wrecked, in terms of funds and credibility and probably resolve. The Government . . .' He stopped, realising for the first time that such an operation, such an elaborate plan involving huge funds, agents operating abroad and illegally on the soil of a friendly power had to have agreement, would have to have clearance at the highest level, '. . . has achieved more in three months against the IRA than in twenty years, more result with some blundering dupe than with internment, shoot-to-kill policies and international diplomacy and the whole paraphernalia of power.

'At best it will take years to rebuild the IRA.' He stopped again, turned away, wiped his eyes and drained the glass. 'If that's true, if I'm right, what becomes of your man and his mates – and me – is almost an irrelevance. What became of Lee was an irrelevance to them. But,' he said, looking at Mary again, his eyes watering, 'not to me, Mary. This – ' he tapped his chest ' – this irrelevance will make them pay. Nothing else matters.'

'Jerry,' she said, putting her hand on his arm, 'let's go into the other room.' She patted the arm. 'Calm yourself.'

'In the grave, Mary. In the grave.'

'What kind of person is he?' Doherty was lying with his shoes off on her settee, waving a cup of coffee.

'No, Doherty.'

'What do you mean?'

'You're looking for an edge, an advantage of some sort.'

'Rubbish, it was a perfectly natural question to ask.'

'You don't make conversation, ask questions without a purpose.'

'You're sensitive!'

'Wary. I've learned to be.'

'If that's some sort of reference to the past, forget it.' He sat up, put down the cup and pointed at her. 'I don't understand. Why are you doing this? Why don't you just tell me to fuck off? You clearly don't like me.'

She pulled the edges of her dressing gown together, in a small agitation. 'Why is it that men always need to know that they're liked, wanted, needed? It's pathetic. I haven't even thought about whether I like you. It's not appropriate, it's not germane. We don't have the luxury of liking, or considering it, do we? I just want to get through this with the minimum possible damage. To me. To anyone. To you even. After that I can consider the emotional questions. If I'm spared.'

'So,' he said, sitting back again, 'what does your Danny want?'

'Well,' she said after a pause, 'I think he's looking for a way out, like you. You'll have to make him trust you, or at least believe you. After that, I don't know. I suppose they'll want to make it all public – '

'To use me.'

'To get back. What do you want?'

He ran a hand through his hair. 'I don't want to be a pawn in anyone's war game anymore. Propaganda or otherwise. All I ever wanted was to be was left alone.' He thumped the arm of the chair and Mary noticed, distractedly, a cloud of dust rise up around his hand. 'I don't know why they chose me. It doesn't really matter now. But I came here because I thought it could end here. One way or the other. Now? Well, it would be useful if I had a period of grace. If his side would lay off for a while.'

'Until you find the man in the picture and kill him.'

'At least.' He smiled. 'Sounds dramatic, doesn't it?'

She stood up, pulling the collars of the dressing gown again, angry. 'Like a man,' she said. 'You are mad. What do you think you're up against? There are no rules here Doherty, no moral imperatives, no white hats. You seriously think that you're going to pierce to the heart of the British secret service and deliver a mortal blow . . . for decency? Revenge?'

He stood up, angry too. His eyes still narrowed. 'Because it will make me feel fucking good! Because vermin like that don't deserve to live. Any reason you fucking like.'

'You haven't a chance. And when they get you they aren't going to tap you on the shoulder and say, come along with me, my son. They're not going to take you to a nice police cell, let you ring your lawyer, and then let you waltz into the witness box and unburden yourself about it all. Do you understand?' She was beginning to shout now. 'They are going to kill you, Doherty. If you are lucky it'll be a double tap to the temple. But they may want to find out what you know, how far it has gone. In which case you'll probably pray to be dead. And it will come eventually. They are going to destroy you, Doherty.'

'Yes? Yes, they will. But not soon enough, I hope. Anyway, it doesn't matter – sooner or later. It'll end for me.'

She looked at him, looked at his eyes, abandoned, and she knew that it wasn't self-pity or delusion, but that he really didn't care. She took two steps across the carpet and put her arms round his neck. 'Doherty, I don't want you to die,' she said into his chest. 'Give it up. Go off somewhere, lose yourself.'

He gently unwrapped her arms, kissed her softly on the mouth and said: 'I tried that. Now, I want to talk to Danny.'

Daniel Patrick McDevitt had been busy. After the meeting with Mary – he had considered briefly that they should go to bed, then decided to put duty before dalliance – he had gone straight to the Belfast Brigade commander, Seamus Monahan, and reported what he had been told.

Monahan was in his early forties, with a round, boyish face, sandy, tufted hair going grey in patches. He was known as the Butcher's Boy, although not to his face, not for any penchant for atrocity, but because he had been an apprentice butcher in his teens, delivering packages of meat up and down the Falls on an old black bike with an iron delivery tray at the front. If nothing else, it had given him an unparalleled knowledge of every street and alley. He was something of a puritan, he neither smoked nor drank, and he had been known to impose his rigorous moral disapproval on others; most famously, when he blew apart the gantry of a raucous, after-hours drinking club with a Thompson sub-machine-gun. He was an intelligent and resourceful chief-of-staff who, like most of his contemporaries, had learned command and tactics while interned by the British, studying classic texts like the *Mini-manual of the Urban Guerrilla* by Carlos Marriguella and, of course, the enemy's chief theoretician, Frank Kitson.

'Bring him in, Danny,' Monahan said as they stood in the door of his terraced house. 'We'll interrogate him, and if he's telling the truth then we'll have a major coup, a star witness. It'll make *Spycatcher* look like a Quaker Sunday school. If he's a plant, well – ' He let the sentence hang.

'I'm worried about the peace, Seamus.'

'You did well, Danny.'

'No. I meant, if we could produce Doherty for them, that would be the conclusive proof.'

Monahan tapped the door frame. 'We should invite some Italian guests, then. Do you reckon they'd send anyone?'

'There are always dispensable foot soldiers,' Danny said, smiling.

Monahan put his hand on Danny's shoulder. 'Trusted lieutenants, you mean . . . Do you know where Doherty is?'

'I can find out.'

'Set up the meeting, take someone along. Let me know

when it is, I'll fix up a safe house where we can question him and I'll make contact with the States, start things moving.'

Doherty had dozed on the couch, the horrors enveloping him when he slept too deeply, and when Mary got up in the morning he stirred into full wakefulness. He rubbed his hair, feeling the grits of neglect in it. While Mary was cooking bacon and tomatoes Doherty washed. He looked at himself in the bathroom mirror. His face was gaunt to the point of cadaverousness, his eyes looked hard and reproachful, his skin was drawn and stained, all of this framed by a tangle of dark hair, long and matted on his head, scrubby and grizzled on his chin. 'Can you spare a tanner for a cup of tea, Sir?' he asked the reflection. The image was coming along fine, the only problem was the itching. If he got to London, when he got to London, he would go to ground, become just another Glasgow dosser on the streets. The cover was perfect. No one would look for him on the streets, in flop houses and hostels. There is no one as anonymous as a vagrant. People choose not to see them, recall them as people, identify them. They have no faces. He would be just another shambling, reeking mess of guttural vowels and alcohol. A role he would fit very securely he told himself. He cleaned his teeth with Mary's toothbrush, made a mental apology to her and went downstairs to bacon and tomato sandwiches and thick dark tea.

He left with her, the pockets of his coat heavy with the money she had changed for him. When he got to Theresa's he quickly packed his two bags, leaving out the Olympus camera unit, the remote control cable and the can of Mace.

He had only seen Theresa once, on the first night, and she had almost refused to looked at him. Lot-like, in case some dreadful recollection might be required in the

184

future. He guessed that she had left the place for the duration of his stay, probably – and rightly – terrified of his presence. Then he went out, leaving the quiet house, and walked down to the railway station, checking his bags into the left luggage and walking across to the ticket office. He was wearing the old tweed cap and his best attempted Belfast brogue, which sounded like a subterranean rasp. He said 'Dublin single.' The clerk gave him the ticket without a second glance. Stupid to be worried, he told himself, how many faces do they see in a day until they glaze over?

He ate lunch in a cheap cafe near the docks, surrounded by lookalikes, mostly youngish men in grimy clothes, eating slowly, prolonging the time and the warmth, wreathed in hopelessness. One man tried to talk to him but Doherty growled, drew him a glance and the man said, 'Fair enough,' and moved away.

After the meal – carbohydrates could have a fatal effect on your longevity, Doherty, he told himself sombrely – he walked until he came across a cinema. A Rambo double bill. Just the thing, he told himself, and bought a ticket. But he had gone blank-eyed by about the hundredth killing and was asleep before Stallone managed to get through a complete sentence. He woke briefly when someone, a man, came into his row and tipped a seat. He watched him warily for a minute or two, but the man sat several seats away. He slept again until a particularly violent on-screen explosion roused him, but the expanse of Rambo's pectorals soon sent him off again.

It was after six when he finally woke. His head ached and he felt parched. He yawned, uncurled himself slowly and made for the exit. Outside it was dark and raining, a soft smirr that quickly soaked his coat, his cap, and which hung in beads from the tails of his hair. He began a slow walk towards the Malone Road, stopping at a fortified off-licence where he bought a half bottle of whisky and a carton of orange juice. He drained the juice and then took a quick nip of whisky, shivering as the alcohol hit his stomach.

He had told Mary to arrange the meeting for eight. There was a Dublin train at nine-thirty and he intended to be on it. He wondered about Danny, his first loyalty, whether it would be to Mary or the Movement. He was betting on the former, probably with his life. Why take the risk? he asked himself. He considered as the whisky flared in his veins. It was because of Mary. He had dipped in and out of her life once before and now, having come back, he could not simply ask for her help, involve her, put her at risk with her own people and then evaporate when she had exposed herself completely to them. He had to do this, pay the debt, whatever the consequences.

The streets grew wider, more prosperous as he approached the house. The curtains were still open, the rooms dark, so Theresa clearly hadn't come back. Anyway, he had told Mary to keep her away for the evening. He opened the door and had a momentary attack of panic that Danny would be waiting in the gloom. But the house was just as he had left it, silent, apart from the ticking of passing time from the Swiss clock in the hall. Six fifty-five. He went up to the bathroom, stripped and began to wash himself down. Then, from some remembered habit, he picked up his underpants and checked their cleanliness before reminding himself that it was a redundant exercise – the bodily fluids evacuate in death anyway. He dressed again, pulling on the damp overcoat to finish, and went down to the kitchen where he poached himself an egg, all that his palpitating stomach could stand. It tasted, he thought, exactly like a jellyfish might. Then he carefully washed the pan and plate, brewed himself a coffee which he fortified with a large slug of whisky.

He put out the main light in the room, lighting a table lamp next to the window and a standard lamp at the fireplace. The light was soft. Then he coupled the remote cable to the Olympus and put the unit on a small nest of tables beside the settee and led the cable down behind, under a rug and, putting his hand down to tear out the base fabric, up through the sofa so that the plunger was concealed in the space between the two cushions. Then he tore the lining of the left hand pocket of his overcoat so that he could put his hand through. He put his hand in his pocket and from inside the fabric grasped the cable release, pressed it and the camera, four feet away to his left clicked, exploded and whirred in the gloom. Doherty got up, checked the unit was primed again and then retrieved the Mace from his bedroom. Then he settled down to wait.

He felt fatalistic now, as he waited sipping remains of the now cold, but strong coffee. At seven forty-four the bell rang. Doherty got up, his bones ached, fatigue seemed to fill the place in his soul where the iron should be, and he went in the dark hall. 'Yes,' he called, skulking in the gloom, pressing himself against a wall in a hopeful evasion of an arc of fire, with the clock's amplified time passing in his ear.

'Danny . . .'

'Right,' Doherty said quietly, his mouth sour, his legs shivering. He breathed in and opened the door.

The shadowy man below him on the step said 'Doherty,' a confirmation, not a question, and walked into the house. Doherty led him into the living room. He seems calm and reasonable, he thought and in the light saw that Danny was not what he expected. Younger, sturdier, shorter. Than? Than me. What arrogance.

Doherty slumped casually on the sofa and motioned Danny to an armchair. He sat down and crossed one leg over the other and leaned on the arm rest and stared, a kiss of a smile on his mouth. He's trying to dominate the room, Doherty thought. So he sat deeper in the sofa and thrust both hands deep into the coat pockets and said to himself, let him.

'You should be dead, Doherty, the trouble you've caused.'

'Yes,' he agreed. 'But I'm not afraid of that. Is that why you came?' And he noticed that he was calmer now. The adrenalin was flowing positively.

'The only reason I'm here is because of Mary.'

'Me too.'

'We're not rivals,' Danny said. And then: 'You're not at all what I expected.'

'Me too,' Doherty said again.

Both men looked at each other, willing the other to break the silence. 'Well,' said Danny eventually, 'what do you propose?'

'I don't know. Excuse me. I'm completely drawn of ideas.'

'Mary doesn't believe you're working for the Brits.'

'I'm not. Not knowingly,' Doherty said, taking his left hand out of his pocket to scratch his hair. 'And you, what do you believe?'

'Well. You certainly did a pretty fucking shit hot job of destruction, for an outsider.'

Doherty moved his lips in a grim smile without warmth. 'A loose cannon. An unguided missile,' he said.

Danny leaned forward in the chair. 'Oh, no. You were aimed all right. That can't go on. A different guidance system will have to be built in. Or –'

Doherty knew the import of the silence but he asked: 'Or? Destruction?'

'You could say.'

'Ah,' said Doherty. 'I had a feeling that was coming.'

Danny got up and moved to the window and looked out. Doherty wondered if it was some kind of signal. 'Tell me Doherty,' Danny said, 'what would you do in my place?'

'Surely you're not looking for absolution? From me.'

'Wittingly or unwittingly you have about ruined the Movement. There aren't any hawks or doves any more – '

'Carrion crow?'

' – everyone's united. Without the support of the people – '

'I sense a little Mao coming.'

' – there's no continuation of the armed struggle.'

'Good-bye to the ballot and bullet game.'

Danny turned and folded his arms. 'Christ, what a smart arse you are, Doherty. Glib, crass – '

'Gullible,' Doherty offered.

'You're a dead man – at my whim, Doherty. Do you realise?'

'I was wondering when it would come to that.'

'You're coming with me. You've lots of questions to answer.'

Doherty hunched into his coat and pushed his hands deep into the pockets. 'No. I don't think so.' Danny snorted. 'But I'll tell you what the deal is. Take the cross-hairs off me for a month, and you'll get more good publicity than you can handle.'

'I don't think so.'

'Let me out – help me get out. I'll make sure that the story breaks, with action and pictures. And if the papers all run scared of the Official Secrets Act, in America and Europe. How – whether it was an approved action or not – and it had to be, didn't it? One innocent was set up, another was murdered. And the by-product, as far as I'm concerned, is that the IRA was covered in blood, opprobrium and inches of shit. But at least I'll be giving you the tools to dig yourself out.'

'And you, you'll flit round Whitehall and the Palace of Westminster – what, visiting revenge on those responsible?'

'I suppose – something like that.'

'You're not gullible, Doherty, you're a stupid, naive,

muddling fool. Or you're a knave, a British knave. I think
the former. I mean, did you seriously think the Irish
Republican Army would pick some random out of the
telephone book and send him jaunting off on a crucial,
dangerous mission. We're not toy soldiers, Doherty. We
take men Doherty, men, who have been born in the
struggle, fired in it, who realise that their chance of seeing
middle age at liberty or alive is negligible, who won't
betray, who won't flinch from being killed or killing, who
can be trusted and relied on. Who won't talk. Not people
like you who prance around the edges, picking up
rewards, juicy bits of other lives and deaths – carrion
crow. Your words, Doherty. We use our people, our
Volunteers, not – '

'Vultures?'

Danny turned back to the window. 'I'm tired of word
games, Doherty. You'll come with me, you'll answer all
the questions that are put, to our satisfaction and then, if
you are what you say you are, we'll call a press conference
and you will tell your story.'

'And then?' Danny shrugged. 'Not a new life and a new
identity like the touts and supergrasses?'

'You'll be looked after.'

Doherty yawned and straightened his arms out inside
the coat pockets. 'That's crap. No, Danny. I don't think
so. I think I prefer it my way.'

The other man shook his head, put his hand inside his
denim jacket and slowly pulled out a pistol. 'You come
now, or you die here.'

'That'll give Mary's cousin a bit of a problem. Explaining my presence. Not to mention getting the blood and
brains out of the carpet.'

'On your feet.'

'And of course you will lose your only chance of setting
the record straight, getting back at the Brits.'

Danny was holding the pistol, in the approved firing
position, in two hands, and Doherty felt his eyes focus

compulsively on the muzzle, which betrayed not the slightest trace of a waver. 'Move yourself, Doherty.'

'Last words, Danny. Never pull a gun on someone and threaten to shoot them without actually doing it. Now pull the trigger, you gutless little fucker.' He waited, watching the trigger finger whiten. Then Danny moved back towards the window, still pointing the gun, took his left hand off the grip and held his hand up in the window. Doherty stood up, his calves against the sofa. 'The help, Danny? You don't fancy your chances on your own? Quite right, son.'

Standing, he drowned in the overcoat, his hair rumpled and tangled wildly on his head, hands deep in the pockets and he felt magnificent, soaring, on the edge of death, truly alive. He heard the door in the hall thump, then splinter and a young lad, looking about eighteen, plainly nervous, with darting eyes and a short Muslim crop, came in.

'Don't tell me. I can make it hard for myself or easy.'

There was still only one gun on view, and Danny's grip and its intensity was dropping in the confidence of his numbers. 'That motion of yours at the window just reminded me of something, Danny. In street fights when I was a kid if someone was in trouble and wanted assistance he called for handers – it was hauners, actually, in the patois. I just thought it was interesting, you putting your hand up like that.'

'As you said, Doherty, hard or easy.'

Doherty pursed his lips and made a pretence of deciding. 'Hard, I think.'

Danny said, 'Right,' and began to move towards him. The younger man started a half second behind. The motor drive and flash exploded in the corner of the room and Danny, whitened and startled, turned, the gun going off, the succeeding flashes catching him full in the eyes. Doherty launched himself, pulling out the can, the Mace stream spraying into Danny's starry eyes and then, over his young colleague's dumbstruck face. The young man clawed at his face, screaming, as Doherty kicked at Danny between his legs and scrabbled for the gun. As he made contact he was first conscious of the intense heat against his stomach, and then the constant, rolling thunder of the explosions, the flailing of his coat as the bullets tore through the material and then the acrid smell of cordite and burnt cloth.

Doherty had his hands on Danny's gun arm, the man's other hand was punching blindly at Doherty's, ineffectual blows. Doherty got a close up of his red, closed running eyes as he twisted the smaller man round then whirled him over his right thigh. The gun went off again, missed and a bullet blew out of the front window. Doherty hung on, twisting and squeezing over Danny, now prostrate on the floor, but scrambling for his feet. The next shot convulsed then paralysed Danny as it split his second and third rib on the left side; the next bullet, fired from his own loosening grip, plowed through his throat, knocking him tumbling back on to the carpet and buried into the floorboards.

The teenager had barely moved. He stood, head in both hands, face streaming, in an awful supplicating fascination. Given a few seconds, Doherty thought, he'll start to cry. The boy's lips were moving, as if trying to appeal. Doherty took the automatic pistol from Danny's now lifeless hand and shot the lad through the right knee. The boy screamed and collapsed, clutching the bloody flesh and the fragmented bone. Doherty noticed that as he did so he moved from the left, clasped the knee with the left hand. He is a southpaw, Doherty thought: I do not have time to search him properly. Then he grabbed the boy's left arm and, as he writhed and screamed on the floor, put the muzzle of the pistol against the bloody hand and blew out the palm.

Cursorily he ran his hands over the jacket of the screaming boy and felt the shape of a gun. He pulled it out and chucked it through the broken front window. Then, thinking there might be another man, a driver, outside, he put Danny's gun into the whole pocket in the overcoat and started to run.

There was no one outside. Careless, he thought. The street was quiet as he ran, he noticed only one person, a woman, at an open door. The area might not have known much violence, but the people knew enough to keep their heads inside when they heard shots.

It was just possible that no one had heard anything, he thought, his shoes slapping the pavement, the gun banging rhythmically against his right side, but it wasn't very likely. The telephone lines would be humming to the RUC now. At the corner he stopped running and began walking briskly. He bet that there hadn't been many Belfast gunmen who made their escape on foot. They would be looking for a fast-revving car, or a whining motor bike, not a lonely nutter on foot. He put his hand into the pocket and pulled out the gun, unclasped the ammunition clip and dropped it down a drain. Then he put the pistol under his armpit in a grip between body and arm and searched, without success, for a handkerchief. Still walking, passing an elderly man being taken for a walk by a Borzoi, he pulled out the front of his jersey. When he was fifty yards in front, he began polishing the pistol with the end of his shirt, inside his coat. He looked at the coat. The heavy weave was torn and gaping at the waist, singed. He could smell it. It was a wonder he hadn't gone up in flames. He continued wiping the gun in his woollen jersey. With this coat and the odd jerking motions under it, it would be just his luck to be picked up as a flasher.

When he was satisfied the gun was clean he looked for a dense hedge and, finding one, pushed the gun into it. He heard it drop, and then lodge. What did he feel? He considered as he walked. Tired. Drained. But exhilarated. He had killed a man and he felt? . . . an overwhelming sense of achievement. Not shame or degradation. Not pride, either. Accomplishment, that feeling of well-being that comes with a particularly difficult problem or physical task successfully, meritoriously completed. Was that sick? Or was it just a by-product of danger, adrenalin overdose? Would the guilt over the death come later? He thought not. Should he have killed the boy, too? That would have been butchery, murder. The other he could justify as self-defence. He had given Danny the opportunity to kill him. He hadn't, although he was sure that in another place, later, he would have done it without a second thought. But the boy, it was probably his first job, the blooding, and after the look of abject hopelessness on his face he couldn't have killed him. He was sure the boy wouldn't talk to the RUC, that much was certain, they never did, however inexperienced. And it would be hours, hopefully days before the Provos knew for certain that it had been him. How long did he have before they realised that the operation hadn't gone off successfully? Long enough to get him on the Dublin train he hoped. He speeded his walk.

And the security forces, what would they make of it? At first, when they identified Danny, they'd put it down to a hit gone wrong, or a Loyalist assassination, some internal feud. They would fingerprint the place, of course, and how long would it take them to attach the prints to him? A day, two days? Longer? Certainly long enough, with a measure of good fortune, to get him out of the city.

His step began to falter when he thought of Mary. When would she find out and what would she do? She would hate him, of course, but would she talk to the police? No. Apart from having to admit to having harboured him, it was against the code. Omerta or the Provo equivalent. The real question was, what would the Provos do to her, about the connection, the line of death, through her, from him to Danny? Mary, Mary, he thought, my

God, I'm sorry. I'm destroying everyone I cared for.
Then, cautioning his conscience, No. No. I am not
responsible, he told himself. What else could I have done?
Then he thought of them, whoever it had been that
dreamed it all up. Had it been planned quite unemotion-
ally in some civil service office somewhere, the talk of the
disposability of life punctuated by coffee, enquiries about
children and mortgages? Had a paper about it gone to the
minister? The prime minister? To be initialled and
returned for action?

He had been walking for about ten minutes now. He
checked his watch. It was just quarter past eight. How
long had it taken, from Danny moving across the carpet
to him leaving by the front door. A minute, probably.
Less? Now he thought about it, he couldn't recall any
feelings at the time. Just actions, beyond control of will.
There had been no prior intent, but in a defensive reflex
his hand had come up with the gun and his finger had
started squeezing. Intention enough for a court of law.

He had no idea at the start of today that by mid-evening
he would have killed a man and probably crippled
another.

I'm sorry, Mary, he thought. Lee. But somehow can't
redeem.

The unmarked Ford Sierra arrived just as the soldiers
were piling out of the two Land Rovers. John Dixon, in
the back seat of the car, looked at the house as the
soldiers ran up the path. A curtain blew out of the main
window, the other was snagged and flapping on the one
ragged piece of glass that remained, like a pale reflective
tooth in the frame. The two detectives in the front seat,
Andy Mitchell and Frank Hughes, got out. Dixon sighed,
opened the door and joined them on the pavement. 'Odd
night for a party, Tuesday,' Mitchell said as they pushed
open the swinging gate.

'A family dispute?' Hughes suggested.

'Sure, Frank,' Dixon added, 'husband comes home, doesn't like the tea, and blows the front window out with his gun.'

Hughes said over his shoulder as they reached the doorway: 'Come round to my place for tea, Inspector, and you'll see it's a perfectly plausible scenario.' A soldier, blackened face, SLR cradled like a baby across the crook of his right arm, blocked the doorway. 'Sonny,' said Dixon irritably, 'get out of the way. Plod is here . . . Show him your plastic someone.'

Mitchell, who had thick blond hair apart from a perfect, circular bald spot on the crown, Dixon noticed, flapped his wallet. The three went into the hall. Dixon looked up the stairs, at the pictures on the wall, seascapes, reproductions, mostly, and then back at the splintered front door. 'Soldier,' he said, 'did you lot kick the door in?'

'No, Sir,' said the squaddie, 'it was like that.'

'Fine. And who's in charge of you.'

'Lieutenant Waddell' – he pronounced it Wad-dell – 'he's in the room. Sir.'

The detectives wandered into the room. It was bristling with soldiers, a blur of camouflage, helmets, radios crackling, large boots stamping around. 'Lieutenant Waddell,' Dixon shouted, craning his head above the melee, 'I am Inspector Dixon and I would appreciate it if you could ask about half of your battalion to stop parading, or any tiny pieces of evidence we may discover will be powdered into the Wilton.'

The lieutenant detached himself, took off his helmet and shook Dixon's hand. Christ, thought Dixon, another fresh-faced stripling.

'Sarnt,' the lieutenant said dismissively over his shoulder, 'clear the chaps . . . but leave one with the wounded man.'

'Ah,' said Dixon, 'we have a live one.'

'Lost a lot of blood. We've radioed for the ambulance.'

'So did we,' said Dixon and as the room cleared he saw the two bodies on the floor, one motionless, the other whispering quietly, with the soldier over him, opening a first aid kit. The dead man was on his back, arms spread in a crucifixion position, the bundle in the corner continued its dull moaning.

'Recognise him?' asked Dixon, pointing to the corpse.

'Danny McDevitt,' the other two said almost in unison.

'Good, you've been memorising the pictures. But, isn't that a fine sight?' Dixon smiled. It was infrequently that a corpse could make his day, as someone else had put it. 'Now what are we to make of all this? And more to the point, lads, do we really care?'

Mitchell was moving around the carpet in a crouch, like an animal on the scent of spoor. 'Can't see many cartridges, Inspector. But there's a camera and cable thing over here.'

'Any sign of the tea, though?' Hughes said, deadpan. And all three burst out laughing, remembering the talk on the path.

The Lieutenant looked mystified. Dixon said: 'Private joke.' Then, to the soldier trying to staunch the wounded man's bleeding, 'Soldier, is he conscious?'

'Just about, Sir. He's been shot in the leg and the hand, and he's been bleeding for a while.'

'We found a weapon outside,' the Lieutenant added. 'Point three-two revolver.'

'His?'

'Probably.'

'Fired?'

'Probably not.'

'Probably? Lieutenant? Didn't you sniff the bloody thing?'

'It hasn't been.' The young man, about twenty-five, Dixon thought, coloured. He had a face that, when he was older, would be called lugubrious.

'Oh, well, bang goes the first theory.' Dixon walked

197

over to the injured man and crouched down beside him.
The man's face was like chalk, but his eyes were open.
'What was this, son, a bit of a disagreement? Internal
feud? Listen, son. You're going to go down for a long
time. Assuming, of course, the ambulance gets here in
time. Do you know how you could get it here quicker?
By talking about this. Otherwise I could tell the crew to
break for a fag when they arrive. Do you understand?
One moan for yes, two moans for no!'

The boy whispered and Dixon bent down to listen, then
shook his head sorrowfully and got up.

'Inspector?' said the Lieutenant.

'He told me to go and perform the anatomically impossible. Foolish boy.'

'Bleeder,' said Hughes and the three burst out laughing
again.

'Oh,' said Dixon eventually, 'I do enjoy my job.'

Doherty sat cradling a glass of Guinness, a large whisky
by the side. Forty minutes to the train. He watched the
screen of the television above the bar, which had the
sound turned down. An American soap, women in dresses
with shoulders that had patently been inflated off-camera,
men with permatans and dazzling teeth – no wonder so
many of the cast wore sunglasses, Doherty mused into his
glass. His bags were at his feet, under the table. He had
retrieved them from the left luggage and checked in the
overcoat, wrapped in a polythene bag. The attendant had
looked at him peculiarly as he had taken it off, carefully
folded it, with the gaping tear concealed, and tucked it
into the green plastic bag.

He checked his watch. Almost nine. Then he unzipped
a side pocket of the leather shoulder bag and pulled out
his small Sony radio, the size of a pack of cards, well,
perhaps Tarot cards, which had brought him the BBC
World Service in more trouble spots than he cared to

recall. He took a swig of Guinness – it wasn't the kind of place you spat in your beer before going to the toilet, not quite, but a good sloppy tonguing of the glass was probably advisable – picked up his bags and followed his nose. In a cubicle, carved and limned with the opposing slogans of the struggle, he tuned the radio into Downtown. The news passed with no report of the shooting. Doherty switched it off, slipping it into his jacket pocket, picked up his bags and went back into the bar. The soap had finished and a man with red, receding hair was mouthing the national news, opening and closing like a goldfish. Doherty kept waiting for the bubbles behind the glass.

At nine fifteen he finished the beer, threw back the whisky, collected his bags again and walked the three hundred yards to the station. Then he checked the platform and walked over to the ticket attendant. Three people were in front of him, brandishing tickets, shuffling forward with bags. Doherty passed his ticket under the attendant's eye and walked up the platform until he found a quiet compartment. Relievedly he swung the bags up on to the rack and slumped down in a seat, facing the engine. At nine thirty exactly the train coughed and moved forward.

Mary was expecting a call. She felt tense, unable to settle with the work she had brought home, correspondence with the Housing Executive about two rehousing cases. She kept getting up, going to the window, switching the TV off and on: she even watered her plants, which flourished on condensation and neglect. And every few minutes she looked at her watch. It was now just after ten thirty. Jesus, she thought, come on. She made another cup of coffee – her ears were buzzing and she felt light-headed from the caffeine binge. The cup steamed on the table, but she got up again and went into the kitchen, uncorked the whisky bottle and brought it into the living room, where she cooled down and spiked the brew.

She felt her stomach in knots. She felt queasy. She bit her nails. She felt pre-menstrual. She looked at the telephone balefully. At quarter to eleven she could stand the tension no longer. She swiped at the phone and began punching in Theresa's number. It was picked up on the fourth ring, but there was no greeting. 'Hello,' she said, her heart beginning to motor.

'Yes?' a male, unfamiliar voice answered.

'Who is that?' she said.

'Who is that?'

She slowly hung up the phone and began to tremble.

Shortly after two o'clock next day Dixon, who had just come on duty, picked up the phone which he had heard ringing from across the room, while he sifted through a filing cabinet, and which refused to stop. He sat on his chaotic desk, leaned across and lifted the receiver, managing to knock the base of the instrument off the desk.

'Damn . . . Dixon.'

'Yes I've heard you called that, John.'

'Thomas?' Dixon said. Thomas Brackenridge was the RUC's best-known forensic scientist and, as such, was a high-ranking target for the IRA. Like most of the senior RUC officers, the most vigorous aerobic exercise he got was checking under his car each morning and then turning the starting key. He knew more about bombs and their effects, fuses, bullet patterns, entrance and exit wounds than probably any man alive: like most of his colleagues, he couldn't begin to come to grips with the psychology behind it.

'John, the shootings last night. Most interesting.'

He waited for Dixon, who had mentally filed the incident as internecine and at the back of his priorities, to draw him.

'I've just had the fingerprint report, it's on its way to you. A very interesting discovery. You simply aren't going to believe it.' He paused again and Dixon could feel exasperation start at the way Brackenridge teased-out a story.

'Thomas, you always amaze me.'

'The fingerprints belong to Doherty – '

'Jesus!'

'No – and I'm not sure we have a match for those.' Brackenridge's jokes were usually ponderous. And he usually joked when he was feeling pleased with himself for displaying some stunning piece of criminal detection. This hardly qualified, but the scientist was clearly elated that the notorious, the elusive fugitive had turned up in his own forensic backyard. He couldn't have sounded more chuffed, thought Dixon, if he had proved that the Turin Shroud emanated from Marks and Spencer.

'Yes,' he went on. 'All over the place. Living room, kitchen, even a bedroom. So it looks as if he stayed there, I should say.'

'Thomas, I'm grateful. Thank you. I must go.'

'Cry havoc and unleash the dogs, eh?'

'Exactly,' said Dixon, hanging up, not having the slightest idea what Brackenridge was talking about.

By eight that evening Dixon was sure Doherty was in the Free State. After the telephone call he had sent out his own teams as well as uniformed men to recheck the bus and train station and the airport. He had also called Military Intelligence at Castlereagh and told them what he suspected. As the reports came back, he had drawn blanks at the airport, the bus terminal, but the six men he had detailed to the station brought back the proof that Doherty had been there. Two of his Branch detectives at the station had questioned the left luggage clerk, the same one who had been on the previous evening. Custom had been quiet and yes, the man did recall a bizarre event. A big man, bearded he thought but couldn't be sure,

201

checked out luggage, two items, some time after eight thirty – he remembered because he had just had his tea break – and then took off the overcoat he was wearing, and deposited it. And a cold night it was, too. That's what stuck in the mind.

The two officers had brought back the coat, in the polythene bag, together with the clerk, who hadn't been able to recognise Doherty from the file pictures, even when the photofit artist doctored the full-face shot to show a beard. Dixon had looked at the green bulging bag with quiet satisfaction, and then with a ball point pen had pulled out the coat on to his desk and opened the folds. He smiled when he saw the torn, charred pocket and then he bent over and sniffed the material. Bingo. The sweet smell of gunsmoke.

'Take the coat and the bag to the lab,' he told Manders, the younger officer. And then to Jones, the sergeant, a corpulent man in his late forties who had survived two bomb attempts and, probably on the third match theory, wasn't the most popular man to be on patrol with, said: 'Check the pubs, restaurants, anywhere that was open last night, within a quarter of a mile radius of the station. Someone might remember something.'

Then he phoned the station enquiry office, tapped his pen irritably as his call was held in line and computerised music dribbled in his ear, and, eventually explained carefully to the initially discourteous clerk who he was and what he wanted. He took a note of all the trains leaving the station between half-past eight and ten – Doherty wouldn't want to hang around, he reasoned – and then, after he had hung up, considered the list. There was one logical departure, the nine thirty to Dublin. Doherty's luggage had been at the station, he clearly planned to get out of Belfast, and after the killings the Provos would have everyone out looking for him. Also, now the police and army. But why had he left the coat? Why hadn't he simply dumped it? Obviously he wouldn't want to walk around with damning evidence on his back, but it had been cold last night and so maybe he hung on to the coat until the last possible moment? Anyway, slinging a coat over a fence would be conspicuous. And once in the station where else could you dump a large item with a fair degree of certainty that it would lie undiscovered for weeks, months? The left luggage office made sense, Dixon thought. But he retained the cautionary doubt that it was all just too pat.

Nonetheless he picked up the phone once more and replayed what they had found to the army. Then he dialled his opposite number in the Garda in Dublin and told him that he believed Doherty was in his patch, or passing through, and that he would wire pictures and prints that evening. To himself, he said, for all the good that will do with you Fenian fuckwits. Then he hung up and decided that he would get a sandwich from the canteen, feeling reasonably satisfied with his day.

LONDON

Doherty was the richest vagrant in Christendom. Most of his fellow guests in Arlington House spent their days begging for coppers for cider, sitting in drinking schools, burbling, arguing, their swollen, broken faces pugnaciously thrust at each other; or else the alcohol poured out in cleansing rivulets down their faces. Doherty walked, at some point each day, to the MI5 building in Gower Street, just to refresh his anger, and spent hours in the library in Camden High Street. He read all the newspapers and followed his own exploits, often totally imaginary, until he faded into newsprint history. And he kept himself to himself, snarling at any overture of friendliness. Even from the few other residents, men in shabby but cared-for clothes, clinging desperately to the edge of poverty.

His exit from Ireland had been smooth. After the train pulled out he took his bags to the toilet and in the bucking cubicle, in the steaming jet of hot water from the pressure tap, he had shaved off the beard, leaving a moustache. He had roughly cut back his hair with the disposable razor too, and then splashed it with water and combed it into a neatish shape. Apart from a few razor nicks, he looked presentable. The moustache, though, he thought, was on the humorous side of gay. Then he waited until the trail stopped at Lurgan and he got off. He had spent the night in a rundown guest house, with a landlord who smoked constantly, wore a shirt without a collar and, in the morning, proffered toast, actually half-toast, since it was only grilled on one side.

In the morning he had caught a bus into Belfast and

then another to Aldergrove. By 10 a.m. he was in the air, sipping coffee, filling in his landing card as Winter. There had been virtually no scrutiny on departure and, he knew from experience, that unless they were on a high-security alert, all he would have to face was a couple of bored Special Branch men idly scanning faces at Manchester. In the seat next to him a middle-aged woman with a baby and a ten-year-old daughter gazed anxiously out of the window. 'You don't like this either?' he said.

'Oh,' she said, relieved about a shared phobia, 'it's ridiculous, isn't it? I just can't help thinking about what's keeping it up.'

'Belief,' he said.

'Oh, don't. Lawrie,' she motioned to the child who was staring at the earth outside the window, 'gets so embarrassed about me.'

'I usually have several large ones beforehand,' he said, 'but this is too early in the morning, even for me.' He put on his most innocent smile. 'Is this business or pleasure? The trip?'

She had a wholesome, open look, trusting. 'Visiting my sister in Manchester. I don't know whether that's business or pleasure.'

'Duty?'

'Yes,' she said, 'terrible, isn't it?'

'Is your sister meeting you?'

'No. She works in the mornings.'

'Look,' he said in his most earnestly innocent manner, 'I'm taking a taxi into town. I'm sure that with those two handfuls and your luggage you could do with a lift. Please,' he said, smiling winningly, 'be my guest.' And he thought, Doherty, you can be a devious bastard.

'Thank you. You're very kind.' She leaned over slightly. 'To tell you the truth I was worrying a bit about how I was going to manage.'

'Don't worry. Well, worry until the wheels are on the ground. After that, no problem.'

Later Doherty said, 'Let me carry the baby,' as they shuffled up the passageway of the aircraft, nodding at the mechanically smiling hostesses, 'it's ages since I've done that.'

'Thank you,' she said again. And Doherty took the baby and the new family walked off the plane and through the arrivals lounge.

Now he walked down Camden High Street again towards Gower Street. He had bought another overcoat in the Oxfam shop and he sensed that it crinkled as he walked. After he paid for it, three pounds, he had gone back to the hostel and undone the stitching of the lining, pulled it back and taped in the remaining dollars and most of the pounds. Then in the library he had borrowed a staple gun from a friendly young librarian with a charitable smile and rivetted up the lining. Understandably, he never took off the coat. He had kept five hundred pounds apart and when he slept at night in is cage, with the insulated overcoat as his quilt, he tucked the roll into his underpants.

Today he walked past the MI5 building and down Gower Street to the edge of Covent Garden. Crossing into Shaftesbury Avenue he almost collided with two policemen – police, like tourists and vagrants, were drawn to the areas of highest conspicuous consumption – one of whom cast an irritable, but unseeing look at him. His stomach had heaved and then he smiled to himself as a line from Burns' 'To A Louse' that was appropriate came into his head: 'O wad some power the gift tae gie us/ Tae see oursels as others see us.' He stopped at the window of a cafe and looked. How did others see him? His hair was cropped to a dark down (he had a phobia about head nits), his skin was still dark and tight to the bones of his face, with sunken, burning eyes and a bedraggled moustache and a scrubland of black and grey on his jaw. The brown, threadbare coat buried him and, looking down, his trousers were loose and crumpled and his shoes cracking and white from lack of attention. As he looked, his attention was drawn past his reflection to a man, fat and gesticulating, with a white apron and rolled up sleeves, moving towards the window, mouthing – he couldn't hear the words over the traffic noise – motioning him to go away. That was how others saw him. When not in motion, a nuisance, something to be shunned. He moved off towards the Oasis and, in devilment, testing the theory, he approached two young, besuited, gelled young thrusters making their way to work. 'Could yies sperr anythin' for a cup of tea?' he said in his best-remembered Govan accent and was passed in disgust.

He walked on, to Marshall Street Baths and, behind the red sandstone and AIDS warnings, took his twice-weekly scouring in the hot soapy privacy of a bath. He bought the *Independent* and the *Guardian* and in the small bathroom, luxuriating in the endless heat, he read them thoroughly. As he finished the pages he dropped them over the edge of the bath. Then, dropping the last page in the pile beside the bath, a wonderful Victorian affair with brass taps and claw feet, he soaped his head and submerged. It was now time to move. He felt tired in the bone. An exhausted inevitability had taken him over. There were no feelings left. He thought about Mary. Wondered, again, whether he should write to her. What could he say? Sorry I snuffed your boyfriend, hope you are well, love etc! He thought about Danny, killing him, and how he should feel remorse. He searched, but there was nothing, just a memory of the time, how vital he had felt. Alive. In death. But that had passed. Then he thought about Lee, the warm, wet, colours of her death. He thought of her family, the bake-brained Christians, the love casualties: he didn't even have an address for them, no mental pictures to conjure, to sympathise with. And finally he thought of Montague, the rose-breeder,

207

the face in the picture, the fate in his life. Maidenhead. It was time to put an end to it all.

He got out of the bath, spilling grey water on to the tiles, dressed slowly and went down into the street. A watery sun was falling on Soho as he walked. By the time he got to Stanford's in Long Acre it had dried the damp hair of his crop. He went in and bought a street map of Maidenhead.

MAIDENHEAD

She closed the French windows, shivered and turned up
the thermostat on the central heating in the dining room.
It was good having the children at weekends, but the
mess! Not just clothes to wash, beds to make but this
weekend, because the weather had been unseasonably
fine with a bright, high sun and low breeze, the boys had
been out in the garden, kicking balls, chasing the dog,
swinging mallets on the lawn in what they called croquet,
but was more like a pedestrian polo, all charges and war
whoops. On Sunday, because Timothy and Benjamin
insisted – Rupert should never have suggested it – she had
to prepare a barbecue, sausages and hamburgers and
small steaks, which they had eaten huddled round the
grill for warmth, charcoal smoke blowing in their faces,
the boys hopping around to keep warm. Rupert had loved
it, the only time he had raised his voice over the whole
weekend was when Ben chased a ball into one of his
bloody rose gardens.

And then, Monday morning, it was trembling lips,
good-byes. Rupert packing them into the car and small
faces waving anxiously until they disappeared into the
distance. Emily had stopped waving, sighed, and begun
to clean up. She felt like leaving everything for Mrs
Watson, who came on Tuesday, but that would be . . .
dilatory? Undisciplined? Anyway, the mere thought of it
made her feel guilty. So she tidied up the garden, put
away the furniture and the boys' bikes and shovelled up
the muck Psyche had deposited on the lawn. Why had
Rupert insisted the damn poodle was called Psyche? From
some radio serial in his youth, she thought, where the dog

was played by some animal impersonator – Percy Edwards? – what a bizarre skill to perfect – or had the dog just been some vinyl bark from the BBC gramophone library?

She switched on Radio Two, filled the percolator with water and spooned in two dessert measures of Blue Mountain, then pressed the start button. From upstairs, as she stripped the Ghostbusters covers from the boys' bunk beds, she could hear Jimmy Young filtering along the hall and chortling upstairs. She threw the covers and sheets into the Ali Baba basket, picked up the strewn socks, underwear, shirts and shorts, added them to the load and heaved the basket downstairs. As she loaded the washing into the machine in the utility room and sipped her coffee she heard the plangent notes of James Galway, 'Annie's Song'. It was a particular favourite. Rupert had taken her to the Queen Elizabeth Hall on her birthday . . . two years ago? . . . to hear Galway and it had been entrancing. She remembered that they had made love later. Which was memorable only for its infrequency. Not her choice. But Rupert seemed so distant and prepossessed now, well for years actually. But, she thought as the Galway flute died away, it had been a satisfactory marriage. There was warmth, and security, and she valued security. She couldn't abide the idea of turmoil, inconstancy, emotional shifting sands, rebuilding. Rupert, she knew, had affairs. She could always tell, not by neglect or discovered sour glances, but by his guilty attentiveness.

What he got up to abroad she didn't want to think about. But she had, on more than one occasion, drawn his attention to articles in the newspapers or women's magazines, about businessmen catching AIDS. She was sure he had taken her meaning. As for her extra-marital philanderings, well, there weren't any. Emily smiled to herself. It wasn't easy to be swept off one's feet in Maidenhead. Anyway, the idea of such instability was unimaginable.

She had been faithful, except for the one occasion. Rather, one occasion spread over several encounters. Five years ago, or six?, in San Diego, while Rupert was in Washington for the week getting up to whatever he and his American peers got up to. Fornicating most probably. Fornication. That was exactly what it had been with her and Robert. She had done, and with enthusiastic, experimental willingness, things she would never have believed she could. He was young, tanned, sculpted, inexhaustible and insatiable. She was? A randy English housewife in her late thirties who didn't want the light to go out? Anyway, she could never wait to see him and when she saw him she couldn't wait to take his clothes off, to get to the only white part of his body and kiss and take him . . . She felt her loins begin to waken and she thought, Emily this will do you no good at all!

She went back into the kitchen and washed the breakfast dishes. Then glanced at the clock. It was almost noon. She felt peckish. Which was probably something to do with transference of desire. She opened the fridge and slid out the remains of the Sunday evening joint, then plugged in the electric carving knife and began slicing the beef. An annoying, familiar whine joined the electric one, then a nuzzling at her legs. That bloody dog. She reached down, grabbed him by the scruff of the neck, thought deliciously for a second about hacking its head off with the electric knife and leaving it in the microwave for Rupert to discover, dismissed the fantasy, decided to put him out the back and that she was not going to clean the lawn again after him, dragged the poodle through the hall and out of the door into the front drive.

On her way back, in the hall, she caught sight of herself in the mirror. She smiled. Good, attractive, she thought. A few laughter lines, but little decay. Shiny hair, good teeth – then she started to laugh, it was like describing a mare. She shook her head and went back into the kitchen, feeling quietly satisfied.

When she had finished cutting the meat, she found the jar of horseradish sauce in the fridge, cut a couple of slices of wholemeal bread and then two tomatoes, spread low-fat margarine on the bread, threw everything on to a plate and sat down at the pine table. She held the knife in her right hand and thought, why not? So she got up, took an opened bottle of Chardonnay from the fridge and poured herself a large measure in the one engraved Victorian glass that still survived from the wedding present. She reached across and pulled over the *Daily Mail* and turned to Lynda Lee Potter.

Half-way through the wine the dog started barking. Oh, no, not the postman, surely? He didn't normally come until after one. Then the barking stopped suddenly, she waited, glass midway between mouth and table, but there was no reoccurrence. She turned back to the paper. The bell rang. She started, then wearily put down the glass, smoothed crumbs from her skirt and got up.

She opened the door and briefly took in a tall, deranged-looking man with a convict hair cut, unshaven, dark, before he was on her, his hand over her mouth, a knife against her throat. She closed her eyes and she felt him kick out, heard the door slam and she knew, he was going to rape her!

Doherty wrote his account of the maelstrom of events in Camden library. It came to ten closely spaced foolscap pages. Then he made three copies. Rather the beatific librarian, who clearly felt a mission to help him, had made the copies. And when he had asked her how much, she had shushed him shyly, her head darting around, inviting him to join the conspiracy. He had tried to insist, but she had started to get even more embarrassed and so he had thanked her and shuffled away, as he felt she expected. This morning, in a post box on the way from the station in Maidenhead, he had posted them. One to Janey in

New York, instructing her, please, to go to *The New York Times*. She clearly hadn't told the police of his days with her. Now he hoped she would help him again. He had attached a brief letter, wishing her well, saying that he would be in touch as soon as he could. The second envelope went to Crenshaw with a promise that he would be in touch, if he could. And the third went to an old acquaintance, the London bureau chief of *Le Monde*. One could certainly depend on the French desire to do down the Brits. Then he had walked towards the avenue – no thoroughfare in Maidenhead seemed prosaic enough to be called Road or Street – with the sharp, seven-inch kitchen knife he had bought in Tottenham Court Road in his waistband. As he walked he felt calm but with a sense of destiny. That, Doherty, he told himself, is the hallmark of the zealot throughout the ages.

It was a fine morning, the warm spell had kept up for almost a week. He had now made four visits to the house, trying to work out a pattern of movement. There was only one that he could discern, the wife did not work. Oh, and his man always returned between seven and seven-fifteen, by car, but because of the regularity of the timekeeping, he probably drove just from the railway station.

Doherty only had his intent and a bare plan, an outline, within which he would adapt to circumstances. Whatever happened, whether he would succeed or whether he was now moving through his last hours on earth, he felt an overwhelming sense of relief that it was all coming to a conclusion. If he could get away, eventually, he thought about South America, Mexico, where he had once taken a series of pictures of Mexican cowboys who, after their gruelling, back-aching work on the poor, thin soil rode into town, tumbleweed following them, to down streams of beer and tequila in the cantinas. It was the Old West, apart from the olive skins and oval eyes. He smiled as he walked. It was a romantic dream.

He had been careful not to loiter around the house on

his previous visits, but had approached it from several directions. He had worked out the network pattern of the streets around, escape routes, checked out the gardens adjoining the house and how he could melt through the carefully tended greenery and away. The mission – he did, he realised, feel almost messianic about his revenge – did not end with Montague. Now, finally, he opened the gate on the short drive of the house.

What he had not taken into account was the dog, the screeching, attention-attracting racket of it, scurrying around in front of him, howling. He put his left hand in his pocket, brought it out in a fist as if it grasped a titbit, and held out his arm, while making clucking noises. The dog, permed, curled, and with a ridiculous ribbon in its headlocks, sniffingly approached. Doherty kept the fist closed and with a couple of fingers tickled under its jaw. Then, and still making deep soothing noises, he moved his hand up, to pat the head, but instead he grabbed the pampered beast by the topknot and almost before the first rasp came into its mouth he had the knife out in his right hand and the blade slicing through the windpipe. The dog's head lolled in his grip, while it shuddered and shook and made gurgling, clotted noises and its blood splashed over his trouser legs and shoes. When it had stopped shivering he threw it with his left hand into the rhododendron undergrowth and walked quickly to the door. He had no time now to consider whether he had been seen or heard. He pressed the doorbell with his left hand, looked quickly about while wiping the blade down his coat with the other hand. Through the frosted glass he saw her moving towards the door, growing larger until, as the door swung open, he lunged at her, bringing up the knife and noticing a look of bewilderment as his hand found her mouth and he dragged her into the hall and kicked shut the door.

'If you make the slightest noise I will open your throat,' he said. 'Do you understand?' From above he could see her eyes rolled upwards, looking at him, her head against the brown material. Her head made a nodding motion.

'Good,' he said, gradually releasing the pressure on her mouth, then grabbing her by the hair at the nape of her neck, holding the knife on the red line at her trachea. She was snivelling, her body was shuddering with terror as he pushed her towards the kitchen. He felt nothing. He told her to sit at the table with her hands on top of it and he looked around. The kitchen was in Habitat country authentic, stripped pine, brass hinges, a large seaclock, set in wood, with roman numerals, dried flowers in baskets, enough hanging cutlery to equip a Chinese Tong. He looked at her. Her eyes were running, she trembled, and she sniffed to stop the mucus. She couldn't take her eyes off him, in some kind of hideous, magnetic fear. 'If you do exactly as I say, you won't be hurt,' he said. And he looked down and saw the red, saturated trousers and the splashes on his cracked shoes. 'The dog's dead,' he said, confirming what she knew, but she started to sob and involuntarily raised a hand to her mouth.

'Are you expecting anyone? Or are you expected?' He raised the knife. 'And don't lie to me.'

She shuddered and spluttered, which he took to be no. He felt a stir of remorse. 'Do you want a brandy, or something?' he said and she nodded quickly.

'Show me where it is.'

'I – I – I don't think I can walk,' she said, and looked down at her lap. 'And I think I've soiled myself.' And then she began to weep deeply, in great shaking gasps, her face covered by her hands.

'Where is the brandy?'

'In the cocktail cabinet in the dining room,' she answered between sobs.

He darted into the next room, saw the cabinet, Chinese lacquered, pulled it open and grabbed the bottle of Remy. In the kitchen he poured a large dash into a blue striped

mug and pushed it at her across the pine table. 'Drink.
And then you can clean yourself.'

She took the cup in both hands and drank it down in
gulps, as if it were the liquid of life. Perhaps it was for
her, he thought. He saw the joint of meat, the electric
carver next to it and he suddenly felt hungry. He put
down his bloodied knife, picked up the contraption and
pressed the trigger, it reared into life and the woman
quivered. He cut a large hunk and picked it up, tearing at
the meat with his teeth, strands pulling away and slapping
into his lips. When he had finished, he washed his hands
in washing-up liquid, ran the knife under the tap and
between his fingers and then dried all three on a hanging
dishtowel.

She sat looking at him, the cup on the table. 'Right,' he
said. 'The bathroom.'

'Are you going to – to rob me?' she said, but he knew
what she really meant.

'No, this has nothing to do with you. I'm waiting for
your husband. He owes me,' he said and he noted the
look of relief and then guilt which passed across her face.
Then she got up shakily and he went with her upstairs.
'How many telephones, and where?'

'One in the bedroom and one in the hall.'

When he heard the running water start in the bathroom
he found both phones and cut the running wires with the
knife. He waited outside the bathroom and when she
came out she wasn't looking at him anymore. 'I need to
change,' she said.

He took her by the arm and pushed her into the
bedroom, and stood in the doorway, looking into the hall.
'Quickly,' he said.

She changed into trousers and a formless jumper and
when she came out she looked at him. 'Please. Why?'

'It won't help to know.'

'My husband's work?'

216

'Later, you'll learn about it all. Now, no more questions. Don't speak unless I ask you something. This will all be over in a few hours and if you do what I say you'll be fine. If not . . .' He didn't need to finish. She nodded, very slowly. 'Downstairs.'

In the kitchen he went through the drawers and cupboards and pulled out a length of washing line. 'Put your hands behind your back,' he said and he tied her hands with a bowline and lots of loops, and cut the rope. 'I'm going to have to examine your house,' he said. 'Where does your husband keep his papers, personal effects? It would save a lot of damage if you told me.'

'There's a bureau in the dining room. It's locked. He has the key.'

Doherty found a chisel and a hammer in a cupboard under the stairs and then shattered the brass lock. Inside, the shelves and pigeon holes were neatly filled with papers, photographs, memorabilia, wads of faded envelopes wrapped in rubber bands. In a drawer he found a heavy, locked green cash box. He put the chisel under the lid and on the carpet thumped the box apart with the hammer. A revolver, a big, heavy oiled Colt .45 tumbled onto the Persian rug, with a scattering of bullets. He picked it up, checked it. It was loaded. He pocketed the shells, checked the safety catch was on and then stuck the gun in his waist band.

In the kitchen he said. 'Upstairs, Mrs Montague.' And he followed her, carrying the rest of the length of line.

It had been a triumphal day. There was no other description. Montague had wanted to turn to his fellow passengers on the train and say 'Watch the nine o'clock news.' And then beam, somewhat enigmatically as they looked at him uncomfortably, their private routines invaded. But instead, he just sat, smirking inwardly, toying with the crossword, as feet scuffled towards his, and people rocked in the passage. Next time, he thought, I will get a first-class season ticket.

Fellowes had called him in shortly after four, carefully screwed the top of his fountain pen, invited him to sit and then had taken off his glasses, which was a sure sign that he was about to impart something 'meaningful'.

'Congratulations,' he said. 'A brilliant operation. It's a pity those outside can never know your part in it. But then,' he interlocked his fingers, 'outsiders don't matter. The minister is ebullient, the prime minister asked him to carry personal thanks to all those involved . . . but the best news is that PIRA is declaring a ceasefire. This evening. Sinn Fein are calling a press conference at seven. God knows how they're going to dress this up as a victory. Watch the news and find out. But there you are. Well done. Again.'

Montague looked beyond Fellowes to the panelled walls of what was euphemistically called the boardroom and at the oil paintings of previous directors, the portrait of the Queen and the photograph of the PM, on which she had written 'democracy, safe in your hands'. He smiled and left an appreciative pause before he said: 'Thank you, Sir. It went exceedingly well, didn't it? Fortune certainly favoured us.'

'Fortune?' said Fellowes. 'Psshaw! Still one troublesome end to tie.' Fellowes fretted with his Corpus Christi tie.

'Doherty? Yes, Sir. No leads, yet. I'm afraid. Disappeared through the gates. Still, we'll get him.'

'Any thoughts? Hunches?'

'Well, it's reasonable to assume that he tried to patch things up with the Provos. And that didn't work.'

Fellowes snorted. 'Indeed. And where did he get the gun, d'you think?'

'No idea. Through Cavanagh. Or in the States, where they are slightly more common even than sexually transmitted diseases.'

'Not as deadly though!' smirked Fellowes.

'The more I think about it, the more I think he probably brought it in with him. Cavanagh is doubtful. No, absolutely unlikely. He ended up killing her beau with it, didn't he?'

'Yes,' said Fellowes, chortling, 'that was an unexpected stroke of good fortune, wasn't it?' He sat back in his chair and picked up the fountain pen, a sign that the meeting was over. 'Anyway, Montague. First class work. Really, between ourselves, the PM is ecstatic.'

'Thank you, Sir,' Montague had said, pushing back the chair and standing. He thought, it would be nice to tell Emily . . . well, maybe some day.

When he got off the train he decided to call into the off-licence. A bottle of champagne, shampoo the younger chaps called it, to have a quiet celebration. He'd hint to Emily that he had done something above and beyond the call . . . drop a few meaningful grunts over the news, watch her eyes widen. Maybe an early night? Then he got into the old Jag. Some of the chaps had laughed at the old Mark 11, until it had started to rocket in value. And now? Well, noticeable envy. He put the car into gear and moved off. The Jag, why did that make him think of Doherty? He mused to the quiet throb of the engine and then it came to him. Doherty had one. Not a Mark 11, a valueless one. He smiled. Their only thing in common.

He swung into the avenue, turned right into the drive and then stopped in frustration. Emily hadn't opened the gates as she normally did. Mustn't let that cloud his sanguinity, he thought, getting out and opening the gates, then driving up the gravel which crunched under the tyres, to the garage, where he doused the lights grabbed the cold bottle and shut the heavy door behind him with a satisfying thud. He walked up to the door, transferred the bottle to his left hand and found the Yale key on his key ring. He turned the key in the lock and stepped into the lighted hall. If a sense told him that there was something missing, the familiar smell of cooking, Emily crooning from the kitchen, it came too late. Something hit him deadeningly in the left temple and the hall rolled over in blurred lights and rushing wind.

Doherty heard the gates, the car on the gravel, watched the lights flicker across the house and then the crunch of the closing door and the tread of his man. He was crouched down beside the door and as he heard the fumble of keys he stood up slowly. When the door opened and he saw the white of Montague's head he brought down the barrel of the gun in a cruel tight arc. The blow connected above the eye, bursting open the tissue and the man toppled against the door and then the floor. And as he went down the bottle he was carrying splintered on the tile floor, a puddle of frothing glass which Montague fell into. Doherty pulled him into the hall, onto the parquet strips and along in a glistening trail of champagne. Then he skipped over him and pushed the door shut, turning the bolt and slipping in the chain lock. He continued dragging Montague into the kitchen, which he had lit with just two spotlights after he had pulled down the Venetian blinds.

When Montague was lying in the middle of the floor Doherty cocked the revolver, knelt and put it to the man's head. With his left hand he felt for a pulse in the neck. It was erratic, but present. He looked at the face. Recognisable, puffier than the picture, certainly around the left side, which was bloody, wealed and contused. The side of his head was swelling noticeably as he looked. Maybe he had fractured the skull? The blow had been a huge one, it had sounded like an axe hitting a wet log, all his hatred had gone into it. He hoped he wasn't dead. That he hadn't crushed the brain. He wanted him to know. Be aware. At the end.

Doherty got up and grabbed the rope, dumped

Montague over on to his face, tied his hands together and then bent the man's knees and pulled his feet up and tied them to his hands, tightly, viciously, grunting as he pulled the knots. Then he sat on a kitchen chair watching. Minutes passed. Montague continued shallow, erratic, breathing. Doherty got up, went to the sink and filled a pan with cold water which he splashed over the inert man's face. The wife was tied and gagged upstairs. He had warned her not to attempt to untie herself, waving the heavy revolver under her nose. She had just blanched and nodded.

He yawned, filled the kettle and plugged it in. He felt totally empty. Very much in control, every sinew and muscle was dancing, but in his brain, his soul, a vacuum. Even the hate had gone. He sighed and then he was conscious of another sighing and he looked back and Montague was twitching. A tic was running in his left cheek, below the grotesquely distended eye and brow. Doherty waited for the kettle to boil and slowly spooned coffee into a cup, poured on the water and went back to his chair with it. The gun was on the table. He picked it up, slipped it into his waistband and pulled round the chair so that he could look down at Montague. The man was conscious.

'You recognise me,' he said and sat down, pulling out the gun and aiming it at Montague's open right eye. Slowly he pulled back the trigger. Montague closed his only sightless eye, cringed, as the pressure increased, as Doherty's finger whitened. Then the hammer released and made a dull thunk as it hit the empty chamber. Montague trembled.

'All the rest are there,' Doherty said quietly.

'You're going to kill me.' Montague's words were slurred, dribbling, punchy syllables. You g'n kill meh. Doherty guessed he was haemorrhaging behind the skull.

'Not like what you did to her . . . Quickly, if you tell me everything.'

'Washn't they . . .' Montague said, his mouth flopping open. 'Naw me!'

'Whether you were or weren't there doesn't matter. You were part of it. Who else was involved? Give me their names!'

'Emmli,' he said, drooling from the mouth, his good eye beginning to close. 'Pills.' Doherty got up quickly, threw his coffee into the sink and filled the cup with cold water which he dashed in the face of the trussed man on the wet linoleum. He fluttered into consciousness.

'Pocket,' Montague slurred.

Doherty looked down at him, mystified.

'Give me the names, you piece of shit. Who thought it all up?' He kicked Montague in the stomach. The man spluttered and gagged. Doherty knelt down and grabbed him by the hair. 'You bastard, you fucking dirty inhuman bastard' – he was starting to cry – 'you killed her. You cut her open. Listen to me. Listen to me.' His voice, even to him, sounded hysterical. He shook the man's head by the air. Montague's face was grey, sheened with perspiration.

'Listen to me.' He looked into his eyes, probing for a response.

'Emm – arrr . . . pocket . . . arrt.' Montague's mouth was hanging open, he was gasping and blood was seeping down his face.

When he had thought about it before, planned Montague's last moments, Doherty saw himself pull the man's head up to his mouth and shout into the ear. 'Your wife. Before I ripped her apart with your carving knife, I tied her to your bed and I raped her. Do you understand? Over and over.' He had wanted that to be Montague's last memory, although it wouldn't be true.

Montague was gasping, mumbling. Doherty dropped down on his knees and put his ear to Montague's mouth. 'Arrt . . . pocket . . . pills.' And then he realised, dumbfoundedly, that Montague was having a heart attack.

Then, totally unexpectedly, as it all drained out of him, on his knees beside Montague, he started to cry. When it had all come out he leaned over and felt a faint breath on his cheek. It stopped. He pulled the man over and felt above the trussed hands for a pulse. Nothing.

He got up and went to the sink and began to splash his face in cold running water. He looked back at Montague, wondering if he was beyond resuscitation. 'It wasn't meant to be this way,' he said out loud. Was it murder, he wondered, if someone died of a heart attack after being assaulted? Yes, he thought, certainly. And then he realised that he couldn't have gone through with murdering Montague. But he had.

Emily Montague had heard the car in the drive, Rupert's step on the gravel under the window and then the door, some crashing and banging and then nothing. How long had it been? She couldn't get her head round properly to look at the clock. He had tied her to the bed post and gagged her with a strip of pillow case he had torn from the bed. She had never truly felt frightened before, she now realised. This was unabated, mortal terror, transcending any other emotion she had ever felt. Her pulse thudded in her temple and her heart raced. She felt sick. She thought she might be sick into the gag, choke to death and she tried not to think about it. And she felt ashamed, that she had disgraced herself in front of him.

Rupert. How was he? Who was this madman with the heartless eyes who had burst into the house. Why? Why? She tried to think of anything, the children, the past, hope? And she tried to regulate her breath to modify her heart rate. She slipped into what she would later describe as a horror-stricken catatonia and then, after how long?, she heard footsteps on the stair. She prayed for Rupert, but it was him.

'I'm going now, Mrs Montague. Don't try to struggle,

you'll only hurt yourself. Within the next hour I'll phone the police and they'll release you. I'm sorry,' he said. And then he went down the stairs, out of the door, out of her life. Physically.

Grant looked at his travelling companion, who seemed to flicker in the passing street lights, almost like a figment of the imagination. Which, in a sense he was, because Lionel Barry did not officially exist. Sure, he was probably on the civil service list somewhere, but his title would obscure his identity. Grant wasn't even completely sure what he was, except some high-ranking officer in Five. That's what the assistant chief commissioner had said. God, he had thought Judy was being stupid or playing a nasty trick, when she told him Ryan was on the telephone. Him! He had stamped into the hall grabbed the phone and barked 'Grant,' and there he was, direct, not even through an emissary, telling him a car was on the way for him, with a senior man from Gower Street and that he was going immediately to Maidenhead to look at the corpse of some bloody agent. Too sensitive for the local Plod.

He looked again at Barry. The man didn't look as if he had seen much secret service. He was certainly in his fifties, corpulent, sleek, with one of those dark blue coats that seems to have a pile. Christ, he should have had a bowler hat, but instead he had thin, white receding hair, combed east to west across the bald bits, and a golf umbrella! Red and yellow. Talk about inappropriate.

'How are we doing driver?' Grant asked.

'Couple of minutes, Sir.'

Grant eased back in the seat. Barry hadn't said anything on the journey. Just a handshake and a 'pleased to meet you' as Grant had got into the car. Now Grant turned to him and said: 'Mr Barry, I'm not quite sure of your role here.'

'Merely an observer, Chief Inspector. And perhaps to

impart the Department's condolences to Mrs Montague, assure her that her husband died in the service of democracy, that kind of thing.'

Great, thought Grant. Is this man taking the piss or is he truly a pompous ass?

'Mrs Montague is all right, Chief Inspector?'

'I understand so.' Worried about the levels of compensation to the next of kin? Grant thought. 'Yes. In shock, obviously. But unharmed.'

'I understand there was an anonymous call.'

'That's right. Not an English accent apparently, could be Irish. But no code word.'

'Yes,' said Barry. It was curious, Grant noticed, neither of them were speaking directly to each other, but into a point, the apex of a far-distant triangle.

'The forensic boys will be there, I take it?'

'Yes. It's only the local force who are being kept out.' And Grant smiled, thinking of the anger this would be causing to the swedes. In the Met, every provincial officer was an inferior, swedes and turnips, but to Grant and the Anti-Terrorist Branch, the plainclothes officers of the Met were spivs,' Arries or Johns, as in 'Allo John.

'I took the liberty of talking to the lab, with Assistant Chief Commissioner Ryan's permission, of course. I hope you don't mind.'

'Not at all,' said Grant, thinking, I'm hardly going to say so, Herbert. And, but I'm damned if I'm going to give you the satisfaction of asking why!

The car pulled up in front of the tall hedges of a pre-war, detached house. 'Here, Sir' said the driver. Grant looked out. A little knot of people at the gate, he could make out the white tape marking the exclusion zone, and a couple of bobbies policing it. Grant and Barry got out and Grant, automatically, dug out his warrant card and muttered 'Chief Inspector Grant,' as he ducked under the tape, adding, 'he's with me,' tugging Barry in his wake. They walked up the drive to the doorway. Two men stood smoking in the little porch. One paunchy, in his forties, the other fifteen years younger, with one of the haircuts they used to serve up at Her Majesty's Pleasure but had now been taken over by the jailers, while the bad blokes favoured long back and short sides. This'll be the pissed-off swedey, thought Grant.

He flashed his card again and paused. No point in being uncivil. 'Anti-Terrorist Branch,' he said. 'Sorry, lads.'

The older man blew a cloud of smoke – fuming, thought Grant – and said: 'Right . . . Who was this bloke?'

Grant shrugged. 'Sorry. Can't say.'

'Right,' said the older one again, resignedly. 'Gave our beat bloke a bit of a shock. He's convinced it's some sort of black magic coven, woman trussed up on the bed, stiff in the kitchen and a freshly-slaughtered headless dog in the undergrowth.'

'No,' said Grant, 'nothing like that. Not sorcery.'

The other man motioned with his left hand. 'Be my guest.'

Grant and Barry walked into the hall and Grant felt his companion falter. Can't stomach it, thought Grant. And they walked into the kitchen, Grant holding out his warrant card to clear the way.

'Headless dog, Chief Inspector?' Grant shrugged.

His first impression was, as always, the activity and then – it's amazing how every scene of crime, every homicide is different, and sticks with you. This one seemed so mundane. Orderly. Pleasant. The body was lying, feet towards him. Because of a photographer shooting pictures over it, he couldn't see the head. He eased round the corpse and looked down at the face. Middle-aged, unsurprising, waxed skin, glassy eyes and a huge sour tear on the side of the head around which the blood had dried, darkened and caked. But it didn't look like a fatal blow. 'Cause of death?' Grant said to no one in particular.

'Heart attack,' one of the men in white coats round the

body said over his shoulder. 'Almost certainly. Probably two hours, three at most.'

'The wound?' Grant said.

'According to the wife an intruder must have hit him. With a pistol probably. His,' he said, nodding down to the cadaver.

'Right.' Grant looked round and saw that Barry was no longer in the room.

Barry and Grant stood in the dining-room. A doctor was with Mrs Montague in the bedroom, sedating her. Grant had talked to her briefly. She had shaken uncontrollably, teeth chattering, but when he asked her whether she would recognise the man again she nodded definitively. 'B – big . . . Wild . . . S – Scottish.' Now Barry was apologising to Grant, embarrassed. 'Not really used to that sort of thing . . .'

It's hardly an everyday occurrence for me, thought Grant, but he said: 'Don't think about it,' and he felt smug, superior to this upper-class spook. 'Well,' he said, looking out through the french windows to the perfectly-pruned rose bed, 'I think we both know who we're looking for. The forensic is just a ritual. Doherty.'

'Yes.'

'What can you tell me about all this?'

Barry was swallowing nervously, Grant noticed, keeping a cap on his supper. 'I don't know how he found out.'

'Doherty?'

'Yes. It had gone perfectly . . . until now.' Barry sighed. 'How did he find out? Montague?'

'More to the point,' said Grant, 'what else does he know? Who else does he know about?'

'Chief Inspector,' Barry gripped Grant's arm, 'you've got to get him before it's too late.'

Too late for Montague, thought Grant.

*

'Christ,' said Fellowes, and it was the first time any of those present had heard him blaspheme, 'we have got to terminate this thing urgently.' There were five other men in the boardroom. To an observer it would have passed for a conventional board meeting, five middle-aged men round a walnut table, coffee steaming in white china cups, writing pads and pencils, attentiveness to the chairman.

'We have absolutely no idea, I take it, how Doherty got Montague's name?' There was a confirmatory shuffling. 'The point is, if he got Montague's name he knows the Department's involved.' The unspoken sentence said, And he can get to all of us. But he said: 'We have no idea what he might to next. Or what he knows and what he might say. And to whom.'

'Director?' John Carpenter, the minister's private secretary, another Cambridge man, said: 'Politically we have to contain this. There is no reason to assume that Doherty knows all about Double Exposure, but proceeding as if he does, then clearly even if he has communicated to his friends in the press, we have the Secrets Act to stopper the bottle. The problem is, I'm afraid, if he gets something out abroad. We can brandish all the writs we like against the media here . . . but if there is a hullabaloo in Washington, if our European socialist friends are jumping up and down in Brussels, realistically some Bolshie here is going to break it. So, I cannot impress too strongly how urgently Doherty must be found. My minister is incandescent, which must mean that the PM's in orbit.'

The stopper in the bottle, Fellowes thought. The truth was that the genie was out and running amok. 'Every policeman in the country is looking for him, all of our people, even the bloody army.' The second oath Fellowes had uttered in public, mild as it was. 'No one's doing anything else. Every man's out looking for him. It's carte blanche for the criminal class just now. Doherty has just disappeared.'

Crispin Dexter, who was wearing his MCC tie as ever,

put down his cup and said: 'The girl in New York. That's where it went wrong. That's what triggered him.'

Fellowes slammed down his fountain pen. 'Thanks, Dexter. That's a real contribution. Unfortunately in a complicated operation – and let's not forget the success it's had until now – in a complicated operation, one necessarily involving our allies, and one using freelance help, one cannot, unfortunately, legislate for some lunatic, a weak link.'

'Presumably the girl resisted, struggled, or something,' said Carpenter.

'Well, that's the story,' said Fellowes, 'but my guess is that our two associates tried something on and it got out of hand.'

'So Doherty got loose.'

'So Doherty got loose,' agreed Fellowes.

'Loose cannon,' said Greaves, in his annoying Midland burr. More like reign of terror, thought Fellowes.

'And the two freelances?' said Carpenter. 'Off the board?'

'Quite definitely.'

'Good. Well,' said Carpenter, 'let's rely on the traditional docility of the British press and a bit of good luck.'

Fellowes held up his hands. 'There doesn't appear to be a lot else we can do at this stage. Unless you would like to join me in a communal prayer?'

Mary was existing in a kind of emotional and spiritual vacuum. She was ostracised, people she had known all her life turned away from her in the street. She had been told not to come to work. She had been told not to attend Danny's funeral, where they carried him out in a coffin with the beret and gloves, and the RUC tried to get to the pall-bearers. And then at Milltown, in the bright air, two young men in masks had materialised out of the crowd – she had watched it on TV – and as the Army helicopter hovered overhead, recording, they had fired a volley over the grave and Seamus had read the oration. Another martyr for the cause. The fools, the fools, she recalled, they have left us our Fenian dead. The hollow rhymes of history.

Then a few days later, there had been a knock at the door. Two young men she recognised. Grim. They told her to get out. Leave Northern Ireland. The threat didn't need to be explicit. She hadn't felt frightened. Dead inside. She didn't know if she had loved Danny, probably not. And Doherty? She couldn't even hate him any more. What had happened at Theresa's? Had Doherty got a gun from somewhere? She had been naive to think that she could act as a go-between. Her naivety had killed Danny. And she hadn't even been able to cry over him.

She went for the whisky bottle. She was drinking too much. What did it matter? The days just hung on her. Shut up in the house most of the time, going down the road for food and drink. Drinking in the day and the evening behind curtains with the TV colouring the room.

She thought about Theresa. Would they charge her? Another parcel of guilt. What made it worse was that Theresa clearly hadn't said anything about her. The police hadn't come yet. She rather wished that they would, it would help vitiate the guilt. She slurped the whisky into the glass, went back into the living room and closed the curtains. The television was laughing at her, gales of canned hilarity leaking out of the speakers. She sat down and toasted the screen, then took a sighing gulp of the whisky.

She had nowhere to go, no money. She thought about the money she had changed for Doherty. That would have helped. But not enough for a new life. And her brother; what would he be thinking of his big sister? He would have been told, certainly. The blood of the past was thicker, she thought. He was probably renouncing her now.

Doherty had washed his hands, sponged the legs of his trousers so that most of the blood was off and what remained looked like grease smears and then had gone up the stairs to reassure, reassure?, the wife. He had taken the train back to London and then the tube to Maida Vale where, in a payphone, he had called the police and told them of the body. Then he had walked down Elgin Avenue, where it had all started, to Paddington Recreation Ground where he scaled the fence, broke into the sports pavilion and spent a non-sleeping night on a bench until the dawn came. Then he had taken a bus to Soho where he bought a packet of razors, a tube of shaving cream and some shampoo in a chemist. And a length of brown paper, some envelopes and a roll of adhesive tape.

When he had come back into the country he had disposed of his expensive luggage, most of his clothing and now what he had left was in two carrier bags in Arlington House. In Marshall Street Baths he soaked and slumbered for more than an hour. Will all Thames Water's oceans, he thought . . .?

Montague was gone. But it wasn't over. It could only end with him. He looked over the rim of the bath at the discarded coat, looking for the shape of the gun in the pocket. Montague's gun. Eventually he got out of the bath and dressed, transferring the gun to the inside pocket of his jerkin. He looked at himself in the mirror. The gun couldn't be seen. Then he took off the jacket and lathered his face and carefully shaved off the shrubbery. Hello, he said to the mirror. Then he tore open the lining of the coat, peeled out ten hundred-dollar bills – this, coupled with the four hundred pounds or so he had left would be more than enough – and finally retrieved a pen and an envelope from his pocket. He wrote 'The silver lining' on the back of the envelope, slipped it into a pocket of the coat, folded it and parcelled it in the brown paper and taped it round. Then he wrote Mary's address on the outside of the parcel and walked to the post office.

Sitting in a cafe in Broadwick Street, spooning coffee into his mouth, he knew he wasn't the stuff of murder. He felt the gun against his body. A prop. He knew now that he couldn't kill anyone deliberately. And, he remembered the phrase used in a different context, they go on for ever. He took another sip of the coffee. He thought of Lee, his responsibility for her death. He shivered. And no way to make it up. Not that sending blood money to Mary was making it up. He just didn't have need of it now. The gun was weighing against his ribs. What was he going to do with that? Once, long ago before Montague, he imagined himself as the death angel, stalking others, going for the prime minister. But death at his hands had brought the reality. Not the murder stuff. It was almost over. Certainly for him. They wouldn't let him live. He thought about it and decided that he didn't mind. He wanted the memories to end. But there had to be a kind of justice, for Lee.

He got up slowly and paid for the coffee and left the cafe.

In Great Marlborough Street he waited for five minutes while one of the retro punks who float around Carnaby Street finished a conversation on the telephone – probably to his dealer, thought Doherty. And then he went in and dialled Crenshaw's number.

'David,' he said when Crenshaw answered, 'I'm giving myself up. The face in the photograph is dead. I meant to kill him and then I didn't mean to. But I'll explain all that. Before they take me, though, I'm going to make sure this all comes out.'

'Your note arrived,' Crenshaw said.

'I want you to arrange a press conference. Short notice. Can you get people like Tony Gifford to come. I'll tell it all to him and then the press. Will you ring round for me – ?'

'Sure.'

'Noon. It's too late to book anywhere. Would your office do? Is that all right?'

'Of course.'

'Don't give away too much. I'll come round now and tell you everything. Make a statement, to Tony if you can get him. Tell the press that there was a killing of an MI5 man in Maidenhead last night and it's connected to that.' And he told Crenshaw about Montague and the address.

'Are you sure about this?'

'What else is left, David? What else?'

'I'll get on. See you soon. And take care.'

Doherty replaced the receiver and went out to look for a taxi.

The small room was packed. Hot and white with the lights as four camera crews set up. Crenshaw had done well, phoning round the news desks, trading on his reputation a bit, saying that this story was the one to bring down a government. He hadn't mentioned Doherty directly, but he had alluded to the war in the States, the ceasefire and he had mentioned the murder in Maidenhead. Which had really caused electricity, because Montague's death had not been notified and when the Yard and the local police were contacted, the explanations were distinctly awry, unconvincing. And, of course, no one would confirm or deny Montague's status as an agent.

Crenshaw had cleared his desk and turned it round to face the room, with two chairs behind it, for him and Doherty. The camera crews had pitched microphones on the desk and had done their sound tests. Wires snaked between feet to lights and powerpoints; battery packs, second cameras, briefcases, news sidearms littered the floor. Sound recordists, cans over ears, checked levels. Print reporters stood, chatting among themselves. The pretty reporter from *Today* was getting much attention. The door opened and the buzz died down. Crenshaw, hair freshly pony-tailed, led Doherty through the room. He was embarrassed, looking down at his feet for the most part, as he moved through the crowd. He caught an eye or two that he knew and as the recognition spread throughout the room in muttered asides the sound level rose, the lights went to maximum and the reporters began to move towards the table, motordrives were firing like hail and microphones from radio reporters jabbed like swords at the two men as they slid behind the table.

'Please,' said Crenshaw, shouting, holding up his hands supplicatorily, 'please. Please be quiet.'

Doherty looked across the table at the faces, the forms pressing into his vision, like, he thought, a distended view through a fisheye. He felt panicked, pressed, claustrophobic. There would be no open spaces ever again, he thought. Just people. And claustrophobia.

'What you are going to hear,' Crenshaw was saying, 'is perhaps one of the most shocking, disturbing and criminally-motivated subversions of democracy by government – the British government – in history. It involves murder, it involves – '

Doherty had lost attention. All he could think of was the wall of people imprisoning him. The lenses in his face, photographers jostling each other across the table to get the best shots. The white light. Faces.

He tried to look up and beyond them. He looked for shapes from the past to come between him and them, the past to insulate him, but all he could see was a young body on a bloody bed.

He took a deep breath, trying to banish the image, shook his head. This is for ever he thought. Then there was a nanosecond of absolute clarity, blinding, fade-to-white light.

The hilarity was over and from somewhere she heard the portentous signal of the news. She finished the tumbler of whisky and went into the kitchen to replenish it. She hadn't eaten today, she remembered, apart from a piece of dry toast with the breakfast coffee. But she still wasn't hungry. She went back into the living room and watched the screen, shimmering pictures of the prime minister. '. . . the keypoints of the by-election campaign, the prime minister reiterated, would be the continuing fight against inflation . . .' the voiceover said. She stood looking at the screen, staring vacantly, mildly drunk now, waiting for a time to go to bed. Two raps at the door. Commanding. She took a mouthful of the whisky and put the glass on top of the television and went to the door. The young men. She knew why they were there. 'Can I get my coat?' she said and went back into the house.

As she took her coat from the hook the TV voice was saying '. . . we're interrupting the by-election coverage to bring you a live report . . . Tony Martin is on the line . . .'; the voice was breathless '. . . there appears to have been a bomb explosion at a press conference in Clerkenwell within the last hour. Several people are reported to be dead . . . Tony Martin was at the press conference. Tony, Tony are you there? What can you tell us . . .?'

CAMPBELL ARMSTRONG

MAMBO

Frank Pagan was sitting beside the world's most notorious terrorist.

Over the years Gunther Ruhr had left a trail of carnage behind him from the Mediterranean to Japan. Now he had been captured. But why had he been in Cambridge of all places?

Frank Pagan had good reason to be uneasy, for a conspiracy of unprecedented scale was under way.

From the foggy flatlands of East Anglia to the steam heat of Cuba, from the chic streets of Paris to the Scottish countryside, the search for answers turns into a race against time as a world-threatening plot comes to a climax . . .

CAMPBELL ARMSTRONG

JIG

Jig the Dancer – clinical killer, elusive assassin, secret weapon of the IRA. The perfect kill, the perfect getaway, are Jig's hallmarks.

Frank Pagan – British counter-terrorist agent. The perfect hunter, a man of singular and chilling motivation. Jig's perfect foil.

Ten million dollars destined for the IRA goes missing in America. Jig is sent in to find and kill the traitor. Pagan follows to hunt and hound Jig, the enemy he has sought for so long.

The perfect match for a dance to death . . .

'*A hurricane of a thriller, having perhaps the most suspenseful and provocative opening chapter in the long and chilling history of distinguished novels about revenge and justice*'
Richard Condon, author of Prizzi's Honour

'*Lashings of lavishly-drawn characters and detonating booby traps . . . Scores a thumping hit*' **The Observer**

'*JIG is an elegantly crafted book and I doubt if we will see anything else as good in the genre this year*' **John Gardner**

'*Unputdownable*' **The Independent**

HODDER AND STOUGHTON PAPERBACKS

CAMPBELL ARMSTRONG

MAZURKA

Frank Pagan is a policeman in disgrace.

Which is why, reduced to a sort of odd-job security man, he is escorting a not-very-important Russian official on a not-very-important trip to Edinburgh.

Where his career prospects take a turn for the worse when his Russian is assassinated – shot at point-blank range – on Waverley Station.

But as he begins to pick up the pieces, the trail leads back to the Baltic emigré community, to the United States and then into the heart of the Soviet Union itself.

It is when the beautiful Kristina walks into his weary life that the facts begin to fall into place and Frank Pagan realises that he is engaged in a desperate race to untangle a conspiracy that threatens to have devastating worldwide effects . . .

'Full of excitement, *Mazurka* confirms Frank Pagan as one of the best new detectives around and Campbell Armstrong as a major thriller writer'   **Best**

'Headline-fresh . . . both pacy and tantalising'
The Guardian

HODDER AND STOUGHTON PAPERBACKS

COLIN FALCONER

VENOM

'I will survive', he promised the black silence. 'I will survive and I will come back to haunt you. All of you . . .'

It began like a page from the Kama Sutra. A beautiful French girl and her Indian lover locked in the white heat of illicit passion.

The result was Michel. Thrown out on to the dangerous streets, he grew to ferocious manhood in the alleys of Saigon. He survived to wreak the most extreme vengeance for every beating and all the betrayals. Possessed of a raw sexuality and the flair of a master criminal, driven by a pitiless hidden violence, he left a trail of blood that stretched from the backstreets of Bombay to the boulevards of Paris.

When the judge's gavel cracks across a Delhi courtroom and the world waits for justice, his destiny will hang on one last ironic twist of fate . . .

HODDER AND STOUGHTON PAPERBACKS

MORE THRILLERS AVAILABLE FROM HODDER
AND STOUGHTON PAPERBACKS

	CAMPBELL ARMSTRONG	
☐ 42219 X	Jig	£4.50
☐ 53065 0	Mambo	£4.50
☐ 49185 X	Mazurka	£3.99
	COLIN FALCONER	
☐ 53550 4	Venom	£4.50
	THOMAS HARRIS	
☐ 20530 X	Black Sunday	£2.50
	GORDON STEVENS	
☐ 42211 4	Peace on Earth	£3.50

All these books are available at your local bookshop or news-agent, or can be ordered direct from the publisher. Just tick the titles you want and fill in the form below.

Prices and availability subject to change without notice.

HODDER AND STOUGHTON PAPERBACKS, P.O. Box 11, Falmouth, Cornwall.

Please send cheque or postal order, and allow the following for postage and packing:

U.K. – 80p for one book and 20p for each additional book ordered up to a £2.00 maximum.

B.F.P.O. – 80p for the first book, plus 20p for each additional book.

OVERSEAS INCLUDING EIRE – £1.50 for the first book, plus £1.00 for the second book, and 30p for each additional book ordered.

OR Please debit this amount from my Access/Visa Card (delete as appropriate).

Card Number ☐☐☐☐☐☐☐☐☐☐☐☐☐☐☐☐☐☐

NAME ....

ADDRESS ....

....